THE JEMENI CHRONICLES

THE
JEMENI
CHRONICLES

a novel

JUSTIN SHABEN

TATE PUBLISHING
AND ENTERPRISES, LLC

Published by Tate Publishing & Enterprises, LLC
127 E. Trade Center Terrace | Mustang, Oklahoma 73064 USA
1.888.361.9473 | www.tatepublishing.com

Tate Publishing is committed to excellence in the publishing industry. The company reflects the philosophy established by the founders, based on Psalm 68:11,
"The Lord gave the word and great was the company of those who published it."

Book design copyright © 2014 by Tate Publishing, LLC. All rights reserved.
Cover design by Rtor Maghuyop
Interior design by Jake Muelle

Published in the United States of America

ISBN: 978-1-63063-143-7
1. Fiction / Fantasy / General
2. Fiction / Fantasy / Contemporary
14.01.21

CHAPTER ONE

He had been walking through the desert for days. He started out running, then jogging; now all he could do was walk. He couldn't stop; he didn't dare try, for he knew all too well the evil that ever pursued him. An evil that didn't sleep, didn't eat, and could not be stopped, so he went on.

The sun beat on him without mercy, making his armor act like an oven. The desert he walked through was once filled with rolling dunes of soft sand with the occasional oasis filled with trees and sweet water. Now though, after being ravaged by the war—he himself had started—the sand had been melted into glassy gravel. The sun reflected off it with such strength that he feared he would go blind. His sword drug across the ground in his limp hand as his belt was torn and could not hold it.

He could not drop the sword, he was certain he would need it before long. It had been weeks since he had seen a single sign of life. Not even a bird of prey circling above waiting for him to breath his last, he was truly alone. It had also been days now since he had a proper drink, and his mouth was as dry as the earth he walked on. Even in what shade he could find, there was little relief from the heat, and the night was even worse. The nights in this place were as cold as the days were hot, and there was little comfort or sleep, as the gravel would cut into him whenever he moved.

Now at the heat of the day he felt his spirit giving up, his body was weak, his mind exhausted, and his thoughts turned to all that had been lost. He fell to his knees and wept. He had lost so much in his own life alone. His mother, several friends, any hope of a peaceful life, and to add to it he was going to die here in this godforsaken place. Never marrying the love of his life, he would never see his children grow up; he would never hold his grand kids. He was going to die here, *now*, alone.

"*No!* I will not be dying! Not today! And not here! I will make it home!!" He cried.

He forced himself to his feet and drove on; he had come *too* far to give up now. He had a chance to change the course of the war; if he could just get to where he needed to go. Plus, it is worth mentioning that this was *the* Michael Rains. Well, that name might not mean much to those hearing this now, but it will by the end.

Michael was chosen for a very special job and some day he will be the one to save everyone everywhere from the doom that had been foretold. But before I can tell that part of the story, I must first tell of how he got there. I must explain his triumphs, highlight and his failures. Most of all I must show just how it would feel to go through what he has so that all those who read this might better understand what it means to have a destiny so great that it changes the lives of all who live, forever …

♾

"Dojee! Dojee!" cried Warbick as he ran down the hall. Warbick's feet pounded the hard carpeted stone floor like a rock slide as people jumped out of his way.

"Dojee, have you seen him?" he asked a passing master. His normally intelligent, well spoken voice was lost amid his desperation.

"No, I'm sorry. He has been spending a lot of time in the meeting hall, what with all the troubles these days, you may find him there," she answered gravely.

So Warbick tore down the hallway, up several staircases, taking some with a single bound. Warbick was a giant of a man, that is to say he was a literal giant from the planet Weatherin, the home planet of the giants. He stood twelve-foot, four-inches tall and was over eighteen hundred pounds of pure muscle. He wore a leather top with scale male on the shoulders, canvas pants with armor plate leggings and heavy fur topped leather boots. He also had a great hammer strapped to his back, which swung dangerously as he bolted up yet more stairs. Finally, he made it to a large metal door and kicked it open, causing everyone in the room to jump.

"What in the name of Hades do you think you're doing?!" Demanded a disgruntled looking satyr.

"Silence, Simein!" boomed Warbick.

"What is wrong?" asked a tall man in blue samurai robes. He had black hair with a single silver streak pulled into a neat pony tail and a neat goatee, his hand resting on the handle of a very finely crafted sword hanging from his belt.

"Dojee, it is Tulsun and Safraiya. Valldiss has…has…killed them…and is now waiting outside the gate with their wee son. He means to kill the boy unless you bring him *The Book of Dragnous*." Warbick was obviously filled with emotion as his body shook with mingled rage and grief. Dojee did not stay to comfort him though, (this was no time for such things). Dojee ran from the room, but not through the door, but passed right through the wall as if it weren't even there. Several other masters, including Warbick stormed after him.

"Are you going to be alright? If not you probably ought to let us handle this? Asked a concerned looking man with a face like a panther and who was near as big as Warbick.

"Yes, I'll be fine thank you, Zezz," Warbick replied. They burst out onto the snowy grounds, as the sun was starting to fall, and out the front gate where Dojee already stood. There in front of him were five men and a single girl who looked to be about eighteen years old sitting on their perspective mounts. In the middle was a man wearing a heavy fur cloak with a hood to reveal a face covered by a mask made of some sort of very shiny metal, the mask had a letter *V* that went along the edge of his mask from his chin up to his fore head. Warbick and the others arrived in mid conversation so they all went silent.

"…Dojee, Dojee, you simple man, I know that your 'little' friend over there told you what I wanted…" He stated in a sweet voice…"So you won't be getting *this* until I have it!" His sweet voice melted into a harsh, cold, hiss.

"What do you plan to do with such a book?" inquired Dojee. "There are only a few people in existence that can read it." His horse stopped the ground in agitation as Valldiss went sort of ridged.

"It is none of your concern what I do with it. Besides that, if I can't read it then what's the harm in giving it to me?" Valldiss had his false sweet voice back, but there was no hiding the fact that he was getting annoyed with Dojee trying to stall him. "…You have delayed me long enough! Now give me the book or I will rip this child's head from its body!" Valldiss changed his grip on the child to prove he wasn't bluffing.

"You don't have to do that, here is the book…" Dojee snapped his fingers and a large, very old book appeared in his hands. "…But you will give me the boy as I give you the book. Any funny business and we will end your reign by spilling your blood all over these grounds!" Dojee's eyes shined dangerously and, if only for a second, Valldiss seemed taken aback by this threat.

"But of course." Valldiss said finally; he stepped down from his horse and walked over to meet Dojee. They walked toward each other, each step made very deliberately as each man had their unused hand on his sword ready to strike, should the need arise. They both stopped at an arm's reach and did the hand off. It was actually quite smooth and each had what they wanted…but neither man stepped back. They just stood there staring each other down.

"You will pay for what you have done this night!" Dojee said finally, through clenched teeth. Valldiss fidgeted a little before responding.

"You shouldn't threaten people who are more powerful than you—they might take it personal!" With these words Valldiss lunged at Dojee. Dojee however was expecting this and was more than ready. Valldiss swung his sword at him; but Dojee easily dogged the sword which missed him by nearly a foot. Dojee answered with a swift kick to Valldiss's face. Valldiss didn't even have time to think, he was sent for a flip through the air, yet somehow he recovered and landed firmly on his feet. Dojee continued his attack with a flurry of kicks and punches all landing perfectly until he knocked Valldiss to the ground.

"If only you had applied yourself to your training you would actually be pretty good. Also you should know that power means nothing if you don't know how to use it!" taunted Dojee. Valldiss freaked out as he stumbled to his feet, and started screaming and slashing his sword wildly like a child throwing a tantrum.

"How dare you! I'll kill you, and the kid too…No, no wait, I have a better idea…I'll take that *brat* and raise him as my son, he could prove useful." spat Valldiss, while Dojee blocked and deflected everything Valldiss did. This time it was Dojee's turn to get angry, but he didn't fall for such bait. He had been fighting for more than twelve thousand years; he wouldn't be tricked by this fool. Plus he still held the baby in his arm, and had to stay on the defensive to keep the boy safe. Valldiss was watching Dojee poor over all this in his mind and realized that Dojee wasn't going to attack because of the child. Though you couldn't see his face there was no doubt that an evil smile had crossed it. Valldiss took a minute to look around to see what was going on around them. All of his men had started fighting the masters that had come to Dojee's aid. Zezz was fighting with Valldiss's third in command Angus. Angus was a very big giant both in height (at sixteen foot) and in girth (with a waist that was at least nine foot wide). See Angus was once *the* strongest giant alive…but he then lost the title to an Oben Groffoot—the former Arena Grand Champion…and…Kinda let himself go. To the right of them Warbick and three other masters (that Valldiss didn't know) were fighting Thive; Valldiss's right hand man, and the only man Valldiss knew of that was more ruthless and evil than he was himself. With all of Dojee's masters busy, there was no one who could come to his side now to help him. Valldiss sheathed his sword and stretched out his hands toward Dojee.

"You seem to value that baby more than I thought you did, but such attachment can be distracting. Allow me to fix that for you!" Without another word, Valldiss shot a ball of red energy at Dojee. He spun out of the way but this time however Valldiss caught Dojee by surprise. Right as Dojee came out of the spin Valldiss's sword swiped at Dojee's face. Nothing but skill and experience could have allowed Dojee to duck just in time. The baby however was not so lucky; the tip of the sword fell toward Dojee's arm where the baby, despite everything, was still asleep. The sword tip just barely nicked the child's arm, this was more than enough of course to wake him and he started screaming.

Normally a child screaming would not have fazed Valldiss, but as the baby screamed something amazing happened. At first everything went very still, and then with a terrible explosion an intense ice blue portal of light appeared in front of the child. Valldiss and Dojee were thrown over a hundred feet, and several of the other masters covered their ears to shield them from the noise. Dojee scrambled to his feet just in time to see the baby—who was now floating in mid air—pass right into the swirling pool of light, the light vanished as well as the child. Dojee stood in stunned silence; Valldiss jumped onto his horse with his new book in hand, and rode off hard with his men close behind. Dojee turned to Warbick with a stern look in his eye. "You must find the boy before Valldiss does, or all hope is lost!"

Warbick just nodded, turned and went back in the castle. Dojee then turned back to see the faint figures of Valldiss and his men fade from view. It was at this moment everything hit him; two people he loved dearly were suddenly gone, and their son had now disappeared. Dojee was overcome with grief; he went down on his knees, tears already flowing from his eyes. There on the ground was one of the baby's blankets and resting on top of it was a locket. He knew it as the locket he gave to the boy's mother as a wedding present. Inside the locket there was a picture of the young family. They were all happy, the boy was in his daddy's arms and his mom was smiling wide for the picture. Dojee looked at the picture for all of a minute, and then he broke down and cried bitterly, and knelt there until the sun was gone.

CHAPTER TWO

Jenna Rains was working late sitting at her nurse's station at Chicago Memorial Hospital. She had just been promoted to RN and was now working extra hours, to keep herself busy so as to keep from worrying about her husband Mark, who was a sergeant in Chicago Police Department. She loved him for his devotion to his job and understood that it was very important, but he was still required to come home every night—something she didn't let him forget. Jenna was hard at work when Dr. Frank Lawry—her boss—walked up to her desk.

"Is there a reason you've decided to work yet another double shift?" he asked with a crooked smile. He was a friend of Jenna's father and was the one who got her the job at the hospital. Dr. Lawry had sort of taken her father's place after he died a few years before.

"I don't want to sit at home and worry about my husband all night," she replied. Dr. Lawry just chuckled and shook his head for a second.

"Now you are going to feel silly, I just got off the phone with your man, and he said to send you home. He is there, and has been waiting for you for the last three hours. Now go home and be with your husband before he comes here and arrests me for slavery," Dr. Lawry smiled warmly. Jenna jumped up and gave Frank a hug then hurried out of the hospital. She unchained her bike from the rack outside and started riding for home. She could not wait for the weekend; now that she was an RN they would be able to afford another car so she wouldn't have to ride bike anymore.

She was only a block away from home when it happened; all at once there was a blinding blue light and a deafening sound like an explosion. Jenna was thrown from her bike and landed on her back. All the windows to the cars parked along the side walk on either side of the street blew out sending glass everywhere. Jenna threw her arm over her face to protect it from the glass but when she lowered her arm she thought, at least for a moment, her eyes weren't working right anyway. Just as she looked at the light, a baby floated out of it and gently landed on the side walk. Jenna got to her feet brushing glass from her jacket and hurried as much as her sore, now bleeding knee, would allow to the child. She scooped the baby up into her arms, and he stopped crying almost immediately, she looked into his eyes and he just starred right back. The baby was young about four to five months by her more than educated opinion. She had started her nursing career in the maternity ward, so she knew a thing or two about babies. However when she found out she couldn't have children of her own; she asked to be moved to a different floor. She sat there on the curb just holding the child, and watching him drift to sleep. By now people had come out of there homes to see what all the noise was about-one had already called the police. In ten minutes flat, Mark was there and ran to Jenna and nearly threw his arms around her when he noticed that she had something in *her* arms. Mark stopped dead in his tracks unsure which question to ask first but Jenna spoke before he could anyway.

"How would you like to be a daddy after all?"

Mark wasn't ready for such a question and seemed unable to speak, and just looked at the child in Jena's arms then back at her. She giggled at the sight.

"You don't have to act so scared he's just a baby." She said, smiling.

"Yeah, okay but where did it come from?" Mark seemed almost as if he suspected the baby of some misdeed.

"Oh honestly he's a baby not a gangbanger! And *it* is a boy," Jenna seemed almost misty eyed. Mark knew that look and that she was already making plans for the child, but he was quite sure the child's real parents would want him back.

"He isn't just a stray cat there are quite a few steps to take if you're thinking about adopting him, like finding his parents." Jenna thought about telling Mark that the boy floated out of a swirling blue light but decided that she might just be thought of as crazy if she did. So instead she just told him something he could believe…

"I found him right here on the side walk…," she said quickly

"All right well that might make it easier if the parents are found unfit…But what about the explosion? Were you hurt—or him for that matter?"

"I have no idea what happened to cause the explosion, and I'm fine—just a scuff on my knee. Looks like he has a bit of a cut on his arm here, but it is pretty shallow."

"It seems like you were both lucky! But I'm glad you're safe, now let's get this guy checked out and see what steps we would need to take to adopt him," answered Mark with a smile spread across his face. He knew exactly how much having a child would mean to her, and he couldn't deny the strong desire to be a father that had been in the back of his mind. She was ecstatic and threw an arm around Mark and gave him a kiss.

The next couple weeks flew by, and with no record of the boy's being born and his not having any blood type that the doctors knew of, the state was glad to hand him over to the Rains. So in what felt like no time for Mark and Jenna, they welcomed the boy into their family as Michael Alexander Rains. Jenna got some time off work which Frank was happy to give and spent the time bonding with Michael who was an uncommonly happy little boy. Time in the Rains' house was now filled with joy and laughter. Mark's mom was thrilled with the idea of a grandson to spoil and wasted no time in doing so. Days turned into weeks and before long nearly a year past and all seemed quite normal…after his first birthday party however strange things started happening.

Only slight things first—like one day, Jenna got a call from the babysitter saying that Michael managed to rip the front of his crib off. That night Mark looked at the crib and decided that it had to be some sort of defect. They bought him a new solid oak crib to replace it; but about two months later, the babysitter called again to say that this time the crib was upside down and sticking most of the way out his bedroom window! This one made everyone very worried because no one had a clue what could have caused that to happen anyway! They came to the decision that the babysitter wasn't keeping close enough tabs on Michael and fired her. Mark's mom eagerly took over the role as babysitter saying she hardly got to see him anyway. This of course was ridiculous as she was there three or four times a week—at least—as it was, but they didn't have time to argue. Several months went by without another incident. Michael was still happy as he could be and started growing fast. It wasn't until one afternoon while Ethel—Mark's mom—was watching him that more started happening. Michael was having a feisty day and was giving his grandma a headache by banging two of his toys together. So in an effort to calm him down, she put on a kids show and put his toys up on a shelf so he couldn't get them. She left the room for about a minute to get some aspirin when a loud crash from the living room made her rush back to find the TV smashed like someone struck it with a hammer; and the shelf that was holding his toys was ripped off the wall and across the room. Frozen by what she was seeing, she just stood there for a moment as Michael turned to her with his toys once again in his hands and a huge grin on his face. Jenna got home not twenty minutes later and froze when she saw the mess that Ethel was trying to clean; while Michael ran to her—he had been walking since he was eleven months. Only two weeks after that Jenna had a day off and her friend Kristine came over with her daughter Jess—who was just a few years older than Michael. Jenna and Kristine where talking in the living room while the kids were on the floor rolling one of Mark's bowling balls back and forth.

"You be careful with that ball Jess, it is very heavy and hard!" Kristine warned.

Well Jenna and Christine got up for just a minute to get a cup of coffee in the kitchen. They stood by the sink a moment talking when they heard an odd, loud, cracking noise come from the living room. They came rushing in, Jess jumped up quickly. "He did it! He did it!" she said at once.

Michael was looking at his mom just saying, "*Uh-oh!*" Pointing at what was once a bowling ball, and was now broken into small pieces! The living room was an add-on to the back of the house and thus built on a concrete block. So to add to it, the floor under the ball was crushed. Jenna and Christine hurried the children away, and then cleaned up the mess. An hour later they got done with lunch and put on a movie for the kids to watch. Michael was getting feisty and wanted to beat his toy bat against the floor. Jenna had put his bat in the hall closet, and it seemed as if he was just going to sit and watch the movie. While Jenna and Christine did the dishes they could hear Jess laughing from the other room—then a terrible crash. They came running afraid of what they would find this time. Michael had gotten tired of watching the movie and went down to the closet—the door to which was split in half! Once inside he had traded up from his bat and chose his dad's very real Police League baseball bat…which was presently sticking out of a hole in the floor! Once again Michael just looked at the scene with wide eyes pointing and saying, "*uh-oh*". Christine decided to go home, and Jenna had a scary thought come into mind. She had to entertain the idea that at least some of this stuff was being done by Michael himself. She voiced this to Mark when he got home who was more than a little skeptical.

"Look, that TV screen was a half inch thick at least! *I* would have a heck of a time *cracking* it, let alone smashing it like that, unless I used a mallet! And you can't think he picked up that oak crib and chucked it, it took two guys to unload it from the delivery truck! The bowling ball…that has me stumped pretty good! I don't know what could do that…But I am fair certain that a child, just a year-and-a-half old, could not! And the closet door and bat being put through the floor…That has me stumped too, but it would take a world class strong man to even have a chance of doing that! I mean you don't think that he is some sort of 'super being' from another world do you?" said Mark, chuckling.

"Okay, then let's hear your explanation for what *did* smash that ball. How *would* you explain the closet door…and the bat…and the large hole that the bat made through the solid maple floor boards…and through a four-by-twelve-inch support beam?" Jenna replied.

Mark had nothing. "Okay, so what do we do then?"

"Well, I think we should start with a doctor visit, he's about do for one anyway, and they may be able to shed light on this," Jenna said, in a way that sounded like she was trying to convince herself.

"Jenna, how on earth could a doctor…"

"*I don't care we're going!*" Jenna said sounding both scared and on the verge of freaking out. Mark knew this voice…It scared him…he would rather be in a shoot out with some gangbangers than mess with her in this state. He called the office to take the day off and they went to the doctor. Michael loved the doctor's office and was quite interested in his surroundings when they were called in. When the doctor came in he started with the usual questions like how were his eating habits, did he run a fever often, had he been sleeping through the night and so on. He then checked Michael's nose and ears, tonsils, breathing and temperature. He also checked his reflexes and paused when he felt Michael's arms. Every time the doctor finished a test he simply made a note and said to himself…

"Hmm…interesting." I would like to do some x-rays just to see how his bones are developing. So Mark and Jenna agreed and they did the x-rays. About thirty minutes later all the tests were done.

Finally the doctor sat down to tell Mark and Jenna what he found…"To be frank I don't know where to begin so I'll just put you at ease and say that your boy is very healthy…In fact I've never seen a healthier boy his age in my twenty-three years as a pediatrician!…" He paused to see their reactions.

"What do you mean?…Are you saying he's unnaturally healthy?" asked Jenna uncertainly.

"Well, yes actually, I am. See at his age some of his larger bones would normally still be somewhat soft and wouldn't fully harden until around three. But your son not only has a fully hardened skeleton but his muscles are very highly developed for a boy his age…for that matter they would be quite impressive for a thirteen year old! Have you felt his arms? Why, he's practically a super hero!" The doctor let out a laugh at his own joke.

Jenna and Mark hesitantly felt his arm and were shocked to find that he did in fact have abnormally firm muscles, they had just never noticed before. Mark smiled and seemed lost in thought all at once. No doubt dreaming of the day he would get to see Michael on a football field smashing everyone out of his way.

"That would explain why and how he keeps breaking things, he simply doesn't know his own strength. And as far as I'm concerned the only thing you have to worry about is if he keeps going at this rate he'll be able to wrestle dad to the floor by the time he's ten!" The doctor chuckled at his own joke again as he followed them out toward the lobby.

Mark seemed very pleased, still in his dream of a son that would one day be a pro athlete so he could pay for his old man's retirement. Jenna, however, was—for some reason—unsure that all the weird things that had happened could be due to Michael's being super healthy, however she decided it was far better news than she was expecting, (not that she had a clue what to expect). However another thought suddenly filled her head. Something that she had forgotten quite on purpose since the day she found Michael. The image of the shimmering light, and his floating through it, and gently onto the ground. Where had he come from? What was the light and how did he float out of it? Wait! Who cares about that? He was her son, her angel, and that was all she cared about.

CHAPTER THREE

Michael grew fast and soon it was time for his first day of school, Jenna was nervous because it would be the first time that he would be in a strange place without someone he knows. Mark reminded her that this was the same for every other kid his age and that she would miss him more than the other way around. As Michael was a very friendly kid, Mark was quite right; just as soon as the door to his kindergarten class opened he was off like a shot and playing without so much as a second glance back. Jenna forced him to say goodbye then Mark forced her to do the same and walked her out of the school.

"But what about his teddy bear, he..." Jenna asked sounding desperate for a reason to go back to Michael.

"—Honey, he hasn't had a teddy bear since he was three, and he ripped the head off the last one, saying, and I quote, '*he gave me lip!*'"

Both Jenna and Mark had to laugh at this, He then dropped her off at her car kissed her good bye and went off to work as she went off to her job. When she picked Michael up later that day he was able to recite the alphabet from A to Z and count to one hundred. He had also drawn a picture that was better than most kids twice his age could do. Within a week Michael's teacher said that he was gifted and should be moved to first grade.

And so began a new trend for Michael of being better than anyone at anything he tried to do. By the age of seven, he could beat his dad at chess, became the captain of his football team, and had received a brown belt in tae kwon do—his father had talked Jenna into allowing him to join the class the previous year.

Michael was an incredible kid and everyone in his classes started getting very jealous at his success. There was one boy in particular who really didn't like Michael, his name was Titus Wickle. He was another far less but gifted student; and he didn't much like his spotlight being stolen by Michael, and so they became quick enemies. Things got heated one day when Titus and a couple of his friends started harassing Alison Carter—a very pretty girl that just so happened to be Michael's first crush—while on the playground. Michael wasted no time in cutting in to protect her...

"Leave her alone you puke!" shouted Michael as he stepped in front of Titus.

"What do you care if I bother a girl or not?...Are you in love with her?" the crowd of kids that had gathered all laughed loudly.

Michael turned to see Alison tearing up from embarrassment and that was all he needed to see. A few seconds later a teacher came hurrying over as shouts of pain filled the air. Michael had Titus on the ground with his knee on Titus's chest, while smacking him around the head. Titus's friends all had black eyes and were rubbing their sore bellies where Michael had planted all *too* well placed punches.

Michael waited outside the principal's office; his parents were in there along with Titus's mom and the moms of the other two boys as well as Alison's mom. Michael was relatively certain his parents were presently planning his untimely death and how to cover it up properly! Titus was in the nurse's office across the hall crying enough that you would have thought that Michael was still beating him. By the end of it all, it was determined that Michael was trying to defend a girl's honor and the principal couldn't fault that fully. However Michael was forced to apologize and was forbidden to fight anyone again and was given detention for a month.

There was no talking in the car on the way home. *Well this is it, good bye cruel world! When we get home mom is going to get her hefty wooden spoon while dad gets his thick leather belt, and they are going to practice their back hand on my back end!* He thought to himself. Mark told Michael to come with him to his study the moment they got home.

"Sit down bud," Mark said in a surprisingly gentle voice.

"You know what you did was wrong, right?" he began. Michael nodded timidly.

"Well do you know why?" Michael had no idea what to say so he just shook his head.

"You are skilled in fighting buddy; you could seriously hurt someone if you're not careful. I'm not going to say that you were wrong for standing up for someone you felt needs it. That is a man's prerogative, and it shows your heart. There is a place for that, but you have a responsibility to learn when to fight and when to hold back. Now for your punishment, you are grounded forever, and you have used up your second chances in regards to fighting so don't let it happen again. As for your mother, she expects you to be thoroughly thrashed so do me a favor and cook up some tears okay? Or I'll be the one crying!"

Michael took these words to heart and was from that point on a model student. He continued to get nothing but A's in school, and touchdowns in football, plus he kept advancing in tae kwon do and now kung fu as well. It seemed hard to believe just how good life had become. As it turned out, his good life was about to be destroyed and all in a single day and by a single word.

The day started normal enough; his mom told him to behave and have a good day at school. His bus trip was the usual helping people three grades ahead with their homework. Michael refused to be moved ahead to higher grades anymore to avoid more unfriendly treatment he would be sure to receive because of it. Michael didn't have friends to speak of. The other gifted students were jealous of how easily he out-scored them. The other athletes thought his being smart was an unforgivable character flaw, one actually told him, "I don't care how good you are at sports! You know math…and spelling…that's…dumb!"

All this meant was Michael could spend more time studying, though he did rather hate that the girls ignored him too ...unless they needed help in their studies. His first two periods went by like normal. But when he sat down to eat lunch, his name was called over the loudspeaker, and he felt a chill in his blood. He knew something was wrong instantly, he could feel it ...

"Michael Rains please come to the principal's office."

Feeling every eye on him, he awkwardly got up and left the cafeteria. His strange sense of foreboding grew as he got nearer to the office. It was made worse by a teacher who was coming toward him from the principal's office, she saw him, started to cry, and said to him, "Be strong young man!" her voice was weak and watery.

There was some kind of terrible news awaiting him, but nothing could have prepared him for what it was. His father was waiting in the office and seemed like he was shaking trying to hold back tears. Michael sat down and the principal started telling him what was happening because his dad seemed unable to speak. Michael's head began to spin

" ...It's about your mother ..." Why was this happening?

" ...They are still looking for the man ..."...What was going to happen to him now?"

" ...It looks like ..."...Tears fell down his face. Why? Why was this happening?

" ...*Murder* ..."

Michael sat outside the principal's office while his dad signed some things. They were going to move—his dad couldn't handle going back home to that house without the woman that made it home. He had already put in for a transfer to Los Angles and that was where they were going. Michael was in a place of disbelief in what was happening. Though he had no friends to be leaving, doing so felt like losing another part of his mom. His grandma died the year prior and that was bad, but this was pain he had never felt. The days leading up to the move were a blur and the actual move even more so, but a week later they had made it. With his transfer Mark got a bumped up in rank and got a nice pay raise, on top of that he also got a large life insurance pay out for Jenna. As a result they were able to get a nice house; which Mark was able to purchase just before they got there. Michael was in a daze for several days but had to get over it quickly because he needed to get signed in at his new school.

"Who knows maybe you'll make some friends here, which could help," suggested Mark.

"Yeah, maybe." Michael found himself hoping his dad was right. He had spent so much time feeling sorry for himself that the idea of making friends in a new place had managed to elude him. Once signed in he was sent to a class for gifted students, and as it turned out his dad was proven right rather quickly. He sat down beside a pretty girl with mocha skin, thick black curly hair pulled back with a light blue head band and a flowery shirt.

"Hi, I'm Penny what's your name?" she asked in a pleasant voice.

"Michael...Michael Rains." Michael stammered. Michael felt a tap on his shoulder and turned to the seat on the other side of him and a boy about his age—that looked rather similar to Penny—was smiling at him.

"Hey Michael, I'm Penny's twin brother Zack, I've been given the job of showing you around today. You and I are in all the same classes so it will be pretty easy."

By the end of the day, it was clear that Zack and Penny were Michael's first true friends, and they couldn't have been nicer people. After school they invited Michael over to their house; this was quite a thing too because Zack and Penny lived in a mansion. Their parents were filthy stinking rich; sadly they didn't want to be parents...just rich. So when Zack and Penny were born, their parents hired a nanny and butler, left each kid twenty million and then split for Italy. Zack and Penny told Michael this as if it were a common story. Michael couldn't feel sorry about himself anymore, here he had been all sulky for losing his mom while

Zack and Penny never even had one—that they knew anyway. In the months that followed life got better, Michael had two new friends and had found a new martial arts school for kung fu as well as jujutsu, which Zack and Penny thought was really cool. Zack ended up joining with the same school.

Life was good and when Mark was made lead detective it got even more so. At fifteen, Michael became a bit of a grease monkey as he got into cars and started fixing them up. Soon he had a side job doing light mechanic work for people around town, even his dad's partner Scott Williams had him work on his car from time to time. Michael was no little boy by this time but was near as tall as his dad and was built like a high flying wrestler. He and Zack were both getting bigger as they had taken to working out almost every afternoon in Michael's garage with the door wide open. Zack suggested they should start doing this when the girls' softball team started jogging by Michael's house regularly. Michael's dad said it was good planning on their part...

"You can get in shape and pick up some girlfriends," he said mockingly. Penny however thought this was just too much "guy-ness" for her so she would just spend that time in Michael's pool. It had been years since Michael had been at the middle of weird happenings or bad news, but this afternoon was going to change that. They had just pulled open the garage, and Penny wished them many happy bench presses and went back to the pool. They started working out like normal but Michael felt strange like he wasn't really working.

"You want me to put on more? Dude you have three twenty-five on there already!" Zack declared the slightest hint of envy in his voice.

"I feel like it's hardly even there, just add what's left," Michael replied

"You want all four hundred pounds? Are you crazy? You just went up fifty pounds last week...! Fine, I'll add it."

Zack added the rest of the weight and got in position to spot. "You know, I don't know if I can even spot this much dude!"

"Don't worry if I die I won't do this again, I promise," Michael jeered. Zack snorted with laughter as Michael grabbed the bar and hoisted it off the bench with ease. He did ten reps and put it down.

"Man I could do even more! I want to try something real quick." Michael grabbed the bar again but this time with only one hand.

"Are you really going to try that? Man, don't strain something I don't want to spend the rest of my evening in the ER!"

Michael ignored Zack and gave a heave to the bar and lifted it at once. "Okay that's scary, this should be hard!"

"What's next man you want me to sit on it?" Zack joked as they switched places, and Michael took two hundred pounds off the bar.

He wasn't paying attention though. His mind had gone blurry and it felt like his brain was trying to remember something from back when he was too young to know what he was seeing. What he could make out was something with a crib and a window…he somehow knew that it was a real memory but that never happens. Who can remember when their a baby? Michael strained his mind to try and think more clearly and it worked…In a way…what he was seeing became clear as day but changed to a much grimmer scene. His eyes snapped open, but he could still see it like he was looking into someone else's memory now, but this wasn't any past that he had heard of. He could see L.A. on fire; people were running, covered in blood…eating…

"Hey! Wake up!" shouted Mark as he helped Zack get the bar up. "Where did you go? I've never seen you space out like that before, you alright?"

"It was weird…I…I don't know how to say it." Michael was quite sure describing what just happened would land him a few mandatory sessions with the school shrink.

"Well that weird something is going to get someone hurt if it keeps happening while you two work out!" Mark scolded.

Zack waited until Michael's dad left back inside before he said anything. He was surprisingly calm considering his near decapitation due to Michael's lack of attention. He began slowly...

"Your dad wasn't wrong about you never spacing out, in class I would dare say you pay more attention than the teacher does...So...What gives?..." Zack paused to see if Michael would answer.

"You wouldn't believe it if I told you, just trust me, I'm fine." Michael assured as they went inside.

They argued as they came into the kitchen, but stopped when the noise they were making caused Michael's dad to jerk his head away from his case file—it was strewn all over the table—his dad give them an angry glare. Michael always wanted to help his dad with his cases but was of course never allowed, that didn't stop him from asking questions.

"Sorry dad, what's that you're workin' on?" Michael asked

"Oh it is just this string of homicides. I had worked some like it...Wait a second! Nice try, you almost got me on that one." Michael's dad had the slightest hint of amusement in his voice but then promptly told them to leave the room before they could try anymore smooth talking.

"Your dad has such a cool job!" Zack stated as they went out to the pool.

"Yeah, all those dead bodies and drug dealing murders must be a bundle of fun!" Scuffed Penny as the boys jumped into the pool in classically poor style.

"I thought you said you would like that job yourself just a few weeks ago?" shouted Michael over the water in his ears.

"Have you even seen your dad these last couple of days? He's been a wreck since this new case started!" Penny explained quickly.

"Penny don't act like you know what's going on, Mark wouldn't tell you anymore than he did us." Zack snapped.

"For your information I didn't have to ask him because I have been listening to the news, or reading a paper or magazine *of any kind at all!*" Penny floated herself over the edge of the pool got up off her floating chair, threw a paper down beside the pool and stormed inside.

"Whatever!…Hey, dibs on the chair!" called Zack diving for the chair, needlessly (as no one else was even near it).

Michael didn't even hear Zack or what he was presently going on about because the front page article had caught his eye at once. Michael hadn't even thought about his mom or what had happened for years now, but this paper forced him to remember it all too well, it read…

The Mysterious Chicago Stabber Comes to L.A.

Roughly five years ago a string of murders broke out in Chicago that proved to be linked to the serial killer dubbed "The Chicago Stabber" who had been at large for over thirty-five years by that time and had claimed over eighty-five victims. This string of murders ended in the death of Jenna Rains wife to Mark Rains who was the investigating officer in these new killings. Now five years later the mad man is back and so far has killed at least seven people in just three weeks time. At this point very little is being released, but we have learned that the FBI has taken over the investigation and that the same Mark Rains who is now the senior detective for the LAPD has been removed from the case due to conflicting interests. No one is willing to speculate as to why the killer has come here but some believe that he isn't done with the Rains family as Mark has a son that he and his wife adopted some sixteen years ago. One thing is for sure; until this murderer is caught our streets will not be safe!—Julie Steiner

Michael just stared at the paper for a moment dumbfounded; he read it again and again as if hoping the words would change by his sheer force of will. It just couldn't be! Not only had Michael's dad never told him that *he* was the one on the case for the guy who ended up killing his mom; but to find out that he was adopted (his parent's never had the heart to tell him). This hit him hard and he jumped out of the pool all at once.

"…Hey you're doing it again, you're spacing out, what's going on man?" Zack asked still oblivious to what Michael just learned.

"I…I'm adopted…" Michael blurted out

Whatever Zack had expected, it wasn't this, he whipped around on the floating chair so fast that it flipped over dumping him in the water. Michael didn't wait to explain it all to Zack; he wanted to hear this from his dad so he went right into the kitchen and up to his dad.

"I thought I asked you to let me work." Mark stated without looking up.

"Yeah, and I thought I was your son." Spat Michael, his dad looked up with a puzzled look on his face.

"What on earth are you going on about?" Michael handed him the paper and quickly saw his dad's look of puzzlement turn to mingled anger and remorse.

"Look…I…It isn't…an easy thing…to tell your child…and there was no sign of your birth parents…we…we thought it would just save you some heart ache…your still my son, blood or not! Now, I'm sorry you had to find out this way, I wish you didn't. But if you could excuse me a minute, I need to make a phone call to this paper so I can have this reporter burned alive!" Mark got up and left the room in a hurry, Michael was quite sure that his dad was hoping to avoid talking at all about the old or new case and his involvement in it.

"He probably blames himself for what happened to your mom, I don't think it would be fair to make him talk about it anyway," said Penny gently.

"How did you know that I was thinking that?"

"Woman's intuition, never underestimate it buddy!" Penny was clearly trying lighten the mood, but Michael just couldn't be cheered right then.

The next few weeks were the worst of Michael's life since his mom died and there seemed little relief in sight. Life went on though, and it seemed like no time when graduation was right around the corner. Penny thought it was quite funny when Michael and Zack both realized that despite their public workouts neither had managed to get dates for the senior prom. She also didn't have a date but that was because…"The right guy never asked her…" So the three of them just went together and had and all-round awkward time, but they could at least all agree that the punch was quite good—as a prank the junior prom punch had been spiked with mouth wash…unfortunately for the pranksters, they ended up having to clean up the large amount of puke all over the gym floor, which still had a slight smell. At their graduation party the following week, they all sat down with Michael's dad, his dad's partner Scott, and Scott's girlfriend Shawna. Chief Winslow—Mark and Scott's boss—even stopped by to wish luck and to announce Scott's promotion to detective, and tell Mark he had been assigned a new partner.

"I'm sorry to mix business with pleasure but he'll be here tomorrow," Winslow said as he was walking out the door.

The next day Michael and Zack got up early and got to work on a 1969 Mustang that a friend of Mr. Rains had brought him to restore. Mark stopped in the garage on his way out the door for work.

"You guys are up awfully early for two kids who just graduated high school! Isn't it like a rule or something that you're supposed to be lazy for the next few weeks and then I tell you to get off your lazy butts and get a job?" Mark had a crooked smile as he spoke

"We are getting a head start on life by getting our soon-to-be billion dollar empire off the ground," Zack said flatly just before a fair amount of oil squirted all over his face.

"You let me know when you're getting close to that first billion. Till then, I need to get to work. Stay out of trouble and good job with this industrious spirit. I like it!"

Mark drove away and Michael felt odd. He felt that he should be going with his dad to work. This was strange and what was even more so was the more he tried to shake these thoughts, the stronger they became. Soon it became obvious that Michael could not concentrate on what he was doing as he started trying to unscrew his thumb with his wrench instead of the bolt beside it!

"Ouch! Well that isn't suppose to come off I guess." He was hoping being funny would stop Zack from worrying … It did not. Zack looked at Michael worriedly, this was the third time that Michael was unable to control his mind.

"You might need to see a doctor or something. I'm not kidding! You never do this kind of stuff."

"I do not need a doctor, I'm fine … I … I just … its going to sound crazy. I feel like I need to go to Dad's office."

"Why exactly? You know your dad said only to do that if there is an emergency," Zack reminded.

"That is the only reason I haven't left yet. I just have one of those feelings."

"Oh … well then maybe you should go. Those *feelings* have yet to steer you wrong."

It may seem strange that Zack would be so quick to change his mind just because Michael had a *feeling*. But time and time again Michael has proven to lead both of them the right way with his feelings. Like once Michael and Zack were working together on a history project that was going to be judged by a historian from a local museum. Michael felt that they should write their papers on the topic of ancient aliens, Zack thought this was a little too *geeky* for a pasty old historian to be into but Zack had no ideas himself. As it turned out ancient aliens was this historian's favorite topic and his main field of study, they got an A easily. On another occasion they were walking home from school when Michael said he felt they should walk a different way that took them through an unpleasant part of town. On the way they came across a guy getting robbed and were able to stop the robber who had been at large for some time, there was even a reward of five thousand dollars out for his arrest. It was this money that allowed them to start the small repair business they had now. These are only two out of about a hundred cases where Michael's intuition worked out quite well. So by now all Michael had to say is "I feel" and everyone would shut up and listen.

So Michael and Zack got cleaned up and hoped in Zack's car (a Nissan GTR) which was his graduation present to himself. They made their way to Mark's office and weren't even half way there when Michael's phone rang, it was his dad.

"Hey, where are you right now?" asked Mark

"On my way to you actually, what's up?" Michael was almost expecting something weird now.

"I'll tell you more when you get here but mainly just watch your back and be safe. Come straight here do not stop for anything else, okay?" Mark said firmly.

"We will be there in ten, but I don't want any kid's table bull. I want straight answers, okay?" Michael could hear snickering in the back ground and knew he was on speaker.

"Hi Scott, Chief Winslow—oh, and Dad's new partner." there was a bit more laughter and a deep voice spoke.

"The name is Tyson, can't wait to meet you."

Michael felt odd again as he hung up the phone. He was certain he had heard that voice before but had no clue where. He also felt as though someone was watching them as they pulled into the police station parking lot, but there was no one in sight.

"Your acting weird again bro," Zack said after a moment turning off the car he seemed downright scared.

"Look will you stop worrying, I'm not sure why I am so out of it lately but I assure you it is not likely to be anything more serious than a large malignant growth in my brain." Michael couldn't help but smile, and this crack had the desired effect as Zack was still fighting off some laughter as they entered the office.

"There you are! I was getting worried," Mark called out all at once.

"Yeah, that twelve minutes since we talked last was a long time," chuckled Michael. His dad was hardly amused.

"This is not a time for jokes, sit." Mark said as they headed in his office. There standing by the window was a man who was the largest person Michael had ever seen. He was at least seven-feet, six inches and had to be close to five hundred pounds. By the way his shirt seemed to be about ready to pop at the seams around his chest it was all muscle.

"This is my new partner Tyson Norfolk, transferred from Detroit," said Mark noticing Michael and Zack's awed faces.

"Don't worry I won't grind your bones for my bread. I am over that phase," Tyson said smiling warmly. Zack snorted with laughter as did Michael. Michael liked this guy immediately. Mark was much less amused.

"Not the time for jokes I said." Tyson made as sheepish face. Scott and Chief Winslow came in and shut the door.

"I understand what you said over the phone about not being treated like a kid so I will come out with it," started Winslow, "there has apparently been some people around town asking for your whereabouts, and some murders to go along with them. We believe someone may be in fact trying to harm you. Now would I be right to assume that this doesn't scare you in the slightest?"

"No I'm not scared, bring 'em on!" Michael said flatly.

"Okay well, listen carefully. Until you learn how to doge a bullet with that kung fu of yours you just keep out of trouble. I can't afford to give you two and your sister a police escort around town until these people are caught. So I will ask a few things of you, first do not stay out after dark, get inside by sundown. Then secondly take these …" Winslow handed them both pepper spray and gave Zack an extra for Penny, "…Now I know you two are both pretty good in martial arts but this is just an insurance, this is not your normal pepper spray. This stuff is extra concentrated so be careful with it, it could put a guy the size of Tyson here on the ground crying like a baby so only use it if you are in serious trouble."

"Why would my sister and I need this though? How could we be in danger?" asked Zack confusingly…

"Well that's obvious," answered Michael, "if I was looking for someone I would ask people if they had seen that person's friends as well as the target. If you can't find the target find the friend then the target will come to you," answered Michael.

Mark, Winslow, and Scott all chuckled a bit; they were often impressed with Michael's knowledge and all around smarts. "You would make one heck of an officer you know that?" Winslow said, but Michael felt a twinge of fear enter his mind.

"Thanks but this isn't my career path. Anyway there is a problem—Penny could be at the mall or a coffee shop or at the beach or even at *our* house in the pool right now. She could be in danger and not even know it." Michael said not hiding the worry in his voice.

"Not to worry we called her first, she isn't going to go anywhere without one of you with her at all times. She is at home right now," Scott informed them.

"Who is this trying to kill me anyway? Is it that 'Chicago Stabber?' Because if it is then it would be the end of his pathetic life if I get my hands on him!" Michael had not allowed himself to really heal from the loss of his mom, nor was he able to express the anger in his heart toward the one responsible. So this explosion was really eight years in the making.

"Now wait just a minute, first of all don't go jumping to conclusions! We don't know that it *is* the Chicago Stabber or not. That was just an irresponsible reporter trying to sell papers.

But the stabber had been around for a long time your mom was likely the last person he got. It's quite possible that *that* guy isn't even alive anymore. I personally believe we are dealing with a copy cat which happens a lot with popular criminals. As far as them wanting you, who knows why, could just be the way this copy cat is trying to legitimize themselves. By picking on the last family targeted by that creep," Mark explained, "secondly I don't want to hear you suggest that you would murder anyone again do understand me?!!" Michael was taken aback by the harshness his dad had in his voice. He must have understood what Michael was feeling and just how serious he was that he wanted to kill the guy.

"This is a dangerous situation and if I feel like you are going to go on some sort of vendetta mission I will lock you in a cell if I have to. I hope you understand my point." Mark got up and opened the door…"Now go home and stay there! *Do not* leave the house!" Zack and Michael left the office in bad spirits—I guess no one could expect much more from someone who just learned that people want them dead.

"Well at least we know we are wanted!" said Zack, trying to be funny

"Yeah, not the kind of attention I look for really." Michael said flatly. They got in the car and made their way home. And Michael felt stronger than ever that they were being watched. Somehow he knew that this was just the beginning of what was about to happen.

CHAPTER FOUR

On the ride home, Zack and Michael did not talk, Zack sent a text message to Penny to have Mrs. Carson, their maid and one of their former legal guardians, drive her over to Michael's house. Michael was angry; he was not a kid nor was he close to helpless. He was benching 550 pounds like it was nothing, the only reason he didn't try more was because his weight bench was only rated for five hundred pounds as it was. But on top of that his kung fu master said he was the most gifted student he had ever had in the thirty plus years he taught. He was not going to be forced to change his life for some sick freak with a soft spot for murderers. When they got home he went to his room without a word and grabbed a check he was given for the last car job he had, said good bye to Zack not giving him time to say anything, and went out of the house. Was he directly disobeying his dad's orders? Yep, sure was. Was he the least bit sorry? Nope, not at all. His dad needed to realize that his boy was all grown up and was fully able to make his own choices! It was a beautiful day so he decided to walk to the bank. It was only about two miles anyway.

It was a beautiful day indeed and it seemed that quite a few people had the same idea to get out and enjoy it. There were moms out with their kids. He walked by some street vendors selling everything from hot dogs and cotton candy to hats and sun glasses. The walk did wonders to clear his head until he drew near his bank. There on the corner before his bank was a man holding a sign and calling out to passers by saying: "The end of the earth draws near! Prepare yourself, it is coming soon!" Then the man's eyes fell on Michael. His eyes went so wide they seemed in danger of rolling out of his head. "You young man, many things await you—some great, some terrible. Only hours remain! Beware of the shadowy figure for his will is to destroy you! He will stop at nothing and you are not ready! It waits in the deep for its master's return, the question is will you make it or will you *burn*!" With that the man ran down the alley beside him, Michael ran to catch him but when he turned the corner the man was nowhere to be seen.

"That is not possible!" Michael said aloud to himself. There was no way the man made it the whole way to the other side of the alley and out of sight in the three seconds it took Michael to round the corner. There were also no doors into the buildings either, that was weird! He tried to shake it off but something made the hair on his neck stand up, and it wasn't just what the man said, but that he had this *feeling*…the man was right. The fact that his mind would even let him consider this made him feel queasy. He went into the bank and up to an open window, the teller was a nice southern lady with thick drawl, "How do you want this, hon." she asked with a grin. "Oh, anything bigger then a nickel is fine with me!" The teller let out a joyful howl of laughter as she went over to drawer to get cash. At that moment Michael heard something that caught his ear—a few windows over he heard someone say his name. He listened carefully. "—No, *Michael* Rains"

"And what is your business with him?"

"He had a rich uncle that just died and left him a sizable sum of money. We are trying to get it to him…"

Michael smelled bull crap from a mile away, he felt reasonably sure all at once that these were the people who had been asking around for him and killing people. He needed to know what he was dealing with so he chanced a look. He knew the voice asking about him was female, but he was not expecting this! She was…well…hot! She looked hardly older than him and was a few inches shorter. She wore a sleeveless black leather trench coat, which showed her fairly defined arms and very tan skin. Beside her was a man a little over six feet and was…well, less pretty. He had two rings in each ear. Michael could see a goatee, a tattoo of a serpent-style dragon which circled around his bald head, and a nasty scar above his left eye. The thing that caught Michael's attention the most—even though it was only visible for a second— was the fact that there was a gun tucked into the man's pants. Michael's teller had come back several minutes before this but hadn't said anything, probably trying not to startle him more than he obviously looked already. But she finally cleared her throat to get his attention.

"…You alright dear? You look as though you've seen a ghost!"

"To be honest, I could be better. I think those two might mean me harm. My dad is a cop, and he said some dangerous people were looking for me."

The teller straightened up a bit and looked at him oddly, then spoke quietly. "You'll forgive me for being so bold, but if you know that people are looking for you then what are you doing out and about? Don't you think a police officer with twenty plus years experience like your father might have known best? Besides that, no amount of martial arts will make you bulletproof, nor will strong muscles—"

"But how could you even know to say…"

"Oh, never mind that. I'll distract them while you take your money and run." And with that she turned to the man and girl, pointed, screamed, then cried, "*Gun!*" The panic and chaos was instant, and Michael slipped out the front door as everyone else either hit the floor or just started screaming as if being mauled by a bear. He made it to the corner of the street when an ear piercing explosion filled the air!

Michael turned to see a huge ball of green…light…or electricity…some form of energy, finish blowing out of the front of the bank. He had no idea what just happened and also could not care less at the moment. All he knew was he did not want to be the next thing blown apart. So he ran hard and fast, he was encouraged to run even faster when he heard feet running after him. After a moment more green stuff started zipping past his head, some of which would hit a parked car blowing it up. Michael dodged and rolled all the while running without a thought to stop. He was getting away from them, so he decided to cut down an alley, change direction, then cut down another alley and change direction again so as to lose them completely. This worked quite well—perhaps a little too well. By the time he slowed down, he realized *he* had no idea where he was either! This street was nowhere near home, in fact by where he was in relation to downtown he was on the opposite side of the city!

I was not running anywhere near long enough to get this far! ... He thought to himself ... *It would take hours to walk home from here!* A low rumble noise brought his mind back to the world around him. Michael looked in the direction of the sound and even from this distance—at least a thousand yards—he could tell that what was coming up the road was not human. It was definitely a male and he was human-like in some ways, but he was way bigger than a natural man. Just by how big he was on the giant motorcycle, Michael guessed he had to be at least nine feet tall and very wide at the shoulders. He wore black leather pants, a black leather vest, and some sort of plate armor over it all. His most stand out features where his glowing eyes which were a bright red and his skin which was so white it almost seemed to glow as well. He had long somewhat wavy jet black hair and a big full beard that made a stark contrast against his skin. When he was getting closer Michael also noticed the man's teeth were sharp and two of them were longer than the rest as he smiled evilly.

"That's it, stay still so this doesn't have to take so long!" he cried.

Michael suddenly realized that his standing there staring at this guy was kind of stupid. However he didn't even have time to try and run because a huge strong hand grabbed his shoulder from behind and tossed him onto the side walk. Michael had to shake his head to see if something had come loose, because he could not believe what he was looking at. Tyson was standing there looking up the road toward the biker; but right before Michael's eyes, Tyson started growing and his clothes started changing. A second or two later he was over twelve foot and was covered in a kind of scale mail armor. In a flash, he stepped over to a nearby light pole and pulled it straight out of the side walk and in the next second swung it like a bat right into the biker as he was about to pass. The biker flew off his bike, and hit the road tearing a huge gouge into the street. For a brief second, Michael thought he was dead but the biker stood all at once looking no more than pissed off.

"Warbick, you should not have done that. Now, I have to kill you too!" cried the biker.

"You may try Axle but you are no match for me, and you will not touch the boy!" answered Warbick. The biker rushed him. Warbick stood his ground and just waited. Axle made to punch him with a nasty spiked glove but was nowhere near as fast as Warbick who dodged him as if he weren't moving and landed a punch, followed by a strong kick to Axle's chest which sent him flying into a parked car across the street tearing it in half. Axle jumped out of the wrecked car to a manhole cover, he pushed his hand though the ground like it were play dough and pulled up the cover along with the top rim of the pipe it sits it and threw it at Warbick who dunked out of the way easily. The manhole cover crashed into a car on the other side of the street making it fly over the curb and into the front window of a closed deli. Warbick stuck his hand out pointing it at Axle and a bolt of lightning hit him sending him flying out of sight. Michael was at a loss for words; he was still trying to process what just happened. He walked over to Warbick who looked at him with kind eyes

"Are you hurt?" He asked. But Michael didn't answer as the sound of a city bus screaming down the street stole their attention.

"Now how did he...? Oh get behind me!" Said Warbick. Michael was all too happy to get out of the way of a bus flying at them at top speed, so he did as Warbick said and rushed behind him. Warbick pressed his feet into the road, and they sunk in at least a few inches as he bent down a bit—this made Michael want to reconsider being behind him, it seemed like he was getting ready to be hit by the bus. There wasn't enough time though for him to run and it is good he didn't try either. As the buss reached, Warbick, he hit it with his hands and with one quick, sharp motion ripped the bus in half right down the middle.

The noise was unbelievable and Michael was quite sure his head was going to explode. This was too much, this couldn't be happening. *I'm dreaming*, he thought. Everything started spinning. *Why can't I dream about pretty girls, or cool cars?* He was falling....*What a freaky dream!* Then all at once everything went black.

↬

Michael had never had such a crazy dream, a white skinned biker named Axle, a giant named Warbick that could rip apart buses with his bare hands! Wow, did he have an active imagination! But of course that didn't happen. He was dreaming the whole time. Right now if he opened his eyes he would see the masterful mess that was his room, the pile of clothes that took up half of his bed the random piles of crap all over his room—containing who knows what—and the whole place having a slight sent of cheese curls. But he didn't want to open his eyes; it felt too good to lay there stretched out on his...wait a second! With half of his bed covered in clothes there was no way he could spread out like this! He forced his eyes open and felt compelled to swear loudly. He was not in his room...He was not in the middle of the street...He wasn't in L.A. any more either...As a matter of fact looking out the window to his right, he could see very plainly that he wasn't even on earth!

"No, no, no! Okay wake up Michael, this can't be real!" he said to himself, freaking out a bit. Out the window, he could see that he was in a very tall building and yet there were car like vehicles passing his window, as well as many layers of traffic going higher and lower than him. Michael should have been terrified but in that moment he was too busy being impressed by the city he was looking at. The door behind him opened causing him to spin around.

"Ah, good you're awake. We have much to discuss please come with me." Warbick was still wearing his armor and a pleasant smile on his face. They walked through a hotel that looked to be the nicest, most expensive place Michael had ever been. There were murals that were made out of gems, statues made of gold, huge ornate vases, and amazing chandeliers made of all different kinds of gems and precious metals. They made their way to a spiral stair case...or actually a spiral escalator. It took a long time to reach the lobby but when they did Michael felt a sudden jolt of the reality of what he was seeing. This lobby was filled with all kinds of creatures, some even bigger than Warbick, others were the size of mice, and every size in between. There was a man a bit taller and much thicker than Warbick in a super nice pin-striped suit with a tail and purple/gray skin. Another man was walking by while floating four feet off the ground. There was a very fat man complaining that the teller gave him the wrong change..."I gave you four gold. I should be getting sixty-five silvers, two hundred fifty coppers! Are you trying to rip me off...?" A manager ran over to calm him down, Warbick continued to lead them both into a very fancy restaurant.

"Welcome sir, how has your journey been? You've been gone longer than anyone thought," said the host who had hurried over to them, menus in hand.

"Oh, I am quite fine. Thank you. This is my friend Michael Rains, the one I've been looking for," Warbick said politely. The man squeaked and shook Michael's hand excitedly. They were led to a reserved table in the VIP area. It must have been late because the restaurant was almost completely empty.

"What's on your mind?" Warbick asked as they sat down. Michael was beside himself! What wasn't on his mind?! Just a few hours ago he was at a bank cashing a check…a very normal thing! Now he was about to eat at a high end restaurant on another planet! This traffic jam of thoughts must have shown on his face because Warbick just chuckled.

"I realize that you must be ready to explode, but I am actually impressed with how well you are handling this experience. But to give you some relief I will answer some questions I know you have. First my name isn't Tyson it is Yolliss Warbick. I'm sure you heard that from Axle, but I wanted you to hear it from me. Next this is one of my hotels located in Percelia, the capital city to our society. We are—when we're done eating—going to meet up with yo—"

"I'm sorry but when you say 'our society' just who are you talking about? I mean you aren't trying to include me in that statement right?" Warbick studied him for a moment and smiled.

"You are so like him! It is cruel that you never met him. He was a good friend." Warbick got a little misty at these words.

"Okay, I give up…Who are you talking about?" Michael didn't hide the irritation in his voice.

"Your father…Your birth father." Michael felt a sting in his heart. He was not expecting that. He had only a few years ago learned that he had been adopted, but for some reason he didn't consider that his real dad might be from another planet!"

"My dad? He was from here?"

"Yes, as was your mother, and so are you," Warbick paused again.

"Okay so what? At a few months old I get tired of the diaper rash and nursery rhymes stole a space ship and made for a new frontier?" Michael jeered. Warbick laughed lightly.

"You are quite funny. You get *that* from your dad as well. But let me answer this question without interruption please as it will take some time" He took a breath then began. "I will start by explaining just *what* you are. See from as far back as history has been recorded there have been people with abilities beyond that of the natural. These abilities can very just as much as people can. There are those that can fly, those that can create and/or control fire; some can see through walls, others can walk through them. Why I even met a man that had the ability to turn whatever he touched into any kind of metal he wanted."

"Oh! Kind of like King Midas?"

"That's the man! Richest man alive, even more than me, and I own two hundred and thirteen planets. I forgot that he was in your dimension, on your very planet in fact."

"Wait, you couldn't have met him personally. His story dates back thousands of years. You would have to be at least that old to have met him!" Michael scoffed.

"As a matter of fact, I am 5,879 years old! As I asked, please don't interrupt me or this will take all night. Now as I was saying this group of people learned very quickly that their kind would not be accepted in normal society. So they started either hiding away from the 'normal people,' or they started ruling over them as gods. Some were so well known you would have read about them in school, such as Zeus, Ra, or Odin. You should know that none of them were from your planet, in fact very few 'gods' ever did come from Earth … Anyway … Where was I? … Oh yes! Soon with the use of their abilities, and limited numbers; they were both provided with the motive, as well as the means, to advance in technology. They went to the stars first, found quite a few planets with life on them. Some were actually very open to the idea of people having powers.

"When people from these planets were discovered to have powers too it became clear that this was a much bigger thing than just one race being *super* like they originally thought. Still other planets were quite the opposite and told them they weren't welcome on their planet. After a while this original group realized that there was much of their own home planet that had not yet been explored as the regular people there were by then just leaving the Stone Age. So they went back to explore, it was this exploration that lead to the single greatest discovery of all time. While exploring a deep cave, a group led by the great Lord Bezrin—the man who founded our society—and a very young Ackatoth—the single most powerful person to ever live and the first king of the Outer Systems—came to an underground chamber that was anything but natural. It was flat rock, a perfectly square room, and nature does not create right angles. This is still a mystery to this day because as far as they knew no one had ever been in this cave before…because it was under the sea! At any rate, getting to the point—they discovered an archway leading nowhere, this archway had a key hanging from a dial on its side. After a long time of every other member of the group messing with it Ackatoth finally took the key. The second he touched it lights turned on, on this stone archway…odd, you might say. He reached out his hand and touched the arch and a keyhole appeared below the dial the key was hanging from. Ackatoth put the key in it and in an instant a brilliant swirling light formed at the center of this archway. As true adventurers they stepped into this light with no fear at all. They were immediately transported to another dimension. It was quite obvious that only Ackatoth could operate this arch—which are now known as gates or portals depending on their size. Just like with everything else, we learned this new discovery very quickly; and soon came to find out that there are an untold amount of gates and portals all over. We soon had a network with an inter-dimensional mapping system. Today there are millions of gates and innumerable portals.

"Now I have so much I could tell you that I need be picky, I could ramble on forever, so I think I should tell you, *your* part in this. The gate that Ackatoth found happened to be something particularly special. Most gates only lead one or two places, his lead to *all* but a five known dimensions. This became an instant problem. Reason being by this time they had found that the person who could control the gate or portal—known as a gate keeper—could use the key to transport themselves from anywhere to anyplace they wanted within a dimension their gate lead to. Meaning Ackatoth could go almost anywhere he wanted. This immediately gave *too much power*—according to the High Council—to anyone who controlled Ackatoth's gate. So to show his good intentions, Ackatoth decided to give himself the largest responsibility anyone person could undertake. He changed his own title and what he was responsible for in being a gate keeper. He said he would from then on be known as the *guardian*, and his gate became known as the Main Gate. He and all following guardians would be entrusted with protecting any and all dimensions his gate lead to from harm and thus became the protector of…well…everything. It was through this act that we found that the sitting gate keeper could choose their successor and/or set the required traits and or powers that the person who would take their place needed to have. Ackatoth said his replacement must have the same base power as he. His power was the ability to control energy, but also to absorb it, including the energy that flows through a Jemeni—the name for our kind. This energy manifests itself in the form of each person's powers, so in short, he could absorb others powers. This is the single most uncommon power there is only fifty-three people have been recorded to have it since Ackatoth. Now I could get into all of the political reasons why this position as the guardian is so important but I hate politics with a righteous passion! So I'll just put it like this—the biggest business there is happens to be inter-dimensional trade. There are minerals, metals, and other materials that can only be found on certain planets in certain dimensions, so they can ship this stuff at an enormous rate. This meant that the person in this position controls forty-eight percent of all economies. Now people don't have to use the Main Gate, but it is far faster than trying to get connecting gates. Plus along with being connected to most every dimension the Main Gate is also a part of what is called the *Super Gate* so named because it was so big you could fit entire legions of ships through all at once—" Warbick paused for a moment for a drink.

Though Warbick had Michael's complete attention the piece of steak on Michael's plate was the single best tasting thing he ever had so he just took the moment to enjoy it. It was also at least thirty ounces!

"…I'm not sure how to say it…So I just will…Where you come into this is, my boss, and mentor Dojee Shinyo believes you to be the next guardian…" Warbick cringed a bit as Michael nearly swallowed his fork.

"Hold up! Time out! Are you telling me that I am going to have the most important job possible and have to fight off any threats that come?! Because that just doesn't fit in my ten-year plan! I am hoping to be alive in ten years you see, so I hate to burst your bubble—"

"—I know this is a lot for you to take in, and it is unfair to say the least that you should have to have all of this dumped on you like this. I hate being the one telling you that your life will never be the same again! But don't go thinking you have a choice in this. You must understand, Axle was just a hired gun and is nothing compared to those who want you dead. When I was but eighteen, I attended an academy, Asendor Academy, the best warrior academy there is. In my same year was a young man named Vando Goz. He and I were friends for quite a while, then without warning he went crazy for power. Vando was the most powerful person in six thousand years, and I guess it went to his head. He since changed his name to Valldiss—which is the ancient elvish name for the *dark angel of death*. He killed your parents in an effort to use you to get something he needed from Dojee. Had he known then who Dojee thought you were, you would have died that day with your parents. Now he is trying to fix that mistake, so we must do whatever we can to keep you safe.

So you are going to be attending Asendor Academy were you will have the protection of not just me but every other of the some 200 masters there, plus Dojee himself whom I am quite sure you will like. Now—"

"—Okay I get you not wanting me to die and all, I even agree with it as well as appreciate the sentiment. But I am not rich, so I can't afford to go to some fancy school, and I also have a cop for a father who has probably destroyed half of LA already looking for me, I need to get home." Warbick just shook his head gently.

"I think not, your father doesn't even know you're gone yet. You see we are not in your dimension, and there quite a few quirks concerning dimensions. One of which is known as *time differential;* you go to one dimension for an hour and six days have past in your home dimension. In others you can spend a year there and only a few hours have past back home. Here two and a half years is the same as a day on your home planet. So by the time your father starts getting worried, you will be ready to bring him here. Besides, you were born here, not but two blocks from this building, in Percelia General Hospital so you are home. As for the money, both of your parents were extremely well paid in their given fields. Thus you are actually quite rich, plus they already paid your way when you were born so you will have no out of pocket expense. Now we must go. I dare say I wasn't picky enough with my words we are going to be late to our meeting." Warbick got up from his side of the table.

"Who are we going to meet this late at night? Michael was starting to feel sleepy again after stuffing himself with that huge steak.

"Hmm...How should I say it?...You've had enough surprises for one day!

"Just say it; I don't think anything could surprise me at this point!" Michael was very wrong—he could not have been more wrong if he tried.

"We're going to meet your uncle..."

೩

Michael's head was spinning not just from the thoughts pouring through his mind but from the city they were walking through. Percelia was the name of the city which covered most of the planet of the same name. And even at three in the morning, the streets were jam-packed with people, big, small, and weird! There was a tiny man that looked just like a garden gnome complete with a long pointed hat and a near toothless smile. He was gilding by on a small silver disc looking quite happy about something. A little further there was a walking talking tree complaining about a man's dog peeing on him and the man said he had to be joking; he was a tree for crying out loud. Warbick rushed Micheal away as that scene started to heat up. After about ten minutes of walking they were coming up to a bar and grill with a man at the door that made Warbick seem wimpy. He was at least thirteen-feet tall and at least ten-feet wide at the shoulders with arms like oak trees. He had a scare that went across one eye which was now robotic and his platinum blonde hair was tied in a neat pony tail. Warbick smiled at him with his arms outstretched as they walked up.

"Hey there Jube what's new?" Warbick said giving him a hug that Michael was quite sure would have killed an elephant.

"Oh, you know Bruce. He takes good care 'a me. Who is this...Wait is that Tulsun's boy?" Jube replied in an extremely deep voice.

"Yes sir he is, and he is having quite a rough night I'm afraid. Had to give him the whole back story to our kind and tell him who and what he was all at once. Add to that some folks tried to kill him..." said Warbick

"Yeah, apparently the guy who said *it could always be worse* wasn't from this world!" Michael added. Jube boomed with laughter as he opened the door for them.

"He likes you; it isn't easy to make him laugh like that. Well done," Warbick said smiling then nodded toward a man leaning against the bar. He was a little shorter than Warbick but just as thick. He wore a tight black t-shirt with a thick gold chain, blue jeans, and crushed velvet shoes.

"Hi Bruce, how are you?" Warbick said giving him a brotherly hug.

"Better now that you're back for good, searching all the known galaxies for that long…" Warbick cut Bruce short as if he said something he shouldn't.

"This is Michael. Michael, meet your uncle, Bruce." Michael was at a loss, he had not considered his uncle would be almost twelve-feet tall and didn't know what to say.

"It is good to see you, all grown up. You have a lot of your grandfather in you I think…" Warbick gave him a sharp look, and he quickly started talking about something else. "…Er…I was your dad's brother, half giant and half elf; and your mom was half human, and half elf so that's why you're not like nine foot or more."

As they were talking a door shut above them and Michael looked to his left to see a young lady about his age coming down the stairs. She was actually a little short not a dot over five-foot-five, and maybe a hundred pounds soaking wet holding a sack of flour! She had jet black hair and fiercely green eyes. She was the prettiest girl he had ever seen.

"Hey there, anybody home?" Bruce had stepped between the young lady and him to get his attention…"That pretty girl is my daughter, your cousin so don't get any ideas. I know your family, but I just want to be clear, you know what I mean?" Michael got an image of Bruce holding an enormous ax and waiting at a chopping block for him.

"Yeah, I think we understand each other just fine," Michael said shaking the picture out of his head.

"Daddy, don't harass him!" She said in a sweet, cute voice that normally Michael would have liked, but right now he felt it was an unneeded liability.

Michael sat down and was brought a white-thick steaming drink. At first he was afraid to try it but after a quick smell, he realized it was just a super cold milk shake and found it quite tasty. The young lady sat down across from him.

"I'm Eliza; it is so cool to meet you finally. I've heard stories of you since I was little. It was quite a thing what you did teleporting without a key or gate or anything and as a baby at that! That's really something! I can't wait for tomorrow, you and I get to go pick out our weapons for the academy. I want to get an ax but I might go with a great sword or war hammer if I find one I like. What kind of weapon would you want…? Oh that's right you aren't use to all this. Well, I can help you pick out something good. Did you know that master Dojee is the longest sitting grand master Asendor has ever had? I can't wait to see the castle it is the biggest building ever built. They say if you could live ten thousand years and spent every minute of every day searching the place for all its secret rooms you wouldn't find even a tenth of what is there! You aren't saying much, are you shy? That's okay, shy can be cute. Not that I can think your cute for me because we're related but it is still endearing. Well I'm tiered, goodnight!" And with that she gave him a hug and a kiss on the cheek, which she then repeated with her dad and Warbick and went to bed. Michael wasn't sure what he just experienced but was quite sure that the kiss was uncalled for!

"What just happened to me? Is she trying to set some kind of speed record?" Michael asked as some of the red left on his cheeks. Bruce and Warbick exchanged looks then just laughed heartily.

"You really are your father's son!" Bruce said wiping his eyes. Warbick gained his composure quickly and stood from the bar.

"Well it is time for me to go. I need to get to the academy and get my classes ready. You will be staying here with Bruce. He will be taking you and Eliza to the academy in two weeks time. Just do as he instructs and don't go into the parts of the city that look like places to stay away from and you'll be fine. Plus this will give you time to bond with your uncle and cousin." Warbick hugged Bruce goodbye and gave Michael a bow and with that he left.

"Well it is late. I recommend you get some sleep. There is a room set up for you, up the stairs last door on the right. Michael climbed the stairs and made his way down the hall his eyes were suddenly heavy again, yeah, he could sleep. He got to his room to find it filled with stuff that obviously belonged to his parents. Including a picture of them, his dad was strong and handsome, and his mother looked young and beautiful. They seemed happy and…There he was. In a picture on the mantel over a large fireplace was a picture with his mom, dad, Bruce, and Warbick, even baby Eliza, and a lady who could only have been her mother. It was such a happy scene, and he was robbed of that life before he could even know it. For the first time a surge of anger built in him at Valldiss—he took from him what would have been an amazing life. He thought for a moment then couldn't help but laugh. In the last twenty-four hours he went from being a normal kid to being one of the most important people alive! His life seemed like it was going to be amazing no matter what he did. He got undressed and went to the bed, which was so big you could have several polar bears sleep on it pretty comfortably. He literally climbed into bed. His head hit the pillow. *Wow, what a day* he thought and fell asleep.

CHAPTER FIVE

The morning came somewhat soon for Michael who was greatly enjoying his ability to sleep as spread out as he wanted on his huge bed. But Bruce wanted him up in time to go out with Eliza on her trek to find her weapon of choice. Bruce explained that while at Asendor you had a primary, secondary, and special weapon. You would then be trained in these weapons for the entire time you attend Asendor or until you master each weapon. Bruce and Michael talked for almost an hour before Eliza got up, they spoke on how life differed on Earth. Bruce had never been there. Michael told him about studying martial arts and that he was quite good. Bruce was impressed by this and told Michael that such training was good practice for Asendor. Bruce then told him about his younger days as a bounty hunter and some of his more exciting missions. His wife Debbie was the bartender, and she advised Michael to be careful of believing everything that Bruce told him.

"…He has a way of adding to the truth. That life was a lot more danger and a lot less glamour than what he would have you believe." She was smiling as she spoke, if you didn't know she was Eliza's mother, you wouldn't believe it. She looked maybe ten years older than Eliza and was just as pretty; but she and Bruce both got late starts on their family as they were both the same basic age as Warbick.

"No! No! The one you shouldn't believe here is Debbie, why she was a trained assassin when I met her. In fact, *I* was her last target, but just one look into these baby blues and she was powerless to resist!" Bruce promptly gave Debbie's butt a pinch.

She slapped his hand but her cheeks went red and she just smiled. Michael thought it was cool to see people who had been married for over two-hundred years still in love like newlyweds.

Eliza was quick with her breakfast and in ten minutes they were both out and about. If three in the morning was busy, then this was just ridiculous. Eliza told him that the city had over six-billion inhabitants and another four billion that move in and out of the city each day. They walked for what could have only been five minutes but Eliza managed to talk enough for an hour. It was almost impressive…almost. They stopped on a corner as Eliza got out a piece of paper from her purse. It was a list she made of things she and Michael would need.

"Okay, we should get our weapons first. They're going to be the most expensive thing we get and also the most important. That way we know how much we have left to spend, however we will need to get some text books too." How much did you get out of your vault?" They had gone to a bank so he could get his stuff too.

"Honestly I don't know, I just grabbed a bunch of gold and silver coins." The money system was still new to him, but her reaction seemed to tell him that this was a lot of money.

"You mean to tell me there isn't a single copper in that pouch?" she hissed.

"There weren't any copper coins in my vault just silver, gold, and platinum, why is that a bad thing?"

"Only if anyone hears you say that out loud! The average person makes two—to three-hundred copper a day, and it takes five-hundred copper to make one silver, three hundred silver to make a gold, and five-hundred gold to make one platinum! You have a fortune in there!" she hissed. She thought for a moment then smiled big.

"Do you think you could help me buy my special weapon, I wanted a plasma cannon but they cost a lot." She gave him a sweet wink. Michael had never been in a position where a girl would use her charm to get something from him, so he was not prepared. He said yes without a thought, as if he had no choice. They walked to the next block and Eliza stopped again, making a funny face at a small shop across the street.

"That's weird! I was down here just yesterday and that shop wasn't there. Let's check it out." They got across the street and went inside and both of them gasped. The inside was far larger than the outside…That does not make sense. It did make Michael feel better that this was something new to Eliza too. But her confusion quickly turned to excitement.

"Do you know where we are?" she squeaked

"Um…I've only been in this dimension for about eighteen hours, so I think it would be safe to say I don't know the answer to whatever question you have." She giggled but didn't answer her own question as she was now too busy admiring a very large machine gun. Then she ran to a rack of huge maces and went for one nearly bigger than she was.

"Hey, be careful that thing has got to be a couple hundred pounds!" Michael said feeling odd having to tell her this. But as you probably already guessed he certainly didn't need to tell her this because she picked it up as if it were weightless.

"No, I would say it is more like five to six hundred pounds. I'm looking for a two ton or more this is so light it would be hard for me to use, so let me know if you find a heavier one." With that she was off looking at armored chest pieces for women, though they were far from bras it still made Michael feel weird so he decided to leave her to it. He walked through the shop and found himself once again at odds with the size of this place. It had isles that broke off from the rest of the shop that could fit a couple dozen jumbo jets, even though from the outside it looked to be only a few hundred-square feet. As he pondered this, he wondered toward the checkout counter, and here Michael became aware of the workers in this shop which were three-foot-tall robots with thin arms and legs and cylinder-shaped heads a bit large for their bodies. One had just picked up the microphone for the loud speaker.

"Clean up in isle three, bring a mop…make that two mops…and a stretcher…make that three…stretchers…thank you!" Michael walked over to read the board that labeled aisle three, which said Grenades and acid bombs. Michael cringed at the thought of what they had to mop up. Michael's attention was then drawn to an argument going on right by the register between a young man a few years older looking than Michael, and a tiny old man. The young guy had a long brown duster coat and glowing red eyes and the man wore red pants, a white shirt, and a brown vest covered in pockets. He also had two or three belts laced together and covered in tools. To go with that old man had a thin, well-trimmed beard, a bald head, and small round glasses.

"Look boy. If ya want ter' bye somethin' tha's fine with me but leave me alone! I don't 'ave one alright!" said the short man.

"Oh come on! I've seen places with better stuff than this, and you're suppose to be the best! My friend speaks volumes of how great that sword is, that is yours right?" The young man pointed to another young man Michael had not noticed who was leaning up against the wall at the end of the counter. He had his face in his hand at the moment. He looked to be between twenty and twenty-five, wore a short black leather jacket, blue jeans and oddly had long dark purple hair. The sword that was mentioned was clearly visible, it was a katana style sword with a simple black lacquered sheath and a handle rapped in some kind of red cordage which gave it a distinct look.

"Yes o'course that's mine! And I *am* the best, but even if I did 'ave a back room filled with me *best stuff* I wouldn't show ya just fer botherin' me." The short man was quite agitated now.

"I could understand if we weren't interested in buying stuff, but we are so just let us look at what you *don't have*. I mean think of the first day you set foot in Asendor with all those other people and their amazing weapons. Would you be able to send us youngsters into that with less than the best? Hey you, wouldn't you like to see what it is he has in the back?" It took Michael a few seconds to realize that the young man was speaking to him, but he didn't know what to say. With all the choices out here it was overwhelming so if there was a room with the best of the best that could make his choice easier Michael would be interested. The young man had walked over to him and put an arm around Michael's shoulder.

"Well, what do you say friend?" He asked smiling.

"Oh Alex, leave him out of it, we don't need to get him thrown out too," said his friend with a reproachful tone.

"No I'm alright. And I say if you didn't have such a room then you would have just showed him what you do have back there just to shut him up. Plus there is too much stuff out here and I don't want some second rate sword to train with," Michael said finally. Alex seemed very pleased with this but the short man's face turned so red, he looked like a beet with a beard.

"Do ya 'ave some way ter pay yourself? I won' be made a foul of now!" He said in a voice of mingled anger and curiosity.

"Instead of telling him, Michael just took off his money pouch and dumped a bunch of coins on the counter. He noticed that there were rather more gold coins than silver. Instantly the shop owner's face broke into a huge smile ...

"That makes ya a preferred customer! Please come with me," the man spoke in a distant blissful voice as if he were in a daze. He started walking and Alex held Michael back long enough to whisper to him ...

"Boy am I glad he didn't ask to see my money because I don't have squat! I'm Alex." He held out his hand which was adorned with a black leather glove.

"Michael—Michael Rains. Nice to meet you." Michael shook his hand firmly.

"Well Michael this is my good friend Ryan, say hi Ryan!" Alex grabbed Ryan by the hand and nearly pushed it into

Michael's when the shop owner came back around the corner still smiling.

"Please this way, my friend." He waited until they all got around the corner behind the counter before following.

"Now I must ask ya ter only touch wha' you're goin' ta buy, and I'm sorry but I 'ave quite o'bit ta do, so call me when you're ready ter check out." He said as he lead them to a bare wall in the back of the shop.

"Um yeah, there is nothing back here. Do you think I'm stupid or something?" Alex was acting smug as he said this and the owner for just a second looked like he forgot about the shiny pile of gold on his counter but then caught him self...

"Why...O'course not, just watch." His smile faded as he turned to the wall and waved his hand at it. Instantly the wall vanished revealing a small ware house full of the finest looking weapons Michael had ever seen. Just as the wall disappeared so did the shop keeper. Alex did as well, with a puff of gray smoke he was suddenly on the other side of the room looking at a sword. Eliza came over to Michael looking like a kid on Christmas.

"Hey, the shopkeeper told me you were back here. This is cool. I never thought I would be here. Slim makes the best weapons anywhere and these are his best pieces. My dad got his favorite gun here..." She kept on talking to no one in particular as they went down the aisles. Michael's attention was now on the only thing in the room that seemed out of place. Way on the back wall was a pedestal on which sat a book, a simple, very old looking black book. It had a light shining on it as if it were a prized item.

"Hey, what's with this?" he asked aloud. They all came over to have a look, Ryan had no idea and Alex was not interested in the book because he had just noticed Eliza. He teleported right beside her and in epically bad style gave her his best line...

"Why, hello there. You are quite a woman, could I interest you in buying me dinner, and maybe some making out?" Michael got a picture of what Bruce may do to him if he found out that

Michael allowed his daughter be hit on...especially that badly. But Michael's fears were short lived: Eliza turned to Alex gave him an odd look then giggled.

"You're funny! It isn't time for dinner yet you silly, but could you carry my axe and mace please?" She put on the same cute face she used on Michael and he had to look away, that thing was powerful.

"Oh you bet, let me just...ooph!" Eliza dropped a large battle axe and a huge mace into Alex's arms. Surprisingly Alex could actually hold it, though it was obvious that she didn't need him to hold them for her, even still he did his best. Eliza reached out, grabbed the book, and looked inside it and a puzzled look spread across her face.

"That's peculiar, it's empty...Why I couldn't imagine why someone would have a...Unless...Oh my...It is...This is *the* book, the Book of Ackatoth!" At these words Alex dropped the weapons he was holding and popped right beside her and snatched the book out of her hand. Ryan also tried to get a turn to look while Eliza demanded to have it back. This soon became a bit of a shouting match and Michael had seen enough.

"Stop it already!" he spat, "what is so great about that book?" The others stopped suddenly and looked at him like he had a head growing out of his armpit.

"What, did you just join this world or something?" Alex scoffed.

"As a matter of fact yes I did, now tell me. What is the deal with that book?" Michael really hated being so ignorant of what seemed to be basic knowledge. Eliza answered as she managed to get the book from the other two by just giving them that cute smile and asking they let go at once.

"Ackatoth made a sword while he was alive that was said to be the most powerful weapon ever made, he then authored a book near the end of his life telling you how to get to it. The only problem is he said only one person would ever be able to read the book...the one destined to have it. Trillions have tried over many thousands of years but most have died and those that didn't and managed to get away spoke of terrible monsters…or something like that, so now it is an illegal road."

"What do you mean? If no one could read that book then how could there be a road at all?"

"Well people tried to find it using history and smarts and so on. And anyone who got close usually ended up dead. You should look at it." Eliza handed him the book, he took it but did not look in it.

"Why should I look in it?" Michael asked. He was still not ready to except that he was the guardian so he didn't want any reason to feel special or otherwise gifted in some grand way.

"You know who you are, just give it a peek. If you see nothing, then maybe Dojee was wrong and you aren't him." Eliza had a different look in her eyes but all the same Michael felt strange.

"Hey stop doing that, if you want me to do something, then convince me, don't use some power," Michael scolded.

"Have I been doing that again? I'm so sorry, its a very new power I sometimes can't control it. You don't have to look at it if you don't want to." Her face went beat red as she looked at the floor.

"Oh, well don't feel bad about that then. Look I'll give it a try." Michael opened the cover and for a moment the first page was blank then words started to form like ink rising through milk. *"Hello Michael, I'm glad you found me. I hope you're ready If not, then we'll just have to see."*

Michael read it aloud, he was glad to see that no one else found it normal that a book would know his name or that *he* was the one holding it. The book went on, *"You are the one so stop trying to run. Without the sword your battle can't be won! You're far away now but soon you'll see, you will be glad that you found me!"*

With that the writing stopped and Michael who had read it aloud was very uneasy. This book knew his name, that *he* was the one holding it, and it even knew his thoughts! He felt like dropping it, but then he had one of those feelings again, he needed, this book. He knew better then to question these feelings so he checked for a price...there was none.

"That is odd, is it not for sale?" Michael muttered. Alex shook his head in amazement.

"You have a room full of awesome weapons and you pick a book to buy...You aren't a nerd are you?"

"Oh, I'm still going to get the weapons I need. I just want this too. I'm going to go ask the guy for a price." Alex shrugged and went back to his vein attempts to hit on Eliza, she was so clueless towards this that he could have actually *hit* her and she would most likely not have noticed. Ryan came with Michael to ask about a spear he liked that wasn't marked either. The second Michael crossed the line on the floor between the back room and the rest of the shop an alarm sounded. Several small doors opened around them and about twenty of the small robots came rushing out and surrounded them both, with small guns in their hands. The wall that had been removed was now back and very much solid. Slim showed up with a pop and looked outraged.

"Just what's the idea of taken that out'a there? Do ya even know wha' tha' is? How hard it was ter find? What would ya even want with it anyway?"

"As a matter of fact it says on the binding that it is "The Book of Ackatoth" and I can read it, so I want it." The second Michael said this Slim waved his hand and the robots disappeared as did his look of rage which turned to shock.

"Ya...read that...did ya? Wha'...wha' it say? His voice shook like he was about to cry.

"It said "Hi" and knew my name, told me I needed the sword and that I am the "one", that's about it." Slim ran over to Michael and gave him a hug around the middle.

"Bless ya lad! You're the new Guardian! Here in me shop, What an honor!" Slim grabbed Michael's shirt and pulled him to the front of the shop (muttering happily the whole way).

"I 'ave something for ya, me best sword ever. So sharp it can cut through most other weapons! Ya won't 'ave much use fer it once ya 'ave *the* sword but it will come in handy till then." Slim got on a ladder and went up to a very high shelf, a moment later he was back down with a long box covered in dust. He set the box on the counter, took a breath, and opened it. Inside was a beautiful katana, it had a dark red dragon motif wrapping around the shiny black-lacquered sheath; the handle just like Ryan's sword was rapped in some kind of red cordage.

"This is yers…No charge! Here ya take back them coins ya gave me too!" Slim snapped his fingers and a bag of coins appeared on the counter.

"So…er…I get to keep the book too?" Michael asked thinking this was all just a joke.

"Ya don't get it do ya? Ackatoth made tha" book and the sword fer only one person, and tha' person would be the only one who would ever be able ter read it. That means he made tha' sword and the book fer you, it always was yers. Now I will come ter Asendor later in the year ter give ya the armor fer yer trip. I'm impressed by wha' you've done two weeks from now. No one will be able ter believe wha' ya did once ya've done it. O'course there is always the possibility ya won't do wha' ya haven't yet. But if that doesn't happen then what will happen will be even more amazin'…" He kept on talking this way for a while, and Michael's head began hurt. Slim obviously had some sort of foretelling ability, but his ability to explain it seemed to lack a bit of details. Eliza and Alex came out of the back room. Eliza was carrying a large gun of some sort while Alex tried to balance a pile of axes and maces that she had obviously wanted also. Ryan had just stood there with Michael this whole time not sure if he should move and Slim finally noticed him.

"Oh would ya look at tha', I forgot I had tha' spear. I've no clue who made it jus' tha' it must O' been a "god" cause it is all but impervious. Plus it gives the wielder the ability ter control fire, birds, earth, and weather. Come ter think on it, it might 'ave been made by Horus. Either way that I'll let you 'ave it fer a discounted price being a friend of The Guardian and all…twenty-nine silver fer it, and you young lady, you'll get a bit o'better deal being related ter 'im and all. Ya can 'ave that whole lot fer one gold sixty-seven silver, as fer you…" Slim looked at Alex and his face went emotionless and stone like…"You don't get a discount. In fact I'm going ter charge ya fer touchin' stuff in a minute. All tha' aside did my "back room" fully satisfy ya? Will ya shut up now?"

"My dear sir, if there is a power that could shut him up…It is only known to the gods trust me," Said Ryan, Alex acted as if Ryan's words were touching.

Michael paid the bill for everything and they went out talking over the amazing prices Slim had given them and how cool it was that Michael was no doubt the Guardian. Alex was also keeping a bit more distance from Eliza after hearing that she was related to Michael. They spent the rest of the day together, got lunch and Michael got some more clothes since he hadn't exactly packed for this trip. Finally, Eliza said that Ryan and Alex should spend the next two weeks at her house since they were going to Asendor as well. So they all went back to the house and were fast friends. Alex was a total goof ball but fun and Ryan was very smart and quiet, Eliza was more talkative then ever and her parents wanted the day for them to leave to come very fast indeed.

Well in Michael's eyes, that two weeks was the fastest of his life, even though he missed Zack and Penny he was having a great time with his new friends. But now, the day had come, he was going to leave here and go to Asendor Academy and he was so restless with excitement he didn't sleep a wink the night before. They had to get up early so they could make the orientation that all first year apprentices had to have. Ryan was reading a book at one of the tables in the pub while Alex had his legs stretched across a couple bar stools with a small, army green duffel bag at his feet. Michael had all his things packed in one of his dad's old suit cases which was big enough you could fit a horse inside it. Since each semester there was seven months long he did need quite a bit stuff, even still he had Ryan put both his bags inside it as well. Bruce came over to the stair case and yelled up to Eliza. "Come on honey we need to be at the gate in twenty minutes!" he shouted.

She came rushing down the stairs with a pile of suit cases stacked at least seven feet high. She deposited these at the base of the stairs and raced back up for more. In total, she brought thirty-six cases two of which just as big as Michael's and one that made Michael laugh. It look just like a guitar case but in the shape of a battle ax! They crammed all this into Bruce's ship and took off. It only took a few minutes and they had already gone about three hundred miles, they came to the only patch of green to be seen and started circling down to the ground. They landed and Bruce grabbed each person's bag out of the storage compartment on the side of his ship and handed each to their respective owners, (Eliza's were tethered together). They hurried over to a very large stone arch way where many other people were gathered. From the looks of it there were at least a hundred other new apprentices starting their first term coming through this gate alone. There was a handsome young man with light skin, silk like hair, and pointed ears who was being given some last minute pointers from his father. A short ways over, Michael heard a young lady's name, as the lady's grandmother called after her to give her a better kiss goodbye.

"Conshen Moonsy! You get back here and give gramy a real smooch or I'll box your ears.!"

Once she gave her gramy a proper kiss she noticed that Michael had over heard her name and came over to him.

"This your first year too?" She asked. She had shoulder length black hair, and large beep blue eyes. She wore a sweet smile and was in fact quite pretty. She also had twin ninja style katanas on her back and wore old world Japanese looking clothes.

"Oh, um … Yes it is. You?"

"Yep. Me too. I am Conshen … as you heard. You are?"

"Michael— Michael Rains. Pleased to meet you. Maybe we will be in some of the same classes."

"I hope so, you seem nice. Anyway I got to go, talk to you later." She ran back over to her parents and brother to say some final good buys. Alex came over to him with a sad look on his face.

"Why didn't she say 'hi' to me? What is it about you that is so special?" Alex whined.

"I guess I really am just that awesome!" Michael said, barely keeping a straight face. The others including Bruce (who had just joined up with them from locking up his ship) all laughed heartily. Michael started looking around some more.

Michael was put at ease a bit to see that most of the new students here seemed to be quite as nervous as he was. But not every student was nervous … In fact a few were downright calm one guy seemed bored. There was a guy about Michael's age that a group of girls ran up to screaming and giggling. They called him Foeseth and he was quite a spectacle indeed. He was over nine feet tall, had wavy blond hair and looked as if he could bench press a steam engine, with arms bigger than Michael's chest, and *his* chest was huge and built. To add to this he was very handsome and … Oh yeah he also had large pure white eagle-like wings, and the tip of each feather faded into orange and yellow flames! Another guy was showing off his ability to create fire by making fire balls and juggling them. Foeseth had been watching Michael talk to Conshen and came over shortly after she left.

"Hello, I'm Foeseth," he said in a surprisingly kind voice.

"I'm Michael, nice to meet you."

"You as well. Now … I don't normally get to know people this way, but do you think you could introduce me to the young lady you were just talking to? She is a true beauty and I would fear to say something foolish on my own." Michael was taken back, he could hardly imagine this young man being afraid of anything, but then felt that he might be a good friend to have. It was also reassuring that he was willing to show his heart like that.

"Um I think I can do that, not to worry." Foeseth smiled, revealing the most perfect smile Michael had ever seen on a man!

"Thank you my friend, I hope we share the same classes! I will see you there then," he gave Michael a nod. And stepped back to join a man who could only be his father looking exactly the same just older, and a minute later Conshen came back over.

"Do you think you could introduce me to your friend there?" she asked him. Michael smiled.

"Oh, I think that may just work out pretty easily actually!" Michael said trying not to let her on to anything.

They finally came to the gate where three men were talking while their daughters and son waited to go through the gate. Two of the men were huge, one at about ten feet tall and just as wide. He had greenish-blue skin and black almost shoulder length hair. The other man was about fifteen feet tall with vivid green skin and dark green hair buzzed super short. The third man look so normal he seemed out of place in the group, He had a blue metal chest piece and a broad sword at his hip. Beside the biggest guy was a young man around Michael's age if not a little younger, he was ten foot plus and looked to have been trained from a young age based on his build and the way he carried himself. Beside him was a girl not any older but just a touch shorter, she was quite pretty for being a ten foot something green girl with dark green hair. But the one that got Michael's attention was the daughter of the normal looking man. She was by far and without question the most beautiful person Michael had ever seen. She had deep red hair that was so long that even pulled into one think braid it still nearly touching the ground. She had perfect milky white fair skin and Michael was pretty sure she actually gave off some sort of glow. As she walked toward him he found it hard to breath and his hands were getting... *Wait a second She was walking toward him!!* Michael started panicking as if she might already know what he was thinking. Then a new thought struck him…she might *actually* be able to read his mind! She *could* know what he was thinking; he had to do something she was…

"Hey! What is up with you? Didn't you hear this young gorgeous lady say "Hi" to you? Oh wait, were you fantasizing about how hot she is? You like her don't you? You little devil you," said Alex all at once with no effort at all to keep his voice down. Michael felt his checks go red but at the moment he wasn't sure if it was from embarrassment or from his sudden desire to beat the crap out of Alex. The young lady however just giggled softly and reintroduced herself…

"My name is Blaze Traigon, What is yours?" Her smile was amazing and it was only by shear will power, that he kept himself from going into another trance.

"I'm Michael, Michael Rains. Is this your first year at Asendor?"

"Yeah, I've been looking forward to this since I was four, I can't wait. But anyway it is nice to meet you, I hope we end up in the same classes! Oh and just so you know there is no reason to be embarrassed for being attracted to someone, especially not a guy as cute as you." She playfully tapped her finger on his nose and walked over to her dad to give him one final good bye. Michael meanwhile was frozen to the spot, he was certain he just felt a spark jump from her finger to his nose!…Alex howled with laughter, the gate keeper stepped forward and blew into a ram's horn he got off his belt, the mournful deep bellow caused everyone to stop at once to listen for instructions.

"Al'righ' here are the rules. No more than three at a time, for those who have never used a gate before, keep your hands at yer sides. *Do not touch the light that will be surrounding you!!* You will lose whatever ya touch it with! Try to keep yer eyes closed and if at anytime ya feel sick, disoriented, light headed, dry mouth, get a bloody nose, start violently vomiting, or you feel intense pain…there's…nothing we can do abou' it. Who's first?

Foeseth stepped forward without hesitation and right through the gate followed by several second and third year apprentices. The crowd quickly started to thin out and before he knew what was happening Eliza grabbed Michael by the arm and rushed him into the portal. The intensity of this experience is hard to describe—it felt like pins and needles on every square inch of his body, and all the while being pressed in on all sides and shocked with about a thousand stun guns! Just as soon as it started however it was over and Michael landed hard on his feet. Michael stumbled forward and ran head first into a rock...or...what felt like a rock.

"Easy does little fella, you could hurt yourself if you do *that* too much."

Michael froze out of shock if nothing else, after all, a rock just spoke to him and he was quite sure that was uncommon even for the Jemini world. He looked skyward to see what exactly spoke, what he saw, he was not ready for. It was not a rock like he thought; it was the largest person Michael had ever seen! He had to be near thirty feet tall and almost as wide, his arms were like volts wagons, his fingers were as thick as a man's leg. He had light gray skin and black hair pulled into a neat pony tail and his mouth was spread into a large smile relieving a two rows of sharp teeth.

"You don't need to be afraid of me, I'm the chief of security here at the academy, name's Pith and I dare say I was a friend of your father's. You're Tulson's boy right? You look just like him, little shorter but you have his chin. Anyway you better run you don't want to be late!"

Michael looked behind Pith and realized that what he had dismissed as an enormous mountain was actually a castle! It seemed just plain impossibly big the sides went as far east and west as your eyes could see and the taller towers vanished into the clouds! Michael looked at it with amazement for about a second until he noticed the group of people way off in the distance running for the gate which from that distance looked about the size of a peep hole on the wall that surrounded the castle. Snapping back to reality Michael ran for it pushing hard, he didn't know what would happen if he were late but he was certain he wasn't going to find out first hand. He was quite surprised by just how fast he seemed to be moving…in fact there was no way he could be moving as fast as he was. It was well over a mile just to catch up to the group that was ahead of him, yet he caught up to and passed them in less than a minute. Michael looked at the group as he passed by and caught a few surprised looks. Eliza was jumping up and down saying…

"That's my cuisine! That's my cuisine!"

Alex had the look of a proud father, and just gave him a thumbs up, while another young man—was the ten-foot-tall young man, waiting in front of him at the gate—ran up to him gave him a nod then started running faster than Michael was. Michael got the idea and started pushing harder still until he matched this guy's speed. The young man smiled and gave Michael an impressed nod then with effortless ease sped off at easily twice their present speed. Michael pushed more…This was crazy he had to be moving at well over a hundred miles an hour and it wasn't that hard. This was nothing compared to the guy he was racing though. Michael got beside him one last time and the young man just put on a crooked smile and with little visible effort he pulled away at no less than five times their new speed. At his speed it only took Michael about a minute to reach the gate which was quite a thing. The front gate was over a thousand feet high and nearly half as wide. Only one side of the gate was open so you could see that each door was a good hundred feet thick at least and constructed out of one solid piece of a bronze colored metal.

Once inside Michael was amazed once again! It was impossible to see all that was going on inside these walls at one time. There must have been millions of people walking around to different tents set up all over the courtyard! Michael was overwhelmed by the site and was starting to fear getting lost in the mass of people that was swarming every which way. Just inside the gate several hundred robots were taking suitcases from the apprentices and bring them up and into the castle. Michael just handed off his suit case and started looking at some the tents to see what they were for. Most of them were elective classes, some of the options were "Taming the Wild: A study of all creatures," "History of The Worlds," "How To Use Not Abuse Your Power," "A None Violent Solution To Violent Problems," and "Violent Solutions To All Your Problems" plus hundreds more. Michael finally looked ahead to see Ryan, Alex, Eliza, and the entire group; they were with all waiting for him. Alex started to clap and the others did too even Blaze and Foeseth as they came over to Michael.

"You ran that fast out of pure instinct! That was very impressive! I have been trained from the age of three and I am the best trained of my race, in my year, as well as son to the most powerful of my race to ever live! And I am nowhere near the natural you are! I can't wait for tomorrow when we get to see you test your present fighting ability! Eliza told us about your martial arts and I for one would love to see it!" Foeseth said giving him a pat on the back. He then nodded to the group and headed over to the tent marked "Killing Stuff Made Easy." Eliza then came over and gave Michael a book named *"The First Year Apprentice's Guide To Life At Asendor"* by Master Miff Crossfoot. The first page read, *"The first thing you must do is get signed in, then pick four electives, there are twenty-nine thousand seven hundred and eighty-five to choose from. (See the following three hundred thirty-three pages)."*

So Michael followed the group to the sign in table while Michael realized that he had passed this group when they were at least a few *miles* from the gate! How did they get here before him? Michael just couldn't imagine how, so he just had to ask…

"Okay, wait just a minute. How did you guys get here before me...?"

"Yeah, you guys even beat me, and I was running at six hundred miles an hour at least!" added the guy Michael had raced to the gate. Alex smiled a bit and swelled his chest as if very proud of himself as he answered, "I just can't help but compete with that kind of thing, I was not going to be beaten to the gate so I told everyone to hold someone else's hand and I teleported the whole group here."

"Well, I think that counts as cheating," said Michael in a mock indignant tone. The group all laughed and moved up the line for the "Sign In and Assessment" tent. From that point Michael could finally see inside the enclosed tent. He could make out the less than inconspicuous form of Warbick sitting behind a folding table the size of a truck. In all the excitement of the day he had almost forgotten about his calling to the most important job a person could have, or his being given a book that would lead him to a sword of untold power. Just seeing Warbick again however brought all these words right back. He was going to be made into a warrior and he was for the first time actually excited about his soon to be job. He was sure it would be considered the absolute greatest of honors by most, and plus it might even be fun from time to time!

Before he knew it, he was the next one in line to go into the tent. All apprentices went in one at a time. Eliza had just gone in and he was starting to wonder just what happened in there. They closed the flap to the tent when each person went in.

"Next apprentice please," said a ten foot tall panther-faced man with a beefy build. Michael walked in (again somewhat nervous) and stood in a square that was obviously where he was meant to stand. After a moment Warbick looked up from his paper and smiled at once.

"Well I don't suppose I need to ask *your* name do I? Well news travels fast around here...In fact (just as advice) I find that if you don't want people around here to know something then don't tell anyone. Anyway your little race here is already popular news. Quite impressive though not really surprising, for one thing your mother was a very fast runner. Plus both of your parents were extremely gifted so it is no surprise that you would be too. I would say that you are most likely full of surprises, of which you have no idea! Now please stand still a moment while I read your power level—that is one of my powers in case you wondered."

So Michael stood very still for a minute while Warbick stared at him with an intensity that made Michael more than a little uncomfortable. After another minute Warbick made a puzzled face and took a note all the while muttering in what Michael thought sounded an almost worried voice.

"So…? What level am I? Is…Is something wrong or…"

"I have to admit, when I said that I was sure you would be full of surprises I didn't expect one immediately or one like this! You should know that there has been only a few dozen people that I could not read, and easily. Even when I first came here and had very little control as compared to now, I could read Dojee's level and tell you all of his abilities without effort. But you!…You I can't read at all, not even a little bit. I can tell you have powers (all Jemini have an aura around them and I can see it) but I have no clue what powers you have. Not being able to read you though, means you either have one of the highest level caps of anyone I have ever met or you have no level cap at all…Meaning you may have near limitless potential! Lets test you some more though so we can have some idea of what we are dealing with here."

So Michael was taken out the back of the tent to a different tent you could not see from the front. The panther man lead him and set out to test him with a bunch of machines. One he had to punch, another he had to push against, yet another he had to pull on a bar. Then they tested the strength in his legs, after which the Panther faced Master (whom Michael had finally learned was named Zezz) took him to what seemed like a very normal treadmill. They started him at speed five and went up until Michael told Zezz he could go no faster. Two hours later the tests were done and Michael felt quite good about his evaluation. He had no idea what any of it meant…But he thought it sounded good, the list that read—

Super Strength Level (approx.): 45
Super Speed Level (approx.): 29
Advanced Endurance Level (approx.): 50
(Masters please note no other powers could be found but are believed to exist, use caution in training)

This last part did make Michael think though, he understood that his parents were both powerful and that usually goes down through to the kids. That being so, he could hardly imagine what if anything he could be able to do, that any of these masters would need to be careful of. This and a hundred other things were on his mind as he headed toward the front door to the castle. These doors were at least eight hundred feet tall and about half as wide at the bottom, they were at least twelve feet thick as well. A few hundred feet above the doors was a huge flag pole baring a coat of arms which was two dragons wrapped around a castle tower blowing fire at each other. He made his way inside to find Eliza, Alex, Ryan, and Blaze waiting for him with two other people. The one was the young man he raced to the gate and the other was the tall green skinned girl who was in front of him at the gate.

"Hi Michael, this is Ben and Rozea. They are really cool, I can't believe that Master Warbick couldn't read your power cap or present level! That is so cool, it hasn't happened to him for quite a long time, you must be super powerful!"

"Yeah or I don't have any powers at all…Wait how did you know that?" Michael suggested.

"News travels fast around here. And what do you mean you might not have powers?"

"It has to be possible that I have no level because I am not who everyone thinks I am."

Blaze giggled a bit, then realizing that Michael was being serious and made a stern face.

"You need to stop selling yourself short! It makes you less cute, plus you know that you have powers just as well as I do. How many people do you know that can normally run at a hundred plus miles an hour!"

She may well have kept on talking but as far as Michael knew she hadn't said a thing since the words "less cute." His heart was beating so fast he was afraid they could hear it. She thought he was cute! Now…he may have been eighteen and a star athlete at school, but somehow he had managed to go his whole life without so much as a wink from a girl. So dealing with a beautiful young woman saying he was cute was more than what he was prepared for.

The group followed the mass of apprentices into the entrance hall…there was no word that could describe the place but amazing! The entrance hall had black, gray, and white marble floors, while the ceilings were covered by murals. There were cases filled with the armor and pictures of former Grand Masters, also large statues of gold, marble, and even gems were all over the room. One statue caught Michael's attention the second he looked in its direction; it was Ackatoth holding a sword over his head. The statue stood nine feet tall and was made of pure sapphire (according to a small plaque on it's base).

"Look that's Ackatoth! Amazing to think that his very hands carved that stone…And also built this castle for that matter! I still think it is cooler that you have his book and can read it!" Squeaked Eliza. Ben perked up and hurried over to Michael's side with an excited smile.

"You have "The Book Of Ackatoth"? And you can read it? That is amazing but you must take care who hears that. Because there are more than a few people that would *kill* to get it! You got that from Slim right?..."

"Yeah, how did you...?"

"Because my dad is the one who found it and gave it to him. Slim is an oracle which just means he knows things before they happen. He said he would find the heir in three-hundred and fifty-two years. So that came true, I have heard that story many times and knew it was about time. I always thought you would be a Clayic though..." Michael just made a face to show that he had no idea what a *Clayic* was.

"Oh, right Eliza said you are new to all of this. I am a Clayic, so is Rozea, basically if you ever see a really big person with green, blue or gray skin they're a Clayic."

Michael thought about what Ben had told him as they made their way into the dining hall. He had never told Eliza or Alex and Ryan that people had tried to kill him...Then something hit him that he had forgotten completely until just then. The day when he was chased from the bank...that man...the one that told him "...*something was going to happen to him, some great, and something terrible.*" He must have been from *this* world...come to think on it, his bank teller somehow knew he had martial art training and that his dad was a twenty plus year police officer without ever having seen him before! Was she from here too? On top of that Penny had on a few cases seemed to know exactly what he or her brother was thinking!

She could have had powers without knowing it! Had there been people from this world around him his whole life? His head was spinning as he sat down at a table across from a Master with a name tag that read Freyja. She was pretty, but was definitely strong—for a woman at least. She had long golden hair and heavy brown leather armor. Eliza and Blaze were talking like long time friends while sitting down on Michael's left while Ryan and Ben talked swords, Rozea just sat there staring at Ben longingly. Michael was looking around the room. This room, just like the entrance hall, was covered in black, gray, and white marble. There were pictures all over some normal in size and some the size of apartment buildings! One painting was of a silly looking man. He had white cottony hair coming out from under a pointy hat just like a garden gnome. He also had a large smile exposing a single, slightly crooked tooth, which was off-center just to the left. His name read Idoe Farsh across a golden plate at the bottom. Michael at once recognized him as the little man who floated passed him and Warbick back on Percelia.

Michael had only just sat down and was pouring himself some ice tea, when everything went strange … like a dream. Everything had a grayness to it and there was a shimmer in the air like a pool of water. He was looking at the same room but somehow he knew it was a different time, many years before. He could see much younger apprentices—somewhere between ten and fifteen. Pith was not there nor was his huge table that was set off to the side. At the far end of the hall was a podium behind which stood a cat faced man like Zezz but this man looked like a cheetah. He wore a sword across his back and a sleeveless red and black martial art gi. He was about to start speaking what seemed like grave news when someone touched his hand. Two things happened very fast, he had just enough time to see that Freyja had tried to shake him out of his stupor. And second, the instant her hand touched his they were both sent flying through the air across the room. She being closer to a wall just flew strait into it and fell to the floor. Michael however was thrown back through five rows of heavy wood tables and landed in a heap more than a hundred feet away unconscious.

CHAPTER SIX

Michael woke with a start in what must have been the medical ward of the castle. His mom having been a nurse he was quite familiar with hospitals, and for that reason he didn't like them much. At the moment he felt like he had been kicked in the chest by Pith. He wasn't awake more than ten seconds before a little old man came in to the room wearing a white coat and *very* thick glasses.

"Now, now young man you've had a bit of a go of it, now you lay down. Though it is good to see that you woke up so fast, I think you'll be alright. And don't you worry your head about Mistress Freyja she is a tough lass, she only has two broken bones, nothing bad." The old doctor's voice was gentle and kind and but a little out of touch as if his mind was not quite all there. Michael decided he must just be *really* old ... even by this world's standards.

Michael hated the idea of being responsible for hurting a Master on his first day ... in his first three hours ... before his first meal ... before having a single class. He didn't sleep well and spent most of the time just laying there wondering what happened to cause such destruction. He thought on it for a while until he remembered the Master's note on his test scores telling them to use caution. Could this be what they meant? For that matter what was "this"? How could touching someone do something like that? Michael's mind was still racing when Warbick came into the ward.

"Get dressed quickly, I need to get you to Dojee, he has some questions for you."

"Isn't he the Grand Master ...?"

"Yes and we don't have time now for questions, you need to tell him what happened as far as you know and ask questions only if he says you can." Warbick seemed very worried and Michael was quite sure he should be too. Michael dressed as fast as his sore back would allow, and they were off. Michael was certain he was going to get kicked out for hurting a master, or maybe worse…an image of pith holding a gigantic paddle board tapping the palm of his other hand waiting for him to come to a podium that looked a lot like a chopping block, only for his butt, and the entire academy sitting in bleachers watching and booing him while Blaze made out with Foeseth, Alex was patting Eliza's pregnant belly as Bruce was loading a giant shotgun…

"Okay enough of that!" Michael told himself aloud.

"What was that?" asked Warbick in a wry tone.

"Oh, nothing, just thinking out loud," Michael said quickly.

"That can be dangerous, now please keep up". Michael knew something was wrong, Warbick was never this grumpy normally. Michael considered the possibility that Warbick and Freyja could be good friends, or for that matter a couple. And now he didn't much like Michael for hurting her. Anyway, it became clear why Warbick wanted to hurry when an hour had passed and they still hadn't gotten to Dojee's office.

"Wow! Dojee must like his exercise! Isn't there a better way to get there?"

"There are faster ways but as a first year apprentice you aren't allowed to use them. That may change soon but…" He trailed off as if he had said too much.

They kept walking through the castle down a stair case around a corridor and down another stair case. They finally came to a stair case at least a mile under the school and there was a metal plate above the archway to it that read—"NO APPRENTICES BEYOND THIS POINT WITHOUT AN ESCORT!!"

"Listen to me very carefully, it is going to take us a very long time to reach the bottom of this case but when we do it will lead into The Hall of Shadows. *Do not* speak at all once we pass the red stare near the bottom and while we walk through the hall keep pace with me and above all *do not look up*, understood?"

"I suppose there is still no time for questions?" Michael asked. Warbick just smiled lightly and started down the steps. Michael followed close behind him. It took just as long as Warbick promised, and Michael was preparing his formal complaint as a paying student having to walk ten miles or whatever just to get to an office! He was distracted from this line of thought when a bright red step came into view. Michael took a deep breath afraid to even breathe too much. Not a minute later the stairs opened up into a hall so big it took him by surprise. There were pillars hundreds of feet wide and way too tall to see the top of. He assumed anyway because he kept his eyes glued to Warbick's heels. They moved very quickly through the room and through a set of double doors just as large as the hall, once through, the doors slammed shut with a thunderous boom.

"At last I can breathe again!" said Warbick, sighing deeply. Michael thought Warbick had made a mistake; this room looked far more dangerous than the last. The room in front of them was a huge cavern carved out of raw rock, they stood on a large ledge over hanging a gigantic pool of lava! Strait ahead of them was a very big rope bridge; on either side of this bridge were two other ledges much larger than the one they were on. Lying on each ledge were dragons! One was about seventy-feet tall, on all fours, and the other was over three-hundred-feet tall but wore a dopy look on its face. Warbick turned to see that Michael had not moved since the doors shut and smiled.

"You don't have to be afraid, they won't hurt you if you're with me, they are told who can come through here," assured Warbick.

"They can understand who is who?" Michael asked, cautiously.

"Well I can't speak for him but I understand quite well, you should hurry now, Dojee is waiting," said the smaller dragon. Michael was taken aback.

"So dragons can talk? Now that I didn't see coming," Michael replied shyly.

"Well my breed can, big ones like Jake here can't but he was dropped on his head as a baby so he is a bit...special...now. So he wouldn't talk much anyway, but that also made him more docile than what he would have been normally. Now hurry along! Go on!" Answered the dragon.

"Teekin I need to get to my dorm wing as I am sure by this time they have torn the place apart. Could you make sure Jake doesn't lick Michael into the lava?" Warbick did not hide the chuckle in his voice.

"Yes, yes. Of course my friend...You go, young man!" Teekin said sounding impatient.

Michael felt strongly that it was a bad idea to let a dragon get angry at you, so he started across the bridge at a decent pace. Half way across the bridge he saw way down near the lava surface was a large stone slab where at that moment there was as Master and a few dozen apprentices who all looked like ants from that distance. Once across he knocked on the double doors to Dojee's office which opened suddenly.

Michael had not put too much thought into what Dojee was going to ask him but spent more time forming questions in his mind, his office though took his attention away from even that. There were book shelves covered with everything but books, instead there were little statutes of gold and stone, many different instruments Michael was quite sure he didn't want to even know what they were used for. There was a display with many different kinds of knives and swords and other various sharp items on the right side of the room and a large map on the other. The room was a large dome with a couple dozen floors; the upper floors were cover with book shelves that actually had books on them as well as other odd end items where ever they could fit. At the back of the office was a big red wood desk with an old looking lamp, and a pile of papers three feet high. To the left of the desk was a door with a sign:

Dojee Shinyo—Grand Master and Leader of the Guardian Search Comity

—Personal Quarters"

The door opened, and a tall man with a long ponytail, a neat goatee, and a streak of silver running through his otherwise black hair came out. He wore a samurai rob of blue and white and had a katana on his side. He looked at Michael and froze for a moment, and then he spoke with a smile.

"You were a bit younger when I saw you last. I forgot just how long you were gone really. Would you like to sit?" Dojee motioned toward a chair in front of his desk and took at sit. Michael sat and stayed quiet for near a minute as Dojee looked at him intently. After a moment's consideration Michael felt there was no reason to not ask a question if Dojee wasn't going to, so he spoke up.

"Okay so what happened to Freyja and I, and why is it that I was thrown through a bunch of thick tables and am already better and Freyja has broken bones?" Michael blurted. Dojee smiled slightly.

"You are right to the point, aren't you? Yes, it is quite a thing you did, hurting an Asguardian goddess! I mean she is not easily hurt by anyone. To answer your question, I have an idea, but it is a bit premature at the moment. So from your end I must know exactly what you saw in your vision and what you felt when Freyja touched you."

"Should I just assume everyone can read my mind around here?" Michael smirked.

"Yes."

"Oh ... I ... I was joking."

"I know ... I can read your mind. Now, your vision.

"Okay well, I sat down for lunch. Then out of nowhere I felt like I was here but a long time ago. The dinning hall was different,

Pith was not here, and the Grand Master was like master Zezz but cheetah like. He was about to start speaking and looked very grim, that's it, Freyja touched me just then." Dojee thought for a moment then snapped his fingers.

"I have an idea come over here with me please." Dojee walked over to one of the random looking book shelves and grabbed a small statue of a gryphon and pulled on it. The shelf spun around to reveal a super computer and some other machines connected to it. Dojee punched some keys and the screen came to life and a very normal looking guy stepped in front of the screen.

"Hello. How can I help you today Dojee?"

"Brains, I'm going to be sending you a blood test. I want an analysis right away, run a trace for any possible oddities and energy out put as well."

"Right, can do. Give me a few minutes," answered the man. Dojee had Michael put his finger in a machine that pricked it and collected blood … It didn't work. They tried a bigger needle that broke on the first try! Brains suggested a skin sample. So Dojee tried to scrape some dead skin off Michael's hand and immediately broke the tool he was using. Brains finally though of a saliva test, so Dojee got a cotton swab for Michael to put in his mouth and saturate once soaked, they stuck it in a machine. Dojee pushed a button, and the piece was on the other side of the screen in a second. Brains took the swab with some tweezers and put it in the machine behind him. A few minutes passed and Brains came back to the screen with a look of sheer awe.

"Dojee, I have never in my life seen such a thing! He is generating more than nine million trillion trillion watts per second! That is a couple hundred times the amount our sun generates! Also he has an anari. That is why you couldn't pierce his skin. His dad had one … I never thought of it. But there has never been a record of a person with an anari ever having a child. This means Michael was born with his—that makes him a new race, a being born with a symbiont! All his children will be born with one as well, and in fact as they have children his new race will spread…"

"I believe you may need to slow down with that, it is quite neat, but *who* he is far more important than *what* he is. What do you think could have caused that kind of a discharge of energy?" Dojee said changing the topic.

"Sorry, didn't mean to make you feel weird Michael. As far as what caused the discharge there is only one option that wouldn't have killed them both. No doubt at this point, he just about has to be the heir of Ackatoth. We need to find that book so we can prove it." Brains seemed grim. Michael thought about it quickly and decided that there was no way they weren't talking about the book sitting in the big suit case in his room.

"Um, just so you know. I have the book of Ackatoth…" Dojee and Brains just gaped at him for a second, so he just explained more.

"Yeah, I was in Slim's shop and it was in the back room he 'didn't have' in plain sight. I read it—it said that I am the guardian so I needed to stop trying to run away from it."

Dojee started smiling as did Brains. Dojee said goodbye to Brains and turned off the computer. They went back to Dojee's desk and sat down again, Michael had a million questions at this point and was about to burst.

"You are quite something I must say! You are a very special person with an even more special ability. When Freyja touched you, you absorbed large amount of her power. Now your base power as best as we are able to see is the ability to generate, control, and absorb energy. Now many people can generate energy blasts that is among the most common of powers. Only one person however has ever been recorded to be able to generate any form of energy they wanted and that was Ackatoth himself. He found that he could use this ability to absorb and copy the energy that all Jemini generate in their bodies naturally. This allowed him to copy people's powers without hurting them. Now *that* is also only true for him and one other, and quite a useful tool, I dare say I could use that! But what you did—purely out of lack of control, which will come in time—was you absorbed some of her power, concentrated it, copied it, then shot back what you didn't need. That is what shot you two across the room. Because there has been no one in thirty-five thousand years to have this power we have little to nothing to go on as far as how long you gain these for. They may be permanent and they may not. Also it is quite evident that it isn't something you get to control by sheer instinct. So we will train you to use this, but we will need to take great care. There was just too much energy there to absorb for your first go, we will need to find someone else for you to practice with, a friend maybe…"

"Alex might like that, plus teleporting might be fun." Dojee laughed lightly.

"My dear boy, Alex is the most powerful apprentice we have had here since Odin, Zeus, and Poseidon…Over one hundred levels above me! Michael could hardly believe that nut ball could be that powerful. It seemed like this was some kind of joke.

"I'm not joking…and I'm sorry for reading your mind so much, you just think so loudly I can't help it. Yes, all of your friends in fact are far too powerful; as a matter of fact Eliza is the only one of your friends that isn't more powerful than Freyja! This is going to be hard actually, but rest assured you will be my top priority this week. If you can't live as a person then how will you live as a warrior? So you will receive special training from myself whenever possible or Master Warbick. Until such time though you must refrain from touching anyone, if you touch the wrong person it could kill you…and them. You might even hurt or kill those around you."

"Okay, that's wonderful news. Now instead of being the guy people hate because he's good at everything. I get to be the guy who gets avoided so I don't kill them! If you ask me that is a step backwards, I mean there was even a girl that I was into, but that's dead now. I could just see her asking me for a kiss and I have to say *Oh, I'm sorry, but your face might explode!*"

"Like I said, it won't be long, here take these gloves, they will keep you from further unpleasant encounters … and they just so happen to be quite stylish!" Dojee smiled at his own joke.

"Okay, that should help some … I guess. Now for the next part of what Brains said, what is an anari and how was I born with one?" Michael was pretty sure he didn't want to know the answer but at the same time he needed to.

"Well that is actually something you are sure to be happy about. An anari is a blob-type creature that has a very interesting ability. They can seep into any porous surface and stay there as long as they want … within reason. However an anari needs a host to survive more than a few years. Not sure why that is, I'm not really a wild life expert but that isn't important anyway. What is important is that you know what they can do—anari give their hosts a large amount of perks. For one, anari and all blobs are basically large slabs of solid muscle so they give their hosts at least a two hundred percent boost in strength. To go along with that anari can breathe under water so their hosts can too. Anari have night and heat vision and thus so does their host. And the host's sense of smell, hearing, and even taste are improved ten fold. The most useful thing though is that once they are in the host they can expand back out of the pours of the skin to form either a protective shell or to form weapons. You can even form testicles up to a certain length, depending on the size of your anari. The way this works is that anari have the ability to change their density at will. One moment they can be as stretchy as any kind of rubber you know of, to as hard as diamond and as strong as titanium! Now as to how you have one, your parents both had anari—your mother had a pink anari, and your father had a black anari and thus was a force not to be reckoned with. There are many types, green, blue, red, orange, purple, gray, silver, gold, pink, yellow, white, and black. All of these types have a few unique traits, except for black which has all the traits just at a slightly higher level in each case. This is because the black type was engineered as a hybrid of all the types and then enhanced. So take all the benefits I mentioned and multiply them by five. Anyway pink are all but immune to fire and the lightest type out of all of them. Yellow and orange are completely unharmed by heat of any kind—you could swim in lava with one of them. Green are immune to acid and blue allow you to breathe under water at depths far lower than the others. Red can't be harmed by energy blasts and gray allow you to take the color of your surroundings like a chameleon. Silver provide the best endurance and gold the greatest strength. White makes you immune to arctic temperatures and can't be burned by lasers. Oh and purples have wings and are the second strongest. So to be clear a black can do all of those things and more powerfully as well…"

"Why would anyone pick anything but a black one then?" asked Michael.

"Oh, because most *kings* don't see enough gold in their lifetime to buy one! Now it was thought that those who get anari can't have children because none ever have before, however it would appear as though your parents proved that wrong. So the anari that they had—being fused to and throughout their entire central nervous system and so on—was now a part of them as much as their liver or heart, thus they had anari DNA mixed in with their own. You thus have an anari from birth…and it would seem without the negative side effects…"

"Like what? The way you say it, these things sound amazing! Why wouldn't everyone have one?"

"Two main reasons, first of all as I stated they are expensive. Even the gray ones—being the least expensive type—are still a few thousand platinum! Second they fuse to your spinal cord and brain stem, then they continue on down through your body until they have grafted themselves into every single nerve in your body and deep into your bone marrow. This is so invasive and painful that one out of three people die before the fusion is complete. Plus not that it is quite so extreme as dying, but anari are heavy, to give you an idea pink are the smallest and lightest breed. They average around nine hundred pounds, so the black ones being more than ten times the size can cause a problem as they can be over nine thousand pounds. Now what we need to do with this is find a friend that can help you learn to use it better, but it seems as though your body has learned to use its anari instinctively so we must see if you can get more use out of it, or if it will just remain a reflex your body uses to protect itself."

"So when will all of this special training take place?" Michael felt suddenly that he might not be ready for such training.

"Honestly you need to relax young man. I have been teaching for quite a long time now, I think I know better than to push someone beyond what they can handle. And I know you probably want me to stop reading your mind but you are too tense. The more anxious you are, the easier it is to read your mind, something to be aware of. Your training will begin tomorrow afternoon, here is a pass that will allow you to use the high speed transport system to get to my office or anywhere else you want in the castle … that isn't off limits to all apprentices of course. Now since you have never used that before I will have someone show you how to get to breakfast."

"Breakfast, huh? What day is it anyway? Have I missed many classes?"

"What? My boy, you were only knocked out for … Oh let's see … About three hours. You will be escorted to your room tonight. I mean … you will need help to use it tomorrow to get to your first breakfast. Unless you would like to walk, of course, I could understand if you would like to spend a little time getting to know Ms. Traigon." Michael went every shade of red.

"How did you know that she was the girl I was talking about, I wasn't thinking of her?"

"Hmm…One does not need to read minds to see what is right in front of them. She is a remarkable beauty, and you wear your heart on your sleeves…"

"Alex told you right?"

"Yep."

"Everyone knows then?"

"And their mothers as well I'm afraid. It seems Alex's way of keeping a secret isn't so much keeping it—as it is blurting it to every living and non-living thing he sees. Dojee had a large grin. Michael liked Dojee, there was something familiar about his humor. They sat in quiet for a moment and something dawned on Michael that was kind of irritating to him. After all of that Dojee didn't even say a word about Michael's vision!

"Hold on a minute here! What about the vision I saw? You should know that wasn't the first time I had one either. What are they?" Michael said, all at once. Dojee shook his head slightly.

"That is hard to say. The grand master you mentioned was Master Covoe Cree—he was the very first grand master appointed by Ackatoth himself. The scene you described is actually quite well known. Covoe was about to announce the start of the Great War. The apprentices were all very young, yes?"

"Yeah, ten to mid or late teens."

"Yes, that would be right. Back then this was a school not an academy. The academy was somewhere else; no one alive knows where that was. The announcement that Covoe was about to give was that the war had reached the academy already and would be there soon and with no time to evacuate the children had to fight…Very sad. The old academy was all but destroyed and its remains lost to time. Ackatoth fixed this castle back to what it was and then some upon the end of the war, making it two hundred times bigger. No one knows why he made it so large but for the residing grand master, but let's just put it like this. This castle is the *last* place anyone wants to attack now!"

"Well it seems you know a lot about this. What is so hard to say about my seeing it?"

"Ha! You don't have the proper understanding of time yet my very young friend. No one has looked upon that scene (except in books) in over fifteen thousand years! I haven't the foggiest how you seen it, unless you've been studying our ancient history back on earth! ..."

"It felt like I was within someone else's memory," informed Michael, unsure if this would help. Dojee's countenance changed the instant he said it.

"Are you sure that is how you remember it? You distinctly felt like you were in someone else's mind?"

"Yeah ... Why ... is that bad?" Dojee didn't answer. He seemed suddenly distracted and deep in thought.

"Hey! You need to tell me what this is about!" Dojee snapped out of his daze and looked at Michael with a disappointed face.

"Michael, there are many things I need to do, most of which you know nothing about, and none of which do I need told by you! Remember your place young one! I have only your best interests in mind. As far as your seeing someone else's memory, I will need time to look into it and that is going to have to be enough for now.

Dojee pushed a button on his desk and a moment later the front door opened and a man came in. He was just a little over four feet tall and nearly as wide, he wore a heavy leather chest piece and had a short sword on his waist. His arms were muscly and hairy, he had thick black braids both in his beard and his hair which were so long they nearly touched the ground.

"Kujex, thank you for coming so quickly." Said Dojee.

"Not a problem, you come with me young one." Dojee nodded for Michael to go with him. So Michael got up and followed Kujex out of the office, Kujex did not go across the bridge between Teekin and Jake but instead went to the right to set of stairs that Michael had not seen before. They wrapped around went down some then went up, curving slightly to the right. After a long time of climbing they finally came to a door, Kujex opened it and Michael found himself in the strangest room he had ever seen. It was a huge room, hundreds of feet wide and tall, along each wall there were a bunch of clear tubes of different sizes. People would walk into one, push a button then shoot off up the tube and out of sight. Kujex walked straight to an empty tube and pushed a button to reveal a panel covered in millions of buttons some barely larger than the tip of a pen and a few the size of Michael's fist. Kujex found the one labeled Men East Wing #120047 and pushed it. The door shut tight and without warning, the floor that they were standing on shot upward at an intense speed. What was really something was that he was no longer standing on the floor and neither was Kujex, they were floating above it. They went down, left, right, up, zigzag, and even a few, seemingly unnecessary, quark screws. More suddenly than it taking off it stopped and the door slid open to show that they were on one of the higher floors in the castle. Just to their right was a magnificent staircase of marble and slate with a deep-red carpet with gold trim that ran down the middle. The walls were covered by warm mahogany and the hall in front of him seemed very welcoming.

"All right you're in room number two zero four. Just go down this hall and through the first set of double doors to your left. Your room should be near the end of the hall, not sure which side—you can figure that out, right?" asked Kujex

"Ah, yeah…I think I can manage—thanks," Kujex seemed to be feeling awkward about something, as if he wanted to say something but wasn't sure how.

"Is there anything else Master Kujex?"

"Oh, well…I…You know…er, I'm glad to have met you…and all…you seem like a…good…um…kid and so on…er…your parents were…good folks…I…suppose…you don't look too unlike your father…somewhat…anyway…I guess...Um...Okay then." Without another word, he went down the stairs and out of sight muttering angrily.

"Wow! That was awkward! You sure do know how to make odd impressions on people don't you?" Michael turned to see Alex standing in front of his whole group of friends—even Foeseth was there to wish him well. They all wanted to know what happened and give him some encouragement.

"Never seen anything like that in all my life! You should have been ripped in half by tables that thick! I would have died if it happened to me—that is a certainty! I only hope I get to fight beside you some day," Foeseth boomed.

"Yeah, you are quite the surprise artist aren't you?" Ben added.

"My father would have been impressed by that, and he has seen just about all there is to see!" squeaked Rozea.

"Yeah, you are kind of a freak, aren't ya?" Chimed Alex, Michael just laughed.

"So what happened? Do they know what caused the blast? Or how you are okay but Mistress Freyja isn't? Did they say how long she would take to get better? What were you looking at when she touched you? Were you in the middle of a vision? Do you get visions a lot? Well...why aren't you saying anything?" asked Eliza in her usual ten words a second talking pace.

Michael proceeded to find a chair in the lounge at the end of the hall so he could tell them the whole story. He told them about the trip to the office and the hall of shadows and what Warbick told him about it, then about the dragons. He then finally told them all that had been said by Dojee and Brains. After he was done speaking, the group was silent for a moment. It was late now and everyone else had gone to bed. Much of the castle was dark, and torches were now lit along the hallway. Michael looked down the long hallway. It was so weird to tell people those things about himself, having alien creatures born into him as a part of his anatomy and so on—it was all still sinking in. Blaze broke the silence at last as she stood up and stretched.

"Well, I for one am honored that you would share all that with us, it shows a great deal of trust. I believe I can speak for all of us when I say we will not betray that trust! I say we are all now bound together by you, the heir of Ackatoth after all! I feel something amazing is going to happen!" Michael did not respond to Blaze, he was at that moment looking strait past her head at something that had appeared at the end of the hall. It brought back to mind something that had been predicted a ways back, while walking to the bank...that crazy guy...

"Beware the shadowy figure for he means to destroy you..." He couldn't remember the rest. But sure enough there at the end of the hall, was a "shadowy figure" if ever there was one. It definitely had legs but otherwise had no distinguishing marks of any kind. It just stood there warring a dark flowing cape staring down the hall right at him. At last someone shook him by his shoulders...

"Where do you go man? Your woman just gave some heart stirring dialog and you missed it!" Alex spat seeming quite put out.

"Why are you so mad about that?" Blaze asked him while her cheeks went beat red.

"Well I can't pick on him about getting all misty and awkward if he doesn't hear you say stuff like that now can I"

"What *were* you looking at?" Ryan asked trying to change the subject.

"I don't know just yet, but I think it might be wise if we get to bed now."

"Well, you heard him, our captain said to bed!" Foeseth commanded. They all said good night and went to their rooms. Michael liked his room; it had a window overlooking the front courtyard a thousand feet below. There were warm chairs and a roaring fire place. It wasn't until now standing in the light of the fire that he realized just how cold it had gotten in the castle. Michael decided his new bed looked too warm and inviting to wait anymore, he would look around his room more in the morning. He got undressed and climbed into bed. The room started to spin into a swirling pool of dreams as his mind turned once again to his dad and Zack and Penny. If only he could have them here to share in all of this too. Someday they would be here. He knew it, but somehow he felt they were better off where they were for now.

CHAPTER SEVEN

The next morning came way too soon and Michael and was woken by Alex jumping up and down on his bed. Somehow this didn't surprise Michael though, as a matter of fact Michael felt that this wouldn't be the last time Alex would wake him up either. Alex was so exited he kept bouncing around the room.

"I love this place, did you know that there are 3,967 different places that apprentices aren't suppose to go on the first fifty-eight floors of this wing alone?! I was only able to sneak around a few of them last night. There are some weird things in this castle! I had a conversation with a statue, had a mother gryphon let me play with her cubs, and I even got to spend some time with a strange shadowy figure! He was actually "What do you mean a shadowy figure? Why would you even say it like that? Did he ask you about me?"

"Whoa! Dude get over yourself man, we only talked about you for like a half hour at most…maybe longer, I don't remember…Anyway he is a nice guy, just misunderstood. I get him though; I think that is why he didn't try to kill me for looking at him. Anyway we need to get to breakfast." Michael wanted to talk more about this *guy* he spoke to, but the second Michael had finished putting on his shoes Alex teleported them both to the great hall and hurried inside the dining hall.

Michael and Alex found seats quickly; Alex sat beside Eliza and Michael beside Foeseth. The breakfast was amazing; there were hundreds of plates of every kind of food you could think of. Piles of bacon, sausages, and ham, platters of pancakes and French toast, as well as large vessels of oatmeal and waffles. There were plates of fresh fruit and pitchers of milk and all kinds of juices, as well as coffee and tea of a hundred different varieties. To add to it there were hundreds of small robots flying about with trays of food on their heads. They all ate heartily and enjoyed good conversation, Ben and Ryan were talking about their favorite arena fighters, while Rozea just starred at Ben and poured syrup on her lap. Eliza was talking to Alex who looked quite impressed by just how many words she managed to spit out in just a few seconds. Blaze was studying in a book called *How To Survive A Werewolf Attack* while Michael and Foeseth talked about what they might be doing that day…

"I know that day one is when they test your present fighting ability, but I don't know how." Foeseth explained.

"I just hope they don't ask me to do something crazy, like wrestle a dragon or worse."

"I don't know the whole story but I know that someone here did fight a dragon whiled at this school." Foeseth seemed almost worried. Michael had a vision of each apprentice one by one having to stand on a rock just big enough for one foot surrounded by lava, while blindfolded— fighting Jake and Teekin with a stick! This pleasant picture was still on his mind as they made their way out of the castle and onto the grounds. There was a large group moving toward two large rings of sand. A master was waiting for the group standing with his arms behind him. Michael could tell this man was a hardened warrior. He was wearing full body armor, had a patch over his left eye and scars covered his face. He had at his side a finely crafted sword that shown brightly in the morning sun. A light dusting of frost on the ground spoke of the approaching winter. Eliza had read that winter on this planet lasts around seven to nine months but sometimes it would go for even longer. The group came to a halt just beside the rings of sand as the master spoke up.

"This is 'Fighting Assessment' I am Master Ortaiga. I will be determining just how good you are at fighting and where you need improvement. You will each step into a ring one by one and spare with a sparing bot. You will each start with a sparing bot set according to your power level. Michael you will go last because we need to do something different for you, as you seem to have no level. Everyone get in line we go alphabetical by first or last name depending on what you gave us." Everyone started getting in line at their appropriate place. Alex was quite pleased being near the front of the line. "Boy would I hate to be near the back!" Alex said aloud, "all that waiting, worrying about how you're going to measure up to all those who went before you! I mean what torture! Could you imagine...Oh wait didn't he say you were going last? Hmm...Well...Good luck with that man."

Alex teleported to his place in line looking sheepish. Michael felt *loads* better now. He sat down in the grass, Ryan, Rozea, Eliza, and Foeseth all sat by him until they had to go up Ben stayed in line because he was so close to the front.

"First up Able Minsoo," Master Ortaiga called. A large young looking man, who's at least twelve-feet tall, stepped up to the first ring. Several manikin-like robots walked out of a shed at the edge of the courtyard to the rings. Three stepped into the ring with Able and Ortaiga went over to them and opened a panel on their backs and looked at a clip board then made the necessary adjustments. A moment later Able and the bots were fighting. It was quickly obvious that Able was no chump! In fact his style was very similar to Muay Thai, and he had his bots in a heap in only a few minutes. Several went up and most did at least somewhat well, however there were plenty that did not do so great. One stabbed himself in the leg with his own sword, and another fainted right before getting punched a half-dozen times by his bot before Master Ortaiga could turn it off.

Alex went up and proved to be better then anyone who had gone up yet. He was fast, agile, and strong, he had ten bots because his level was so high, and each one was set on its highest difficulty. Even still they stood no chance and were destroyed in no time. There were so many apprentices it became easy to spot a good fighter from a bad one. Michael also felt much better about going last now because he used this time to see what the others did and learned from it. Ben went up and proved to be even better at fighting than Alex, being so fast he also had the new best time, Rozea cheered. Blaze went up shortly there after and was so smooth and graceful she seemed to dance about more than fight, yet the sword in her hand was ridiculous. It was about five-feet long and about ten-inches wide and at least an inch thick at the spine of the blade. Though it had to be over a hundred pounds of shiny metal with a hilt in the shape of an eagle's head and the blade coming out of the open beak. She used it as if it were as light as a feather. She finished just one point two seconds short of Alex's time but seemed quite pleased. More went up and more did well, yet some did so badly Michael felt they had gone to the wrong school! There was one who breezed through his bots in two minutes flat, but the one right after him tried to use her axe while holding it upside down. Another threw his knife at his bot and missed very badly having it fly out of the ring and stab right into the foot of an unlucky Pith as he was walking by.

After about an hour Eliza went up and punched each of her four bots in half. It lacked any kind of style, but she didn't need it. Her one punch one kill style got her a great time! A while later Foeseth went up. He walked to the center of the ring and spread open his arms, which were immediately coated in fire. Foeseth was given seven bots and in a few punches all of them had melted holes punched strait through them. More went up, one had a solid time and good form, the next several were the worst thus far. One was given two bots, and she got the stuffing knocked out of her by the time Ortaiga stepped in. Another two each knocked themselves out, and another one shot off his bow with his eyes closed nearly hitting Master Ortaiga in his good eye. Ortaiga had a few choice words for him. Rozea went up and proved very good with a bow and arrow. Ryan went next and got the fifth best time overall.

Michael was about to go up now. It had been a half hour since Ryan had his turn and it was now quite lonely on Michael's side of the ring. It seemed like no time when Master Ortaiga told him it was his turn. Michael stood and stepped into the ring. It was funny at this point he wasn't nervous—he was excited. This feeling was made better by the fact that everyone seemed very interested in how he was going to do because everyone got quiet. Ortaiga started Michael with three bots at half-skill level each. They came at him at what seemed to be much faster then what it looked like from the sidelines. Michael was ready however, he had competed in martial arts since he was twelve so he was used to it by now. He took them down more easily than he thought he would. He used every bit of his heightened strength to break apart the bots. Michael did so well that he received a round of applause from the group of onlookers. Ortaiga went and got more bots and sent them in the ring with Michael; this time he had eight, and each of them was set to the highest level.

Michael was just moving right—this was what he was built for, fighting had always come the easiest out of the plethora of skills he mastered. Michael felt really good and something weird happened as he destroyed his last bot with a single punch. It felt like an odd tingle in his hand as his hand hit the bot's face, and he saw a blue energy spark jump off his hand and into the bot which promptly exploded as if it were hit with a live grenade. Ortaiga stood from his chair with a start.

"Do you think you could reproduce that?" he asked in an uneven voice.

"Yea, give me more; I can do way more than eight! I'm feeling really good!" Michael exclaimed.

Ortaiga stood there a moment then smiled, making his scared face hard to look at. He went back to the shed again but this time came out with a different robot this one had a shiny blue coating and was about seven-feet tall. It was obviously much stronger and better made, so Michael got ready, but Master Ortaiga had some instruction first.

"This is a fighting droid. The difference between this and the bots you just fought is that these can and will try to kill you. This is no joke. These have settings that are challenging for a sixth year apprentice! So you will start on level one. If you feel like you can't handle it, say so or you will die, clear?"

"Yes sir." Ortaiga open the back panel and set the level to one. The droid sprang at him at once. It was fast and much stronger than the bots. Michael wasn't sure what he did to make the energy come out of his hand but he felt that he needed to try anything to do it again because this droid was a bit out of his league. He just focused on the feeling of the energy coming off his hands as it hit the last bot. To his shock, this worked very well—too well. All at once Michael started pulling energy out of the droid, and then let it go, all be it a bit sloppily. Skill didn't matter though, first the droid was already shutting down for having the energy sucked out of it, and on top of that the energy blast hit the left arm of the droid and tore it in half. Unfortunately it didn't stop there, the blast kept right on going and blasted a hole, three-feet wide right through the wall surrounding the castle! Ortaiga jumped to his feet once more this time with a look of stunned silence. Even Alex was without anything to say. It was only seconds until Dojee and Warbick were on the scene as well as Pith.

"What happened? Is anyone hurt? Demanded Pith.

"No, no. The wall has had better days though," answered Ortaiga.

Dojee studied the wall and then what was left of the droid. He nodded his head in understanding and walked over to Master Ortaiga who just nodded while Dojee whispered in his ear. Ortaiga whispered back and Dojee seemed to finally have enough information.

"Michael, did you blow a hole through that wall? Purely by instinct?"

"I…well…yeah. I didn't mean to destroy the wall…"

"No, no. You have nothing to apologize for. That is amazing! You should be proud if you aren't. That wall is eight hundred and fifty feet thick and you blasted straight through it with a simple ball of energy. There isn't a *master* here who could do that…Not even me…Well with energy anyway! Yet again you surprise me. I want to start our training class early today in light of this and see if the surprises will keep coming!" Dojee patted him on the shoulder and went over to the wall to see what would need done to fix it. Ortaiga gave him an approving nod then went around and handed out course studies for everyone based on their skills and ability to use those skills. Michael found himself yet again at the top of his class, the course study he was given read—

Michael Rains (Advanced Learner)
Learning to know your powers, (class room) 33456
Monsters, beasts, and freaks, what you need to know, (class room) 6600980
History of the worlds, (class room) 500
Weapon training 101, (class room) 14
Snakes, Weasels, and Rats: A Study of Politics, (class room) 41002
Advanced training, (class room pending)
Guns, blades, and bombs: A look at the finer things of life, (class room) 3341
(please note you must choose at least two elective classes by the end of the week or they will be picked for you)

Michael loved the sound of these classes even the history class should be interesting for him having very little overall knowledge of the world of the Jemini. He and the rest of his friends all looked over everyone else's courses. They all shared "Weapon Training 101" and "Learning To Know Your Powers," but only Foeseth, Ben, and Alex had "Advanced Training." Blaze and Rozea had the class on monsters, while Alex and Foeseth had "Guns, Blades and Bombs" and only Eliza had "A Study Of Politics"

"Man, I never heard of a first year apprentice having that many classes out of the gate. I hope they don't burn you out!" Ben said concernedly.

"Yeah, and your special class with Dojee isn't even on here," stated Blaze, seemingly disappointed.

"I think it was meant to be a bit of a secret. I guess he might be afraid of other apprentices getting jealous of my getting 'special treatment' or something."

"I could understand that, I mean *I* hate you already! Is there anything you could even *let* me be better than you at?" teased Alex

"Oh Alex, don't be ridiculous! You're way better at being annoying than I could ever be!" Michael retorted. Alex acted moved beyond words and rest of the group shared a laugh as they made their way to the castle to get to class.

⁊

Michael, Blaze, and Rozea sat down a little late to the "Monsters, Beasts, and Freaks" class. The master who had just started his opening lecture was more than irritated at this.

"Yes, well now that you three are here I suppose we can continue. Well all right then, as I was saying—there are an unspeakable number of vicious and deadly beasts out there. Creatures that will rip your head from your body as soon as look at ya! So if you ever find yourself in a wilderness of some sort you must know what to look for and how to avoid dying…or worse. In this class I, Master Edgar G. Witt will teach you what things to watch out for and how to know if you are likely to run into something dangerous. I will also attempt to instruct you in how to handle such a beast should the option of running and or hiding become unavailable. All right no time like the present, so let's get going. First we are going to start with some rather misunderstood creatures…fairies…" Master Edgar paused to see everyone's response. The room filled with light sniggering and giggling. Master Edgar smiled slyly and nodded.

"Just as I thought. You all grew up hearin' stories about fairies I wager. I suppose you also think they just play sweet songs on their flutes and set up tea parties hmph! Only slightly close— they do play sweet songs and act all nice and friendly. They seem so cute and innocent with their wee wings and rosy cheeks, but that is just what they want you to think. My first encounter with these freaks was in fact my very first adventure. I was a part of a team that was exploring an unknown planet at the time. We had two 249 people in our group until we came upon a fairy nesting tree. They drew the men in close ... then, with no warning ... they started tearing the men apart, eating them live!" The class let out a gasp, one girl shrieked, while some of the guys in the room still thought he was making it up. Master Edgar heard one of them whisper as much. "Oh, I would have thought the same thing, before I had to witness a good friend of mine having his intestines ripped out! I may seem crazy to you but I've been out there, and I have seen things that would give any one of you nightmares for the rest of your lives!"

The class went on for about forty minutes in which time Michael realized that Master Edgar believed all creatures want to eat you! Why he even tried to convince the class that he was once bitten by a slug, and that squirrels will tear you limb from limb if you get too close! When class ended, Blaze said goodbye to Rozea and Michael, and went to her next class, which was a good ten-minute walk away from them. Rozea had a free period, and then she would be going to "Advanced Archery Training" under Masters Balo Hamerswell and Sif Dromgar. So Rozea decided to walk Michael to his "Politics" class.

"So ..." started Rozea, after a moment of silence.

"So ... Do you think that someone dangerous might be at this school?" She bit her lip as she spoke as if afraid he might be angry that she asked. Michael however was so not expecting this question so he didn't say anything; he just stared at her like she had three heads.

"You saw something last night in the hall, it scared you! I know that look you had in your eyes. You saw something you didn't like. We know who and what you are and obviously so does the people who were trying to kill you before. So what if what you saw down that hallway was a bad guy? ..."

"Well ... I hadn't thought about it. I don't want to make people worry for no reason."

"Well you need to think about it!" Rozea shrieked stopping in her tracks.

"...Look, you have a bunch of people that look up to you now, and you must by now see just how big a deal it is that you are the new guardian! There are a lot of people who wanted that job and every single one of them are going to take it personal that you got it over them. It will more or less put them in a killing mood, to put it bluntly. So what did you see?"

"I saw ... A dark ... figure ..."

"Like a ghost!?" gasped Rozea.

"Um ... Are ghosts real?"

"Yes, very ... But not what you might think. They aren't the reanimated spirits of the dead. They are a race of beings from somewhere in the dimension called the Underworld. Some believe they were genetically engineered by Hades himself but that has never been confirmed. More to the point if it was a ghost then we need to let a master know right away, someone could get hurt. We had better have a fair amount of proof or we'll get in trouble for trying to cause a panic. Come on follow me!" Rozea took off at full speed. She had a huge stride being ten-feet tall or so, but Michael was able to keep up with her much easier then he could with Ben. She took them both to the end of the hall where they were talking the night before.

"Okay, so where over here was this figure? If we can determine where it stood then we can use stuff around there to figure out how big it was and so forth."

"Yeah, my dad does that kind of thing all the time as a cop. But I don't have time for this now, I'm already five minutes late to class!" Michael protested.

"Oh, just tell them you got lost, after all this castle is the size of a continent!"

"You want me to lie…to a Master who might just be able to read minds…and may or may not be able to turn me into a rat or something? Are you nuts?" Michael spat indignantly.

"Oh stop acting like a kid! You do realize that you're getting personal lessons from Dojee, right?"

"Yeah, so what? That's not a license to do whatever I want. Even if I would get special treatment I can't misuse such a privilege. That would be the fastest way to lose what—if any—respect I might have from Dojee or any other master for that matter."

"Okay, maybe so, but if you know that something bad is happening, or something dangerous could be lurking about then don't you think that it would be your responsibility to do something about it?" Rozea seemed almost desperate.

"Why is this so important to you? I doubt that anyone is going to try to kill me while in this Academy. I mean with Masters like Dojee, Warbick, Zezz, and Kujex, plus all the others, it would be suicide!"

"Yes but there are plenty that *would* die to kill you, Valldiss isn't the only one who would send people after you. You were told there were only fifty some people that had the ability to absorb powers right. Plus just what do you mean *why is it so important to me?* You are a good friend, am I not suppose to care if you die?" A tear rolled down her cheek.

"Look, I'm sorry. I get that you care about what happens to me, but I don't think this is too likely anyway. I'm the only person since Ackatoth that absorbs powers through energy. And you need that power to operate the gate."

"Not everyone knows that detail, and many that have heard it don't believe it. I know this stuff from my dad. He and Dojee are good friends and I overheard them talking before. Most believe you just need to be able to absorb powers. Most likely because no one wanted to believe that it would be *that hard* to find Ackatoth's heir. All that aside do you think that any power hungry fool that wants your job is going to care if they can't actually control the Main gate? As far as that goes they may well want you dead for just for that reason. You know, the 'If I can't have it no one can' mind set. Now just stop stalling or we'll both be late to our *next* class, where was this thing?" Michael let out a huff and started looking around them while remembering what he had seen.

"It was right here by this light or well straight across from it anyway. Yeah, right here," Michael said making up his mind and standing on the spot.

"Was his head at the same height as the light?" Rozea asked putting stuff together.

"It was actually a little higher. So what would that be, like seven feet, maybe more?"

"Well if it was floating off the ground then that doesn't matter."

"This thing definitely had legs—that I could tell for sure. I just couldn't make out anything defined otherwise."

"Hmm … Ghosts don't have legs, they float around. The plot thickens! We need to keep an eye open for this thing, if it was looking right at you, then I dare say you will see it again."

"It may be worth mentioning that it disappeared instantly, so *it* either is a person with powers, or there is a secret passageway around here. Eliza had said that there were so many of them in this castle it would take thousands of years to search them all." Michael started to feel around the wall when he noticed that one of the small engravings of dragons that ran along the trim on the wall was a little crooked. He pushed on it and at once the wall slid to the side without a sound reveling a door made of some sort of metal. The door wasn't closed the whole way and Michael could feel cool damp air blowing out of it.

"Well mystery solved as far as where he…Oh okay or she went…" Rozea had given him a nasty look.

"…Anyway let's see where this goes." Michael was about to open the door more when Rozea grabbed his shoulder to hold him back.

"You can't just go wondering around the secret parts of this castle. You know better than me what it was like to get to Dojee's office, that Hall of Shadows, what if there is something dangerous in there?"

"Yeah and what if there was and someone let it out? It's like you said at this point we need to take care of any danger that could threaten our fellow apprentices." Michael was a bit surprised by his own bravery, but at the same time he had to start embracing his fate didn't he? Rozea seemed both impressed and inspired.

"Who needs archery training anyhow, I'm already the best archer on my planet; let's see what we have here!" She drew her bow off her back and got an arrow ready; Michael drew the sword that Slim had given him. He hadn't messed with it since the day he got it, (he had accidentally lopped off a post of the bed he was given by Bruce)! It was so light it was hard to tell it was there; he grabbed the door handle and started pulling on it. It opened slowly as it was seven inches thick of solid metal.

"Boy is that a tick door! You might want to reconsider going down there alone!" Michael and Rozea whipped around to see Ben, Foeseth, Eliza, Blaze, Ryan, and Alex who was grinning from ear to ear.

"What are you guys doing here?" Rozea asked looking directly at Ben and putting on a pretty smile, Alex answered.

"I can hear anyone I want at anytime I want no matter where they are. Dojee asked me to keep this youngin' safe, so I always keep an ear out for him. When he didn't show up to his politics class, (good call by the way) I listened for where you were and what you were doing. I went around to gather the troops as it were. Oh and this is Conshen Moonsy, she and Foeseth have a thing or whatever. So when I made up the bull crap story that he was needed by a master somewhere for an emergency she tagged along, hope you don't mind. Conshen went as red as a beet, and Foeseth looked like he was weighing the pros and cons of murder.

"You shouldn't have done any of that! Now at some point people are gong to wonder what nine of the top students at this academy are doing out of their classes. We could all get in big trouble!" Wined Rozea.

"We are wasting time I'm going down these steps because I feel like I should, and trust me these "feelings" have never been wrong yet. Come to think of it, it may be some sort of power." Michael didn't wait for them to respond. He was always more for action then words. He went in the door which opened right into a spiral staircase going down. It was completely dark and twice Michael nearly fell missing the next step.

"Excuse me let me lead, please." Conshen had made her way to the front of the group then at once started to glow exactly like a glow in the dark toy. Foeseth followed suit and made flames engulf his arms casting yet more light. With their way now lit enough to safely walk they made their way slowly down the steps. As they went lower and lower the air got colder to the point soon there breath was pouring from their mouths like billows of smoke from a dragon's snout. They went on for several minutes and at last the landing came into view but with it also came a distant soft light and the sound of voices. Michael motioned for everyone to stop moving and to be quiet. They leaned forward to hear who was talking and what they were saying.

" …So you didn't tell him how much danger he may be in …?" said one voice.

"No, I don't believe he is in that much danger. He may have been hurt by absorbing some of Freyja's power but he also was completely better in about three hours! You or I would have been bed ridden for a week, or at least in Freyja's state. Do you know that she was given a three month relief from use of any weapon;

her ribs are so weak right now such stress would break them worse than they are. Do you know how hard it is to break the bones of an Asguardian?" This voice Michael knew at once as Dojee the other he had never heard before. What was this, how was it that *they* were down here and what of the shadowy figure? These questions were cut short however when a voice behind the group let their secret out.

"Hey now, what are you lot doing down here?" asked a tall gray skinned Clayic.

"Well...? This is a Master-only zone so how did you even get down here?" He seemed almost as curious as he was angry.

"The door was open...Well the metal one was anyway," answered Michael

"Really? Hmm...And whom or what were you looking for?" He asked this time far more interested than anything else. This talking was enough to get the attention of Dojee who came to the stairwell.

"Now how did you get down here?" Dojee made no attempt to hide the chuckle in his voice. Michael and the group came out of the stairwell into a warm well furnished room that was obviously a master's lounge. There was a huge warm fireplace, large squashy arm chairs were here and there and a handsome sofa sat in front of them. On this sofa sat a person covered in short tight fur with three sets of horns, one large set just like that of a ram the other two were much smaller and curved only slightly but ended with sharp points. He had hooves and his legs bent backward like a goat as well, though sitting down Michael could tell he was quite tall. Behind the sofa was an over seven foot tall blue skinned man with four swords on his back and two more on either side. He was tall and thin though what muscle he had was very well sculpted and he crossed his arms over his chest as he turned to see them.

"So, we have some adventurers, aye? How did you all get through the door up there?" Said the blue skinned man.

"Yes, and what pray tell were you looking for?" Asked the horned man. Michael spilled the beans, he told them about the prediction that the man by the bank gave him. Then of seeing a shadowy figure, then their deciding to come down here to look for it, he even remembered that Alex had mentioned speaking to a shadowy figure later that night when he was sneaking around."

"Oh thanks a lot, see if you get a birthday gift from me!" Alex squeaked.

"Well why were you not in bed? You looking for trouble?" Asked the blue skinned Master.

"I haven't slept in … That's it actually … I haven't slept. As in, I never sleep, besides it seems like such a waste of time just lying still on a bed for extended periods of time, boring!"

"You and I can discuss that later," Master Dojee interjected, "Now for the matter at hand, I am impressed by the bravery of just rushing to face your foe. That is useful. However, (and I must stress this I'm afraid) it may not be the best idea for a group of very powerful, yet inexperienced Jemini such as yourselves to just blindly search for something that could have been too much for you. It is unlikely to say the least that you would ever face harm within these walls but in this case you had no idea. Since all of you seem aware of who Michael is then you should also be aware of just what kind of resources his enemies have at their disposal! Don't walk around in fear, just use some good sense. I assure you I will have Pith conduct a complete investigation …"

"I'm sorry sir but if there are really thousands of hidden passages throughout this castle then that would just be a waste of time," offered Michael.

"Hmm … Do you have something in mind?"

"As a matter of fact I do. We set a trap for whoever it is, you must have a room full of all kinds of stuff that Valldiss would wet himself to get his hands on …" Alex let out a snort of laughter. "…You pick out something just too good to pass up and put it someplace where it would seem easily stolen. Then just sit back and watch. If they're smart at all they will assume a trap, but if the take is ripe enough…"

"Well, well. That *is* a decent plan. But there is a bit of risk, if we underestimate this culprit even a little then we could end up just giving Valldiss a valuable item," Dojee answered. Michael thought hard a moment, and then another idea came to him.

"Who knows just what the *Book of Ackatoth* looks like?"

"Ha! I think I know where you're going with this, the only people who have ever seen it and are still alive are Hull (the man who found it) Slim and now you and your friends."

"Well then what we do is we make several copies, like four maybe. Then we put the real one in there, you then let it be known more or less publicly that you have found a group of five books and that one of them is the Guide you just don't know which one yet. You then have each book put in a different place, and have each one watched by hidden cameras that only you can control."

"That might just work, but I want to add a little touch, if I may. Everyone but Michael leave the room please." The three masters had everyone out of the room in a few seconds and shut the door behind them.

"There now, you are quite bright, aren't you? There is still a small risk with your plan here. If the real guide is in the group of books then it could still be at risk if picked first by a lucky guess. I say you pull yet another fast one. This will only work if you tell no one. You will keep the real copy with you at all times. We will *say* that the real one is in there. The allure of the idea of getting that book should be more than enough…"

"What is the big deal with this sword anyway? Does anybody know what it does? What if it was all just some kind of 'going out with a laugh' practical joke?"

"Hmm…never thought of that…don't think it is likely though. See Ackatoth was something of a genius when it came to making weapons, if you can find one of his swords today, It is worth a king's fortune. He taught Slim everything he knows, so it is unlikely that the sword is a dud. However some go as far to say that he who wields the sword will have all of Ackatoth's power. That of course would have to be wrong because no one was more against people getting power without the capacity for it than Ackatoth. See Ackatoth had gotten to the point where he could actually give powers to other people.

"Now that is not unheard of, Odin can do that to a point as well as Zeus and Poseidon, some others like that. But they are all limited in a major way. Many of the powers they give are temporary, only lasting a few hours, maybe days. Others can only give you the most basic form of the power and that will take years to level up to anything worth having. And others the powers themselves would have limits; such as you could only use them at night, or in water, and so on.

"But Ackatoth, he could give you any power he had up to whatever level your body could handle, and with no limitations in using the powers. Ackatoth had to learn the hard way though, that not all people can handle having powers. The point is he has actually made some of the worst dark lords alive today. That is unprecedented and also the reason for the interest in his sword. This was the sword *he* used every day, and everyone agrees on one thing concerning it, whoever has it will be unstoppable. I don't think so again but that is not important. Of course Ackatoth wouldn't be fool enough to make such a thing—if it is anywhere near so powerful—easy to get and only one person at a time would be able to use it. At least that is what I would have done if I were him. Since you are the only person to be able to read that book since Ackatoth, it would appear that he did just that. You are meant to have the sword, and you will. Now enough of this, you need to get outside for your next lesson, should be 'Getting To Know Your Powers.' Oh and just so it has been said; don't come down here again..."

CHAPTER EIGHT

L ife, for the first time in over a month, was almost normal. Just as always when it came to learning anything, Michael was leaps and bounds ahead of his class. Unlike back home though, these people were not jealous ... at least not openly, in fact he was just about everyone's favorite person. It was almost freaky at times. Michael greatly regretted letting Alex know that he was getting weirded out by everyone being so nice to him. Because from that point on Alex did the best he could to make Michael feel "more comfortable"—basically he mocked him openly for being such a "stupid little genius." Blaze started going out of her way to sit next to or near Michael every chance she got, this was special treatment he was more than happy to receive! All this aside, life was great and Michael felt for the first time in his life that he was where he belonged. This thought was often met by a sting of guilt that his dad, Zack and Penny couldn't be there. But he knew why they couldn't come here yet, and that they would understand.

The castle was a place Michael was quite sure no one could ever get used to, just as far as the size was concerned. Though, at this time of the year no one—including Michael—wanted to stand around in the corridors much. Most of the castle was made tens of thousands of years ago and the newest parts still near fifteen thousand years. Back then they didn't use mortar to put the blocks together they just got really big bricks of stone and let gravity hold them together. Though this makes for a long lasting building it meant that at some points the frigid air from out side could sneak in through the cracks. The winter rains had come which were mainly just ice storms that coated everything in a thick sheet of glassy ice. Everyone dreaded the weapon training classes because by the time they were done, their joints felt frozen stiff. Michael's personal training from Dojee had been going quite well too, and Michael looked forward to these classes most of all. He had proved to be a natural at producing energy as well as controlling it. He did so well with this part That Dojee decided that it was time to try absorbing energy. True to his word Dojee worked with Michael to help him learn to control absorbing, so he could shake a person's hand without killing them or something. This was tricky at first; Dojee had Michael practice this with Kujex, who (though very powerful) also had a very high endurance so he could handle a bit of a jolt if things went wrong. The first few times Michael would wake up across the room looking through the hole his body just made through a nearby book shelf! While Kujex would have to come back down stairs after flying up to one of the many levels of Dojee's personal library! After five tries Michael managed to only cause Kujex to shake a bit, while steam poured off his forehead. Three days later Michael could shake Kujex's hand with no effect at all. Once Dojee was certain of Michael's control he had Kujex stop practicing with them, and they started working with Warbick (who was far more powerful than Kujex). These practices went well as with the ability to stop absorbing already fully mastered; Michael found it much easier to learn how to gradually absorb powers. He also found that he was getting stronger, Kujex was quite strong himself, but Warbick was a hundred times his strength at least. With every second Michael and Warbick shook hands, he could feel his arms getting bigger, his legs beefier, and his chest thicker. He also now knew all of Warbick's powers which were, super strength, super jumping, power reading, and electrokinesis—the ability to generate electricity—and higher than all of them was a very high level of invulnerability. It turned out that powers weren't all he gained; Michael gained all of his head knowledge too. He knew Warbick's darkest secrets…his worst fears…his wife's name…

"Okay, we can stop there!" He said indignantly.

"I'm sorry, I didn't know I could see your thoughts and stuff while doing that," Michael felt bad, this was obviously something Warbick didn't want to think about.

"It is all right, just don't ask about it, please," Warbick gave Dojee a bow and left the room.

"I take it you saw his wife?" asked Dojee wisely.

"Yeah, but you don't need to tell me, I know when something is off-limits."

"I'm sure he would appreciate that, but I dare say that it is a story that you should know. Many years ago Warbick was writing a peace treaty between Asgard and Olympus, at the time Ares a long time rival of Warbick's had his eyes on Athena. Athena however was far more interested in Warbick, as Warbick is a very kind man...And Ares...is not. Well, when Warbick and Athena married something in Ares' head came loose. He broke the treaty by killing Mordur, Odin's grandson...Warbick's first son. These lines have since been mended, however Athena was stricken with grief and Mordur—being the spitting image of Warbick—she could not bear to look at him, they have not seen each other since. "Dojee took a break from talking to sip his tea.

"So why did you tell me about that?" Michael felt that this wasn't stuff he needed to hear just then...Or ever!

"Because you are developing strong ties to young Miss Traigon, and I want you to be properly informed about how life is, and what yours will be like...I myself have had every one of my children...And my darling wife, herself...All systematical hunted down and killed by Valldiss. So you need to know what you are doing, what you're getting yourself into. Don't misunderstand, I am not saying that you should not marry, if you feel that, then go for it and best to you...But I strongly caution you...If there is any chance that you would be unable to handle the pain that comes with the death of a wife...or...a child...Then do yourself a favor and let that part of your life go, it may make a very important decision very hard at some point. Anyway, listen to me, a grumpy old man burdening you with such things, at such a young age. I suspect you only mean to date her ... for now anyway. Tomorrow, you will not be having this lesson in my office, I am going to give Masters Warbick and Zezz the task of training you with your new found powers gleaned from all of these classes. I am going to be leaving the castle for a few days—nothing bad has happened—I just have some work that needs to be taken care of."

"Master, what happened with the trap you set for this mysterious caped villain?"

"Hmm ... Well, don't tell anyone, but I believe they may do something if I am not here, one of several reasons I am doing what I am now."

So just as Dojee said, he left the next morning leaving Warbick in charge, and for the most part nothing was different. Classes were as normal and things seemed to go without a hitch. Michael had a new least favorite class, that being his class with Warbick and Zezz. They pushed him hard and gave him no room for excuses. They would spare with him for an hour strait at full speed. When they gave Michael a break he would run to his water bottle and even puke sometimes, while Zezz and Warbick just stood there barley breathing hard.

"You guys are just crazy! I mean, are you sweating at all?" Michael gasped

"I believe I felt a drop or two." Zezz jeered, Warbick chuckled.

"You just need to build your stamina, you have already gained a fair amount from Kujex and myself, if you hadn't your heart would have given out after that hard of a workout." Warbick said encouragingly. From there they started helping Michael learn to use his powers, he had gained a few from Kujex; magnokinesis— the ability to generate/control magnetic fields—electrokinesis— the ability to generate/control electricity—and an ability called "rock skin" with which you can—as you might have figured—make your skin as hard as rock. The first two powers were very easy for Michael to get the hang of because they were energy based. The rock skin seemed to be a bit harder for him but even still he got the hang of it by the day Dojee was due to return. They also worked on the super jumping Michael gained from Warbick; Michael found quite quickly that getting high in the air wasn't hard...but that the ground is! Landing was rough but Warbick showed him how to use his legs to properly handle the shock without hurting himself, or how to roll out of it. On the third and final day Dojee was to be gone Warbick and Zezz had just called it a night after a four hour training session. Michael had done very well this night; he even managed to knock Zezz down and landed a hit on Warbick...right before being knocked across sand ring. Michael headed inside with his sword under his arm while he put his belt back on. He was walking to the high speed transport system; because he would rather die than walk a bunch of stairs after a workout like that. Michael felt an odd breeze blow past him, this should have been nothing out of place in these drafty halls but this did not feel right...he wasn't alone. He drew his sword the second the sheath was tied on; he looked around quickly to try to catch a glimpse of what was around. He was standing at a central hub leading to six different halls; he only ever took the one to the far left. He had never gone down the other halls and had no idea where they went. His class with Warbick and Zezz went late, so no one was up, and the halls were eerily quiet and still, while a mist of fog coated some of the floor from extreme cold. It had started snowing very hard when Warbick said to come in and the castle was getting colder. Michael looked down the hall to the far right and saw very clearly a dark figure standing there in front of a door trying to get into it. Michael didn't think twice, this guy was after one of the books for sure. He didn't look to see where he was going or take notice of the sign to the right of the hall that read—

"ATTENTION!!! NO APPRENTICES BEYOND THIS POINT TRESSPASSERS MAYBE EXICUTED!!!"

Michael ran fast and hard, he didn't even remember to be sore after a hard night's work. He wanted to catch this punk, and ask a few questions…with his foot…The figure didn't seem to be having luck with the door and also didn't notice Michael until it was too late. Michael lounged at the guy…okay or girl…and hit them right as they turned toward him. The *man's* hood fell down to reveal a metal mask and broad shoulders; the guy didn't like being tackled, and punched Michael full on in the face. Just as the fist hit him, Michael could feel something seeping out of his face…his anari. He didn't feel pain, and spun right back to his feet as the large man shook the pain off his hand.

"I've dealt with your kind before" He said in what sounded like a thick Russian accent.

"I seriously doubt that buddy, now give yourself up so you don't have to die!" The metal faced Russian just chuckled as he pulled out his right arm—which was robotic—from behind his cape and had a double edged sword blade fold out of the forearm. The man stood at least seven foot but was fast for his size. Still it had not been for nothing that Michael had been getting special training from two of the best fighters in the history of the Gran Arena! He out maneuvered the Russian at every turn, his anari was still protecting half of his face, and he wanted it to come out the rest of the way; the second he said this to himself it did just that. The anari came out and coated him entirely; it felt weird to say the least. First he started getting taller, then he felt it come out of his mouth and coat his teeth and tong. He also felt large wings come out of his back and his legs now bent backwards. Michael was quite sure he must have looked fearsome, because the Russian stopped dead in his tracks.

"You…Have I…You can't be…Look…You don't have to kill me…I…Didn't know…" With that the man fumbled with something on his belt, while folding his blade away. Michael didn't want this guy to get away clean, he swung his sword at the man's natural arm just in time to sever it at the elbow. He let out a howl of pain as he disappeared in a flash of green light. The noise of the man's cry had gotten the attention of some masters. Zezz, Kujex, and Sif—Rozea's archery instructor—all came rushing down the hall at Michael, weapons drawn. It was at this moment that Michael had the realization that he did not look like 'Michael Rains' anymore. Instead he looked like some eight or nine foot winged monster covered in an anari that only a few people even knew he had. So these extremely well trained, battle hardened warriors, meant to kill the dark scary thing in front of them…That being him! He immediately told the anari to go back in, this started working, but a good bit slower than what he would have liked. Zezz was about on top of him when he realized that it was Michael that he was about to cleave in half with his huge axe and skidded to a halt.

"By Odin! What the…? You…What is this? What do you mean by being in the hall of forbidden artifacts? If a security bot caught you, it would have shot you to death!"

"The shadowy guy I saw…the one Master Dojee set the trap for…He was here. He tried to get into this room, but I stopped him, got his arm too…" Michael kicked the arm over toward Zezz, who stepped back a bit.

"Did you forget about explaining how it is that a young man such as yourself has an anari? Just what was the big idea in not letting the masters know you had such a thing?" Snapped Sif.

"No I didn't forget. You know I'm getting pretty sick of this kid's table bull crap! I am not a kid and I don't have to tell anyone, anything, that I don't feel needs to know, masters included…! Not to mention it was Dojee's call not to tell you all so if you have a problem with take it to him!" Michael didn't mean to be so harsh, but he knew that there were far more important things going on here than him breaking a rule or not doing something she felt he should. She was taken aback by this and didn't seem to know what to say, Zezz spoke slowly trying to calm everyone down.

"You are right, Michael. I feel that we all need to change the way we treat the apprentices around here, I should not have questioned your being in this hall the way I did either. It is sometimes hard for us to remember what it is like to be a young adult. We have come through so much, that with each year people your age start to seem younger and younger than they really are. What is important right now though, is that you tell us what you gained from this man." Michael felt an immediate sense of respect for Zezz; it meant a lot to be treated like an adult.

"Okay, well he was Russian … or he had that kind of accent anyway. He was seven foot plus and mostly robotic. The weirdest thing was when I brought out my anari, he acted as if he had seen it before. Of course that is impossible; because that was the first time I ever brought it out the whole way. But I mean he was afraid of me in that form …"

"Well I should hope so, I nearly wet myself when I saw ya lad!" boomed Kujex.

"Yes, you are quite a sight in full-anari form; you may want to take a look at that when you get to your room, so you know what others are seeing. But back on point I believe I have heard of a man that would fit that description, a hired gun really, and very skilled if it's the same one. Let's get this arm to Brains for analysis right away." Zezz grabbed the arm and lead them to Michael's dorm room on the way to Brain's lab.

"You get some sleep, my young friend. You have done well tonight, but just be more careful about what halls you run down. I don't want to have to punish you, after all the rules are designed to protect you … Of course, I'm not so sure *you* need much protecting … but the point remains … just be careful." Zezz, Sif, and Kujex all went on to Brain's lab, while Michael went into his room.

It was amazing to Michael how things around this castle seemed to either move in slow motion or at light speed. He was being treated by Zezz—the third highest ranked master at Asendor—as an equal! He beat a mercenary—who had a reputation for being very skilled—with relative ease! And to round things off, he had a nine-foot monster under his skin ... not something too many people get to say huh? Michael looked in the mirror on his closet door, and made the anari come out. He was at least nine feet tall with his anari fully covering him. He had horns much like and ox, and his legs bent backward at the knee. The wings on his back were ten foot long each and looked very powerful. The most unnerving part were his eyes, the anari made them silvery and metallic looking. Michael had to look away. He put the anari away and climbed into bed and turned out his light, the room was quiet and still. Michael felt odd, as if this encounter tonight had changed something, he was sure things were about to change ... but when ... How? Would things get better or worse? Then his thoughts went to what Dojee had told him. Was he going to have to be alone, just to keep his friends safe? Would he never have children of his own, just so he wouldn't have to loose them? No ... that seemed wrong, he could not, *would not*, let himself live in fear of what could happen only. His thoughts went back and forth on this as he drifted into a restless sleep, but elsewhere people were not so sleepy.

Ryan was wide awake lying in bed, he felt sick, it had been so long for him—so long since he had tasted that sweet, sweet flavor on his lips—but he couldn't ... not here. There were no animals for him to ... He laid there for a while, if he could just go without for long enough he could get off of it for good! But that was hopeful thinking; he wasn't going to make it! He needed an outlet or someone would get hurt! All of a sudden it hit him; he would sneak down to the kitchens and get what he needed there they had to have some raw meat there, right? Ryan got dressed in all black, to help him blend into the shadows, and left his room. It helped that it was so cold in the halls—no one lingered in them for longer than they needed to. He moved relatively unhindered all the way to the kitchens and found a cooler filled with all kinds of meat hanging from hooks. This would do nicely…he let go. It a few minutes he had two pig carcasses striped to the bone and felt not just better, he felt alive! He had to get out of there though, the chef would get in there early for breakfast. He went out the way he came in, and was out of the kitchen as the baking team made their way in to start the bread, biscuits, and muffins. Ryan had to get back to his room before four thirty, because he and Ben—whose room was across from his—were suppose to meet for a morning workout. Then they were to study in the library where Rozea and Eliza would be joining them before breakfast. Ryan feared more than anything, his secret getting out. No one ever treated him the same after that, people hate, and fear his kind. Ryan moved along a hallway for a few minutes then, went down another, in about five minutes he realized that he had made a wrong turn somewhere and had no idea where he was. With the size of this castle suddenly at the forefront of his mind, he knew it could take him an hour just to find his way back to something he knew. This thought was interrupted by the sound of someone walking down the hall in front of him. Ryan peeked around the corner to see who it was. It was without a doubt—as far as he was concerned—the shadowy figure Michael had seen those few weeks back. It had a long flowing tattered cape, and a hood that conveniently hid their face from view. It stood right outside a door marked Masters Only. Ryan was quite sure this was no master and if it was then they were still up to no good or why would they need the disguise? Ryan snapped into action mode, he was the oldest of his group of friends (twenty-eight) and had been through a lot in his life so he was more than familiar with danger. The figure made it in the room and Ryan came just to the door as it closed behind the phantom. Ryan was about to throw the door open ready to kill should he need to, when a voice called him from behind.

"Now what are you doing up this early in the morning? Not up to anything bad are we?" It was Master Balo; he taught advanced archery as well as advanced weapon training. He was a big guy (around twelve foot) and always had a large mace on his back, but he also wore a wide grin and had a kind nature, Ryan liked him.

"No I was out for a walk, couldn't sleep really, anyway as I was on my way back to my room, when I saw a suspicious character go into this room." Ryan said in a whisper.

"Hmm ... Suspicious character you say? ... What did they look like?" Balo was suddenly very serious.

"Have you heard of Michael Rains seeing a 'shadowy figure'? Because I believe he is in there. Balo did not ask another question, he just put a hand on Ryan's chest and gently but forcefully pushed him back against the wall. His mace already in his other hand Balo reach over to the door knob and with one smooth motion flung it open. There was a loud bang and flash, followed by a cloud of smoke, Ryan was immediately scanning the cloud with his night vision—one of his powers. The cloaked man was right beside him trying to sneak by; Ryan sprang on him like an angry cat—bad idea. This guy was *way* stronger than Ryan was—which is something because Ryan was quite strong. The guy also had to be twice his size and threw him against the wall like a rag doll. Balo was not so easy to deal with though. Balo was the master of metal and earth, basically he can control metal and dirt (of any kind) with his mind. He was also an Argonaut back in the day as well as a champion of Asgard, so he has seen more battle than any twenty average people have! The hood fell off the face of the figure to reveal a gray skinned man, with a ring in his ear that looked like a metal lion's tooth. He had black greased hair and a thick neck, with almost no nose just a flat nub with two slits for nostrils. To add to this he shook himself to loosen two large vein covered wings, the tops of which were covered by sharp armor plates covered in blades.

He came at Balo with these wings like deadly weapons, but Balo was far beyond this fool. Balo ducked out of the way of the wings as if they were sitting still and knocked the guy in the chest with his mace. That was all it took, one hit from Balo's mighty mace was enough to bring down many foes and this was no exception. The intruder coughed against the blood filling his mouth, Balo quickly grabbed a small round device from his belt and called Warbick, as well as the Medical ward to get someone down there ASAP. In ten minutes flat the place was like a crime scene; the hallway was taped off and security bots were dusting down the area for prints. The medical team had their hands full trying to make sure the poor little thief didn't die terribly; by drowning in his own blood! Dojee (who had just gotten back to the castle) was ashen faced and looked both sad and enraged.

"He is lucky he met you and not I, Balo, or he would be a pile of ashes right now!" Dojee spat. Warbick had asked Ryan to give them his account of what happened. Ryan was sure to make it known that he was only out for a walk, and had nothing to do with the disappearance of two pigs, that were apparently purchased to celebrate Kujex's birthday—Rotisserie pork was his favorite meal. The chief had come to Dojee moments earlier practically crying, Dojee reminded him that he could just order more and the chief excused himself sheepishly.

"I would say that this guy might have had himself a bit of a snack before trying to rob us blind!" Balo suggested. They all seemed very willing to except this conclusion, and Ryan was all too happy to encourage it. Dojee finally calmed down a bit and looked to Ryan again.

"We are indebted to you! There are quite a few valuable items in there, as well as a few dangerous ones. I feel you are owed something…hmm…I have it! How about, we cover the rest of your tuition for the rest your time here?"

"I ... That is very generous ... Really?" Ryan was beside himself, just what was in this seemingly random room that could be so important that his foiling the theft of such items would justify them covering His tuition. He had five more years and Asendor is the most expensive school there is?! Dojee seemed to know what was going through his mind because he smiled and nodded his head.

"Trust me when I say that you absolutely deserve such a reward. This man is not just a thief—he is also an assassin who works for Valldiss himself. I have no doubt that this man was after one of the weapons we have in there to use it to kill a certain young friend of yours." Dojee had a grave look back on his face.

"Wow ... Do you really believe that?" Ryan asked.

"It would make sense, there is nothing in there worth stealing but the weapons we keep in there," answered Warbick.

"Well that is a problem then isn't it?" Ryan stated, frankly.

"What do you mean?" Dojee asked seeming almost afraid of the answer.

"Well, the door is labeled 'masters only' so I'm guessing that only masters know just what is there ..." Ryan paused for just long enough to see that what he was saying had sunk in, "... this would mean that there has to be a traitor within the masters of this academy!" Ryan just sat there a moment, Dojee, Balo, and Warbick all cringed at the word "traitor" but as what he said sank in, they seemed to realize that Ryan had to be right.

"Dojee, if there is a master at this academy ... that could be involved in this ... then we must find out who and fast or we could be in for a real problem! They could grow desperate if they don't start getting the results, that I am sure Valldiss expects from them. They could even become violent, and that could cause all kinds of problems for this academy!" Balo explained.

"Yes, I agree, this must become a priority ... so ... I can kill the little weasel!" hissed Warbick.

"Hmm...I know this may sound crazy but I think I may ask Michael what he thinks we should do. It was his brilliant idea that caught this guy in the first place, plus I feel he would be quite angry if we didn't tell him someone tried to kill him."

"With respect Master, isn't that speculative? I mean he didn't get past the thieving. Do we really know that Michael was his target? If so why did they not send a more skilled combatant?" Inquired Balo

"Well with myself not even being here—and obviously this fellow would not have been sent for me. I can think of no one at the school who would have enemies enough to send assassins in the night. As far as him being a wimp, I suppose Valldiss may have assumed that Michael growing up outside of our people he would not know how to fight. Thus why risk sending and losing a well trained assassin if a lackey could do it?" Dojee explained.

"You believe Valldiss to be that foolish?" Balo grunted.

"I believe Valldiss's ego is so large at this point that I would not be surprised if he has no sense left at all. He is mad with power and lacks true vision. That is why he established his little council of evil war lords." Dojee shook his head at his own words.

"If you wish I could go get Michael for you." Ryan offered.

"No, no. Let the young man sleep and you do as much as you can you want to be well rested for your training with Ben." Ryan was about to ask how Dojee knew his plans, but then decided that the answer was obvious, and just shook his head and went off to bed.

By the next morning, it had become school wide news that not one, but two 'shadowy figures' had been found and engaged by apprentices in the same night. Michael now shared his popularity with Ryan and was quite pleased to do so. When Dojee was informed of Michael's encounter happening only an hour earlier and only a few floors away, he established a ten o'clock curfew, and the buddy system was now in effect at all times. Dojee also decided that Michael needed to buddy up with someone more experienced; as news of his handling the Russian would certainly have spread to Valldiss's ear by now, and he may try using a more skilled guy next time. Thus Michael was pared with Kujex who only taught one class and thus was the most available. Ben picked Ryan before Rozea could blink so she ended up pared with Blaze and Alex with Eliza. Conshen and Foeseth were side by side most of the time anyway so it was not a stretch to be forced to be together all day long. Dojee pulled Michael aside after breakfast to ask him for his opinion for what they should do about someone trying to kill him.

"You want my opinion on what we should do? I mean, I'm hardly...I just..."

"You were the one who had the idea that caught both of these men. Don't sell yourself short, after all you are a man, and are...'*tired of this kids table bull crap* are you not'?" Dojee smiled as he spoke clearly amused by this statement.

"Look I didn't mean to disrespect anyone, I just got a lot of that over protective stuff from my dad—being a cop—and it got to me. Plus that wasn't the time for correction..." Michael blurted but was cut short.

"Now, now, no need to be so defensive. I am on your side; after all it seems you're quite a sight when your anari is fully drawn out. Wings and everything, just like your father's, but the back bent legs, claws, teeth, horns...well let's just say you probably don't need a buddy, but you will have one all the same. I know I said I would have someone help you learn to use your anari. However it would seem you don't need it, amazing!" Dojee put a hand on Michael's shoulder. "Here, walk with me. There is a place I like to go if I wish to be alone, or just to think."

They walked up stairs for a while, down a long curving hallway to an upper wing of the castle, and to a set of double doors with a large key hole. Dojee reached into a pocket inside his robes and pulled out a key. "Here, you have this one. I have another in my office. Now let's go out here and talk." Dojee waited for Michael to unlock the door, he opened the door to find a beautiful courtyard. There were trees that looked like a cross between weeping willows and cherry blossoms. To the far left, there was a small fountain with a piece of bamboo that would fill up with water, dump it out, then it would stand back up to be filled again. At the other end of the courtyard, there was a huge picture of a battle scene that looked to be thousands of years old. There were dragons, trolls, and many other creatures all killing and battling each other. At the middle of this courtyard was a training mat. Dojee walked over to a bench by a small pond with a few orange and white fish swimming happily. Strangely, though this courtyard was very high and outside, there was no cold breeze to be felt.

"So Michael, I am sure you have an idea for just what to do, to further confound these fools that keep entering this academy!" Michael did have something in mind, but he thought it was too crazy to mention! He wasn't ready ... But that wasn't true! He had been getting none stop training at a very advanced level. Maybe it wasn't crazy ...

"Well?" Dojee pushed.

"I did come up with an idea, but it is a bit nuts."

"Hmm ... Sounds good so far. Tell me, after all the worst that can happen is that I say no."

"Okay. I was thinking ... about something Slim told me before I got here. He said he would be bringing me armor for when I go on a trip, but he didn't say where to. I think it is pretty obvious he meant I would be going for the sword. I have been thinking ... maybe what I should do next, is go get The Sword of Ackatoth. It will draw these men out in the open and make them easy targets. If I am what they want, then they will come after me ... And they better be good! However without this book, anyone who *would* try to catch me wouldn't survive the trip. I think I can do it ... No I know I can!" Dojee was quiet a moment reflecting on what had been said.

"I see what you meant by nuts. You are suggesting that I let you—a well trained but completely inexperienced fighter—go on a trek that could and in fact has claimed the lives of warriors far beyond yourself. You want me to let you go; with powers so extreme that you could easily kill *yourself* trying to use them, if you were not careful. And you want me to send you, alone in the hopes that the men that may be sent to *kill you*, would follow you out into the *wilderness*, and hopefully die before they reach you; so you can have some chance—though slight at best—of surviving the trip yourself. I am afraid I was wrong, I could say something worse than 'no'. I think you may have lost your mind young one!" Dojee had a hint of laughter in his voice.

"I didn't mean I would go by myself. You have a few masters here that have gone on dangerous journeys—Balo, Kujex, Warbick, Zezz, Ortaiga, and many more. I think that it is more and more obvious that you have a traitor in the ranks of masters. That is the only way that two people would get in this academy undetected, someone would have to be on the inside. So if you suggest that you want a few masters to go with me and my team, and one or more people are a little too willing to come, it may raise some needed flags."

"Your team? Do you mean you want to bring your friends?" Dojee said intelligently.

"We have been getting special training...all of us. I cannot believe that is a coincidence, can you?"

"You do have a point, you and your friends are the most skilled first year apprentices that have ever stepped onto these grounds. But I am not sure you are ready." Dojee seemed concerned now.

"How about this then, give me and my friends intense advanced training, specifically for this. If other apprentices start complaining, then tell them that it is a special class for super-gifted fighters. No one could argue with that, and you save face all the while getting us ready."

"You want…harder training…than what you are already getting? That, is quite something. Is there more to this then just catching traitors? I won't help you go on some sort of ego boosting, foolhardy attempt to prove yourself to your friends!" Michael didn't know what to say. He was going to say no right off the bat; but the second he thought it, it seemed untrue. He felt that he hadn't been ready for any of what had happened to him in the past few months. He was tired of lessons—tired of feeling like he was not cut out for the job he was born for. Maybe he felt if he could get the sword now, it would be what *he* needed to trust himself and his abilities. Dojee nodded in understanding.

"I know you have felt inadequate in comparison to all those around you. But that is why I doubt you are ready. You do yourself the greatest injustice when you think that way. You learn half of everything you do as if by luck; however you seem to master things just as quickly. Your last sparing match with Zezz went two hours longer than it was plannedand you knocked him down! There is no other apprentice at this academy that could last thirty minutes with Zezz at his pace. There is a reason he is one of only two people to win the Grand Area Championship without ever losing a fight. In fact he has never been defeated in battle, of course he never fought Warbick, that would be a good fight, but Warbick would win of course. As he was the only person to win the Championship (in his weight class or any other) without ever taking a hit! And if I remember correctly he told me in the match you and he had just after Zezz you managed to hit him once before getting knocked across the sand ring! So you are easily the best fighter out of every apprentice here, and that is roughly sixteen million people! So all of that being said, you must understand, you do not need to prove your abilities to anyone. That said, you did say that you believe you can handle this mission, and that is the first step, so here is what I will do. I will have a few friends of mine come to help train you all. And I will train you now myself; I know I said I would be training you before and didn't do much. This is different though, a major event, so I will make the time. Now there is one thing you may not have considered, some or all of your friends may not want to go. Even if that is a slim chance, do not assume so. Though we will do whatever we can to prepare you, and send the best people we can spare, it is possible some of you may not come back from this trip. I hope that is not the case, and I don't even want to think that it is too likely, but it could happen so do not take this lightly. Oh and one final thing, since this was your idea, and since you are the only one that can read the book, then you will be in charge of the group. I hope you understand the importance of that." Michael felt something in his throat that seemed strangely heart like! He was not expecting to even get Dojee's approval for this, let alone be put in charge! Though, he *had* all but asked for it. He thought it would be odd for the masters—who have been in wars and fought in real battles for thousands of years—to take orders from such a young guy. Michael was going to ask Dojee about this but Dojee wasn't done with the surprises. "I almost forgot you will need this to pull your friends out of their classes." Dojee held out his hand and smiled warmly; in his hand there was a badge. The badge displayed—"Michael Rains, Graduate First Class, and Leader of The New Asendor Special Task Force."

Michael thought this had to be a joke! This was a six year academy, and if he were to believe this badge, he had already graduated—not only that but with a first class rating. Eliza had talked about this to him one day, through one of her thirty minute straight talk-a-thons. She said that the usually good students get is a sixth, maybe fifth class rating. There are almost never more than two people within the same graduating class that get a first class rating! Michael just starred at it for a moment.

"It won't bite you, I'm almost certain!" Dojee said chuckling. Michael took the badge. It was heavy and shiny, and looked to be made of the same metal as the great gates to the main courtyard.

After a second, Michael noticed that the badge had a clip on the back of it that would attach to something else.

"Oh yes, that badge comes with this." Dojee went into a satchel he had on his side and pulled out a gauntlet with some sort of screen on it and a notch where the clip slid in. Michael took the gauntlet and put it on and put the badge in it. The screen immediately came to life and text appeared on the screen.

"Good morning, Mr. Rains. This is Brains. I have made this gauntlet to the exact specifications Dojee asked for, and I hope you enjoy it. With your badge in it, all but a few doors throughout the entire castle will unlock as you touch their handles. There are quite a few other features on this unite so take some time—when you have some to spare—and try some of the stuff out. That's it for now and welcome to the team sir." The screen flipped to a menu screen then went black. Michael looked up at Dojee.

"Okay, just so I know, what am I a leader of again?"

"Oh, that is a long story, but I suppose you should know as much as possible so I will walk with you to get your friends and tell you on the way…" Dojee cleared his throat, "When your father was here, his class was—at the time—the greatest we had ever seen, Warbick, Zezz, Sif, Freyja, Kujex, Bruce, and a few of my friends you haven't met yet, all graduated with your father—your mother graduated the following year. Now according to the Academy bylaws, an apprentice must be in a job for no less than two years before they can be considered for a job at Asendor. Tulsun and his classmates had only been here for one year. This being true, your father, and his class mates were so gifted that I made a special exception for them. I told them to come up with a job that the group of them could do for Asendor, something worthwhile. Your father came up with the *Asendor Special Task Force*. The idea of this group would be to act as an aid to myself or any grand master, whether in sending them on missions to protect someone who had a threat made on their life. Or in some cases, they fought small wars to free planets from tyrannical leaders and evil armies bent on domination. Under this banner many small groups were formed to be more effective at specific tasks. Your father started Dagger Company, a hard hitting anti-war unit, specializing in assassinations and sabotage. In this group was your father, Kujex, Brains, Zeaga—your father's closest friend—Sif, Freyja, Ortaiga, and Zezz.

"Warbick started 'The Eight Man Army' a group of men all with a minimum strength and endurance of one hundred. They mainly saved planets from being destroyed by war. They started with Warbick, Biff, Raylin—you haven't met him yet—Jube, Mendiss—he teaches hand-to-hand combat to the sixth year students—Jet—Brains best friend—Hull, and Hercules. Those last two were not students then, they were already very well established they just liked the idea and signed up. There were many other groups as well but you get the idea. Well they became very popular people and developed enemies right quick! I remember Zezz tell me that he once had seventeen attempts made on his life in the same week, he got out shortly there after. Something about the shipping costs on dead bodies being sent back to where they came from being very high. They kept going even after a fight between Hull and his oldest son Dane, who had joined a few years earlier, caused a falling out within 'The Eight Man Army.' But only a year later your father and mother, being killed…It was just too much, I shut it down. Now though it seems only like poetic justice that you would lead an all new task force. This is what I was up to those three days I left, I needed to meet with the members of the board for Asendor, and they are rather spread out. I *could* just make a decision like this myself, but the checks and balances are there for a reason. Anyway when I told them that you had managed to strike Warbick after only a few short weeks of training they all agreed at once! Now I hadn't actually thought that your first adventure would be one quite so dangerous…but that just goes along with your pace of learning doesn't it? Just so it is clear any of your friends that want to join the task force may, and they will graduate today in fact. But all who join now will be going on the trip too. Ah, here we are. You should find Blaze and Rozea in here and from here I must leave you, I have a great deal of work to do to get you ready for this."

Dojee gave Michael a tap on the shoulder and walked off for his office. Michael wanted to ask how Dojee told the board members something that happened when he wasn't even there … But then he remembered that this was Dojee for crying out loud! Michael knocked on the classroom door, the low sound of talking in the room stopped and Master Edgar opened the door.

"Oh, so you show up now, do ya? Just what do you …? What is that on your arm?" Edgar spat looking confused.

"I need Blaze and Rozea please," Michael said pleasantly.

"Just wait one second, you can't …"

"Grand Master Dojee gave me this badge, and he said I would be able to use it to pull them out of class. If you have a problem with that, please take it up with him, now I am on a bit of a schedule so …" Michael ducked his head into the room just long enough to catch the eyes of Blaze and Rozea. Master Edgar wanted to object further but seemed to think better of it and just let them go, shutting the door to his class with a snap.

"What's going on? Why are …? Is that a Master's badge?" Rozea blurted.

"No, it is my new ID badge. I'm the leader of the New Asendor Task Force." I graduated … with a first class rating … no big deal." Michael couldn't hold back a smile as he looked at their faces.

"Michael that's amazing! I'm so proud of you! But is that why you pulled us out of class, because I have to admit, I am starting to fall behind on my work from all of our interruptions," explained Blaze. Rozea looked at her as if she were crazy.

"Blaze, you are currently working on term papers for our second semester … of year five … Master Ogal asked you to help him grade papers in history class the other day! You scored a two hundred-and-fifty on that automated quiz in Advanced

Computer tech," Master Gage didn't even know that it was *possible* to score a two-fifty on that test! He spent the next twenty-three minutes trying to prove that the computer made a mistake! My point is you can afford to miss a class!" Rozea said, seeming disgusted by Blaze's being brilliant. "...That being said what *did* you pull us from class for?" Rozea asked gently.

"I need some people to join the New Asendor Task Force, and you two are the first I got to. If you would like to join you may. But do not make your decision yet, we need to get the others so that I can tell you all at once, there's a bit of a catch." The girls went with Michael to get the rest of them. They didn't even get to Alex's class when he came up to them with the rest of their friends in toe.

"So what's going on? What's the big deal?" Alex asked. The others seemed to be getting impatient.

"Let's go someplace more private, follow me." Michael led them to the courtyard that Dojee had shown him earlier. Once the door was shut and everyone took a seat on one of the benches, Michael finally told them what was happening.

"Okay, here it is. Once upon a time there was a group here called The Asendor Special Task Force. My birth father started it back when he was young. Now Dojee has given me the right to lead the New Asendor Task Force, and you all have the right to join me," Michael paused to see their reactions. They all seemed both shocked and excited. "There is one little thing I need you to consider though. I am going to be going on a quest to find the sword of Ackatoth..." The group gasped..."I know that this journey is going to be dangerous, so I do not want you to make this choice lightly. Just so that it is clear, if you join the task force now, you will be coming with me on this quest." The others seemed lost for words. Eliza had a look of confusion. Ben was dumbstruck while Rozea was deep in thought, as she stared at him. Ryan looked impressed, and Foeseth had the look of a proud father....Alex was smiling like a dope.

Foeseth was the first to speak, "I am honored by this, and I believe I will join you. But I am not sure I understand. How we will get our classes done if we are travailing for who knows how long?" Michael chuckled. Foeseth had a sort of innocence to him, odd for a big strong warrior with flaming wings but...

"You wouldn't have classes. You are all being offered the opportunity to graduate, today! Dojee said that we are the most gifted group of apprentices he has seen at this school! So this is a big deal, the last time something like this happened it was with my dad, and Masters Warbick, Zezz, Kujex, and the rest of that crowd, most of whom are masters here now! But that class had been here for a year by then, so we are the first to graduate this soon, at least since before Dojee was here!" Alex didn't need a lot of time to think about it, and spoke at once.

"You can count me in; all this studying gives me a headache!" The rest of the group just looked at him in disbelief while Ryan spoke his mind.

"You haven't so much as picked up a book since we got here! You've spent most of your time exploring the castle and trying to find a way into the girl's dorm!"

"Both, noble pursuits!" Alex said defensively, Ryan clapped his hand over his face, Ben and Foeseth just grinned while the girls giggled.

"Anyway, I'm on board too. You didn't think I was going to let you do something that dangerous...and cool alone did you?" Ben stated finally. The rest of the group agreed with this in unison and they all shared a hug.

"Okay, now what?" asked Rozea. Michael wasn't sure, Dojee hadn't told him to meet anywhere so he decided the best thing would be to start training and wait for someone to get them. Michael shared this with everyone, none of whom even questioned it. Michael guessed they all felt that they could use some practice for what they were going to do. Ben and Rozea got some bo-staffs and started sparring, Michael couldn't tell if Ben was just really good or if Rozea was just distracted, fantasizing about him. Blaze must have thought along the same lines because she called over to Rozea.

"Hey, don't take it easy on him! Hit him in the face!" Rozea snapped out of her stupor and started fighting hard. Blaze had started sparing with Eliza, and they were quite well matched even though their styles could not be more different. Michael paired up with Foeseth—with one hit Foeseth knocked Michael across the mat they were on. It seemed that Foeseth was a little bit out of Michael's weight class. To go along with his size though, he was also very fast and found creative ways to use his wings in a fight. At the far end of the mat, Ryan and Alex were about to practice, but Ryan wanted to lay down some ground rules.

"Look you and I have never had a strait match against each other so let's do it right. No powers, that is to say I won't slow down time or use energy blasts you don't teleport or...do anything else like that. Only physical powers, strength, speed, agility, and so on."

"Are you sure about this?" Alex asked, seemingly genuinely apprehensive.

"Of course, why wouldn't I be? I have been trained in hand-to-hand combat since I was five!"

"Okay, but remember you asked for this." Alex took off his coat. It was the first time Michael had seen him take it off since they met. He then proceeded to take off his shirt to reveal a body like stone. Alex was thin, but super cut and the muscle he had seemed very tough. To go along with it, he was absolutely covered from the neck down in scars. One particularly nasty scar went from his right shoulder all the way down to his hip. Ryan took off his shirt too and though he was in very good shape he looked kind of sad next to Alex. Ryan came at Alex in great form and surprising speed, but Alex countered Ryan and flipped him over his shoulder in a second. This happened several times, Ryan was bruised and gasping for breath and Alex wasn't yet sweating. By this time everyone had stopped fighting and were all watching the fight, they were all looking on in wide eyed amazement. Michael was not quite so surprised since he knew that Alex was so powerful, but he was impressed all the same at his skill. The group decided that it would be fun to take Alex on one at a time, and so that is what they did. Rozea went first and was beaten in seconds, they were doing best out of three and it was just incredible how fast Alex kept the line moving. Blaze went up and Michael shot Alex a "you better be careful" glare. So Alex beat her lightly, and took his time. Foeseth went next and proved to be Alex's toughest opponent yet, even still he was beaten in ten minutes. Ben went next and was proven to be just as good as he seemed to be with Rozea, and was able to match Alex blow for blow. After about fifteen minutes, and to everyone's surprise, Ben came out the winner. Alex congratulated him and went over to the nearest snow bank on one of the battlements of the castle and stuck his hands in it to ice them. Michael got up and joined Ben, he was a lot bigger than Michael, but so were Zezz and Warbick so Michael had already gotten use to fighting huge guys. They started at full speed and it was to Michael's surprise just how well he was doing. Michael was fast, strong, and accurate with everything he threw at him and in less than ten minutes had Ben pinned! The group cheered and they all slapped five with Ben and Michael in support. It was clear Michael had learned a lot and was in fact on a different level than the rest. You would think, after so many years of being the best at whatever he tried to do he would be use to it, but something about this was different. These people had been trained since children in combat. Then again so had he, he started his first taekwondo class when he was six, it was still an odd feeling though. The group sat down and Michael would take them one at a time and show them some ways they could improve their fighting. He showed them better form when punching and how to defend more effectively, as well as countering maneuvers that would help them all out a lot. Michael was suddenly very grateful for all of the painful training Dojee, Kujex, and Warbick gave him so that he could control his ability to absorb powers. Michael wouldn't have been able to share in any of this without it, he owed them a lot.

"Well is that a sight or what?" Balo had just walked outside to the court yard followed by Warbick, Zezz, Kujex, and Dojee. They had wide smiles and were quite pleased with seeing them all taking the time they had to train. Dojee had them all sit down so he could say what he needed to.

"My, my…look at you all, such fine warriors! No doubt in my mind that you all are shining examples of your parents being the greatest of their age. But moreover it is because you all have put forth tireless effort to get to where you are. This is unprecedented, and I have checked our records, no one—not even Zeus or his brothers—graduated this early from this academy! Foeseth, Ben, and Alex—I present you all with first class ratings. This is also a record as never has there been four first-class graduates from the same class! Blaze, Eliza, Rozea, Ryan—you all receive a second class rating. I hope you all understand just how special you are, and also I hope you are ready. I have no doubt that you can do this—or you wouldn't be here now—however there is more to this journey than just physical ability. For example, Conshen Moonsy, she is also a very skilled warrior and I have offered her the right to graduate at the end of this semester, but she herself said she felt that she would not be ready for any true action. If you can say that you do not know that you are ready, then you are not. *You* must know that you can do this for yourself. I had the pleasure of finding yet one more person who deserved the right to graduate early and he was more than willing. This is Able Minsoo he has been right on the tail of Foeseth and Alex here in grades, and is one of the top one hundred most powerful Jemini to attend this academy since my first year. I think you will all like him. So take some time and shoot the breeze with him tonight after your first training session with me (which will take place in the next ten minutes). Now each of you come up here and receive your badges so we can let the other Masters get back to their classes."

They all went up one at a time. Alex made himself look like he was crying and tried to blow his nose in Kujex's beard. Dojee had to quickly step between them to keep Kujex from punching Alex in the face. The rest went fast and all the masters but Dojee left. Just as they left, two more people showed up. The first was the blue skinned master that they had seen in the master's lounge. He seemed taller in the light of the day (over seven foot) and had several swords under his arm plus he had four strapped to his back and two on each side. Behind him one more person entered the courtyard. He was nine feet tall and covered with a super shiny armor like Master Zezz. His face was black and had odd markings and green glowing eyes. Michael could tell at once that this man had an anari. His eyes were then drawn to a very nice set of swords on his back plus a large broad sword at his side.

"Ah, good you're here. Everyone, this man here is Master Slairin. He teaches swords to our most skilled sixth year apprentices," Dojee pointed to the Blue skinned man who bowed deeply as he was introduced. "And this is my good friend Zeaga; he was crowned with the title of greatest swordsman alive a few years ago. They will be helping me train you all …" Dojee's words were cut off as the door to the courtyard burst open. The other Master that they had seen in that underground masters' lounge came stomping out toward Dojee. He was taller than Slairin, and his ram horns were adorned with a kind of armor that rapped them in shiny metal. He had his left hand on the handle of a curvy sword at his side and in his right hand was a piece of paper. As he walked toward Dojee, he locked eyes with Michael for just a minute. There was no doubt this man hated him—maybe even wanted to hurt him! He walked right up to Dojee fuming and breathing heavily. Dojee was not about to let such disrespect go without a word.

"Simein, what is the meaning of your intruding like this, as if I, or anyone here, owe you something?" Dojee spoke firm enough to let everyone know that he was not joking around.

"Oh, but I was owed something! I am one of the senior members of the board for this academy, and you did not come to me! You did not ask *me* if it was alright for you to graduate a bunch of children before their time!"

"That is because I didn't, and don't, *ask* anyone for anything! I simply informed the others that I had enough proof of their skills to justify such actions!" Dojee lost a bit of his cool as he answered and rightly so in Michael's mind, calling him and all his friends *children* right in front of them all! *What a punk!*

"You did not bring this before me! I demand to know why!" Simein spat as rage pumped through him.

"This very action, you are taking now answers your question. You are a grump, and hot headed. You do not see the opinions of others, only your own! And just to be clear, you are not a senior member of the board, you may be older than some of them, but you lack wisdom. I fear *you* were the one not ready for the promotion given! Now get out of my face before I make you!" Dojee had an edge to his voice Michael had never heard before (most likely because he was not dumb enough to put himself at odds with him before). Simein looked as if he had just been spit in the face, he looked around the courtyard and his eyes fell on Michael again.

"This is the supposed leader of the new Task Force? A child?" Michael had heard enough of that.

"I am not a child! You should do your best to remember that. Because if you speak out of turn to me, my friends, or Master Dojee again I'll punch you full on in the mouth!" Simein did not take this well...he punched Michael right in the face...This proved to be worse for Simein than Michael though, as Michael made his anari come out over his face. Simein's hand looked like it was broken, but he twisted the bone back into place and it healed instantly. Simein drew his sword...Dojee stepped forward with his drawn...

"I do not know what it is you think you're doing, but if you intend on trying to hurt Michael, I am afraid you will have to step over my dead body to do so! Now do yourself a favor and walk away before you do something foolish!"

"*How dare you!* I will leave for this betrayal, good luck trying to find someone to replace me! Out of respect for my students will I stay until the end of term! You Michael stay out of my way until then or you will be sorry! Michael felt an unnatural anger towards this man and this threat was more than enough to put him over the edge. Michael brought his anari out completely, none of his friends had seen this yet and so they all gasped in horror. Michael walked straight to Simein—who was stricken with fear—and grabbed Simein's sword out of his hand. Michael made as hot an energy as he could come out of his hands turning the sword to liquid instantly!

"Unless you want me to do the same to your face I suggest you never threaten me again!" Michael felt a very hard slap on the back of his head, followed by a second. Zeaga had slapped him across the back of his head and at present had a look of an annoyed father correcting their child. Dojee had the same look but was looking at Simein; he stepped in close to Simein and whispered something no one could hear. A moment later Simein apologized to them all but didn't make eye contact as if afraid to look at them. Dojee then turned on Michael with a look of true disappointment on his face.

"Do you know what you just did? You just did something very foolish! Not only did you try to pick a fight you didn't know you could win. But you followed that by using your power—which you barely have control of—in a way you never have before! Do you know how hot you were just a moment ago? ..."

"N ... no ..."

"Well, you were hot enough to instantly liquefy metal! That sword wasn't just any sword either; it was made by Loki, Simein's father! I have seen that sword withstand blows from Aires's sword which burns at around ten thousand degrees! Let me put it to you like this, if you had pushed it any hotter, you could have caused what has been come to be called "The Fire Storm Effect". Basically you could have set fire to the planet's atmosphere causing a chain reaction that would have destroyed all life on this planet!"

"I ... I just ..."

"I know you were stepping in to defend my honor and then your own, and you were right to put him in his place for talking to you, and about you in that way. But you must realize we do not know what you can do, what your limit is. We do know that you seem able to do things by sheer luck and instinct, which most fully trained and experienced Jemini, could never do. That leads me to believe you may have more raw potential power than anyone else has had since Ackatoth! In a few hundred years I could see you learning how to destroy entire planets at will! There are those who could do that now, but they had to learn control. In the future just let me handle a situation like that, or you could hurt someone you love and that would destroy *you*."

"I'm sorry. I didn't mean to put myself or others in danger. I just let my temper get the best of me.

"That you did, and that is the other problem. Simein is a god-level Jemini with over seven thousand years of fighting experience if he had any reason to think of you as a threat he could and *would* simply kill you. You may be powerful but you are so young you haven't the proper understanding of just how valuable experience is. Also you must never pick a fight with one of my Masters again or I will strip you of the title I just gave you. All that said I do have to admit, though. You do have quite a knack for doing things I thought couldn't be done. You did manage to scare him, not many could say that! And just so you know, I told him that if he ever did pick a fight with *you* again, that I would *let* you do what you wanted to him! I would just make sure no one was anywhere near you two!" Dojee, finally smiled warmly again.

"Now, back to more important matters. Michael run and fetch "The Book of Ackatoth", we need to know where it is you are going, now don't we?"

Michael ran to his room and was back in ten minutes flat and promptly opened the book. There was nothing for a few seconds, then once again like ink rising through milk words appeared on page one.

> *Hello Michael. A long time have I waited for you, alone in the dark.*
> *Now hear me clearly, before on this journey you embark.*
> *While for the sword you and your friends shall plunder,*
> *Its guardians will awaken from their long peaceful slumber.*
> *You will leave in five weeks to start on your great quest*
> *Do not dare argue with me, just trust that I know best.*
> *The way is cold, the way is dark, the way is dangerous too.*
> *So be sure you are ready for this trip, or it will claim you."*

Michael finished reading aloud and everyone was frozen, Dojee was ashen faced. He looked from Slairin to Zeaga and they all shared the same look, a look of worry and doubt.

"Five weeks isn't enough time for us to train these young ones as they'll need!" Slairin hissed.

"Yes, I feel the same. However at this juncture I'm looking at the bigger picture. I must get the sword, I'm meant to, always have been," answered Michael.

"You are…dead set on going then? No matter what the cost?" Dojee asked hesitating as he spoke.

"Yes. I am the guardian and I need my sword!" Michael felt a surge of courage fill him, at this point he was just too excited to be afraid…but that was about to wear off though.

"So be it. Prepare your selves my friends. You are all in for a tough few weeks and far worse after that!" Dojee went to a weapons rack and grabbed a wooden sword. "Time to train."

CHAPTER NINE

True to his word these five weeks were horrid. None of them had worked so hard in their lives. Even Dojee, Slairin, and Zeaga all felt tired. They were all learning very fast, and by the end of the third week it was hard tell that Michael and his friends were recent graduates Ben was now nearly as good as Michael, while Alex and Foeseth were right behind. Rozea was now vastly improved with the sword and Eliza could dodge any attack with ease. Ryan was now by far the best swordsman of the group, and Blaze had become twice her normal speed with her great sword. And then there was Able, he didn't much like swords. He preferred to use his hands. Zeaga simply replied, "Then the day your enemies share that sentiment you'll be ready for them, now pick a weapon!"

Able ended up picking what are known as war blades. They were basically a "J" shaped piece of metal with a handle inside the hook of the "J". They are held with the long part going the length of a person's arm so that they can punch with *it* instead of their fists. With these Able became nigh unbeatable, to put it another way Michael was the only one of the group who did, and it took nearly an hour to do it.

They all worked on mastering their powers better as well. Ben was fast, everyone knew that, but it turned out that he also had the ability to charge his hands with electricity; so that getting punched by him felt like getting punched by a cattle prod! Eliza—aside from her super strength—could hover in midair, and she had mind controlling abilities as Michael found earlier. Rozea had strength too, but her main ability was super enhanced reflexes. She could dodge a bullet without trouble; on top of that she could shoot yellow beams from her eyes that could melt straight through steal like butter. Foeseth turned out to have the highest level of fire casting or pyrokinesis since Apollo and Aries! It was so extreme he couldn't even use a tenth of his potential, or it would kill anyone near him! Ryan had the ability to slow down time, and he also had enhanced reflexes and night vision. Blaze could Phase through solid objects and could shoot energy blasts from her hands and super strength. Alex obviously could teleport—but he also had many other abilities which he refused to share with them. Able had super strength beyond anyone there as well as speed enough to run over a hundred miles an hour, agility that allowed him to flip twenty feet in the air, and endurance enough that a standard knife couldn't cut him! To add to all of this he could fly and he could generate lighting blasts at levels enough to destroy cities with ease! Michael was being taught how to use his new powers from Kujex and Warbick. He was getting quite good with his magnokinesis and lightning abilities from Kujex. The super jumping was still hard for him to land, but he had learned how to roll out of it at least. They also proved that Michael had a notable level of regeneration. During one of their last practices before the trip, Michael and Able were sparing and Able got a little too close with his war blades. Michael's anari didn't even have time to come out before the edge hit his arm cutting him to the bone. Everyone came over quickly to see if he was okay and watched as the cut healed in mere seconds!

"You are full of surprises Captain Rains!" he said between gasps.

"Yeah, it seems that way doesn't it?" Michael and Able got along quite well as did the rest for that matter. It wasn't even the second day, and you wouldn't have known that Able had just met the group. He was very smart, yet he was still fun loving and liked to kid around. When it came to hand-to-hand fighting though he was just ridiculous! He managed to just barely beat Michael once, and even held his own against Zeaga and Warbick in one training match!

Michael and Blaze were getting closer, but he still wasn't sure just how forward he could be with her, or if she thought of him as a boyfriend or more like a brother. Foeseth and Conshen were head over heels for each other and Able had his girlfriend flown to the academy so he could propose. It was well done and all of the girls cried. Kujex watched this from a distance and looked very grumpy but if anyone tried to talk to him he would jump and shouted at them while wiping at his eyes, "I am not crying. Now get away from me!"

Alex was crying too, to a degree that was hard to tell if it were fake or not. He then added to this display ... "My little man's growing up ...!" Between fake sobs. This little event made Rozea all the more desperate and she finally got tired of her so called "subtle" tactics. She walked up to Ben the day before they were going to leave.

"Oh my, you certainly are strong to lift such a big axe ...!" She said in a sweat, over the top voice. " ... Do you think I could feel how big your arms are?

"What, this? You use a great sword that's just as heavy—if not more so. Besides that if you want see the strong ones around here look to Foeseth and Able. I might catch up to their level by the time I stop growing though. And you can see how big my arms are why would you need to feel them?" Ben answered, completely clueless. Rozea let out a shriek of frustration and stomped off. The entire group had their faces buried in their hands. Michael had taken to checking the book regularly to see if it said anything new, but it hadn't since he read that they had five weeks. He opened the book again and just as before there was nothing on the second page, at first. All of a sudden words started appearing in their eerie way. Michael called everyone over so they could hear as he read,

"Some clue you seek, so you take a peek, at what may lie ahead.
Fear sinks within you like a weight made of lead.
What fun would it be, if you could see, the things that are to
come.
You will do as you're told, because not to would just be dumb.
For if you don't do as I command, then you never again will
see this land.
In the cave are things so dark, that they would make you cry.
So if you test me, do not doubt me, you will surely die!"

Michael stopped reading and felt as if something nasty was crawling under his skin. This book seemed more and more like it didn't want him to make it. *Just what kind of a man was Ackatoth anyway? After all he made the book and the sword!* Dojee and the rest there, obviously felt the same ominous air flowing about them. They all shivered and Slairin sat down as if winded.

"There is still time for you to change your minds you know, you do not have to do this!" Dojee said at once with a tone, almost asking them not to.

"Dojee, I am not going to let an old book scare me! I am going for that sword if I have to do so alone." Everyone just looked at him as if he were not right in the head. "...Look I have this...power, I guess. It's a feeling I get and no matter how strange, dangerous, or downright stupid the *feeling* is if this feeling says to do something, it has always turned out right. Even my meeting you all was because I *felt* like I needed to take a walk to my bank. I met people sent to kill me there, and I ran in the direction I *felt* and it lead me to right where Warbick was or at least close enough for him to find me. Either way if I had not done as this *feeling* had lead me to do, at any one of those points, I may well have never met any of you! I might have died back on earth! So now this *feeling* is telling me I need to go for this sword, so that is what I will do!" Michael was not sure how this would be received, but was surprised to see that everyone's faces were more relaxed.

"Michael, I wish you would have told me about this ability sooner. We could have practiced it more," Dojee said with a relieved voice. "By Zeus! Do you know just how useful that is going to become on this trip? You may know of the leader of the Argonauts, Jason. You have heard of him, yes?"

"Yeah. Are you telling me that he had this power too?"

"Quite right you are. Balo could tell you many stories of just how it saved his life. It makes me feel better about this whole thing, really!"

"Master Dojee that reminds me I was wondering who out of the masters would be joining us?"

"Oh…well…That is a good question. We *were* going to have some of them go with you weren't we? I shall make a list of those from the staff that could go with you and their skills, you will get to choose."

"Well, if I could, I would like it if Master Warbick could join us."

"Hmm…I would think he would be honored by that, and would like to come, unfortunately he is not available. I could have to leave the castle again and as he is my second in command, he must stay here. Like I said let me get you a list, shouldn't take more than an hour." Dojee hurried from the private courtyard, which had become their permanent training spot. The day was moving slowly, and the team was all enjoying their breakfast. The following day they would be leaving and they all seemed to be getting tense, except for Alex that is. He was so excited that he could hardly sit still. Michael finished eating and decided to take a walk around the castle. It was odd really, he hadn't even been there a whole semester yet, and it felt like he was going to be leaving his home. He didn't pay attention to where he was going. He just walked. He figured he would just use the nearest high speed transport system to get back. He walked throughout parts which he had never been to before, there were classrooms over here as well as many dorm wings, lobbies, and a few libraries. He met a master named Cross, who had a nasty scar over his left eye and oddly enough a patch over the other. He was in charge of the armory and despite missing one eye and having a patch on the other he seemed to be able to see just fine!

Michael had no idea how long he had been walking, but it helped him clear his head. He was about to turn back when he saw the next hall. There were magnificent stained glass windows that went up at least a hundred feet on the left side of the hall and to his right were portraits of former masters and grandmasters in order of there arrival. He thought the hall looked interesting. There were trophy cases; by the window, there was a fountain a little ways down. Rays of sun shown through the windows casting red, blue, and yellow light all around. There were statues every so often, cases with weapons belonging to great heroes of old; there was a tall shadowy figure at the end of the hall. There were flowers in vases of all sizes and colors. He saw a large picture of a very young Dojee, and there was...um...*Hold on a second!* Michael stopped dead; the "shadowy figure" was just standing maybe two hundred feet away with its back to him. It was quite out of place in the hall, and kept looking down each end of the hall it was in. It stayed there for just a moment, then almost like smoke on a breeze it floated to the left and out of sight. Michael hurried after it and came around the corner just in time to see a door, way down the hall close with a heavy metal thud. Michael ran to the door it was locked, Michael tried to use his new badge to open the door but it didn't work. The screen on the gauntlet flipped on and said,

"...There appears to be a problem, there is no door here. You are advised to acquire corrective lenses."

Michael felt like smacking the thing! Of course there's a door here! He was looking right at it! Michael didn't want this thing to get away, there seemed to be an infestation of shadowy figures around here and he wanted it to stop! So Michael quit subtlety and grabbed the door and started pulling as hard as he could. The door groaned, but stayed quite locked.

"What are you doing?"

Michael nearly had to change his shorts, as he jumped two feet in the air. Blaze was standing there looking both confused and intently interested in what he was doing.

"What are you doing way over here?" Michael asked.

"Well, for one thing my dorm is only two halls over. Plus...I was looking for you," she said bashfully.

"Oh...well...I, um..." Michael stammered.

"Anyway I asked you what you were doing first, now spill it!" Blaze added in a sort of playful way.

"Alright...You won't believe this, but there was another shadowy character and who or whatever it was ran down here and through this door. My badge doesn't open it so I'm trying another approach." Michael admitted

"That door is made of mallieum, one of the three unbreakable metals, and also the heaviest substance there is. You would have an easier time going through the wall!...Oh don't actually try going through the wall! Just step aside." Blaze shook her head and muttered something about boys as she phased her arm through the door as if it weren't even there! Michael heard something click with a heavy thud and the door swung open.

"Wow! It slipped my mind that you could do that, it really is a handy trick!" Michael said, trying to sound flattering.

"Oh...it's nothing really...You know we should go after this thing if we're going to." She said turning red. So they hurried through the door which closed on it's own as soon as they got through it. They rushed forward down a huge spiraling staircase more than big enough for Pith to fit in. Both of them thought this was weird because there was no way he would have fit through the door above—not without remodeling the castle anyway. They kept going down for what felt like twenty minutes with no sign of catching the phantom. At last the stairs came to a landing, and they found themselves in a dark tunnel not unlike a sewer. There were old lights along the tunnel ahead—several were blown while one was flickering sporadically. There was a drip somewhere deep in the tunnel, and they could hear the mumbled sound of distant voices. Michael motioned for silence as they crept down the tunnel; they stopped at a few hundred feet from a side opening in the tunnel. They could see a soft yellow glow—such that can only come from many lit torches—in the antechamber ahead. It must have been a big chamber too, because even from this distance the voices from within were easily heard by way of the echo.

"...I don't know how! Either way, someone told him we would be here. There *is* one person that roams the halls every night—but only late and he is impossible to catch! In any case, two men have been compromised—one had most of the bones on his right side broken by Balo." Michael couldn't recognize the voice. It sounded altered in some way.

"Failure is not wise—we expect more from you! What is happening now? Is there any news on how the boy is developing?" This voice was deep, cold, and harsh—something about it sent a chill down Michael's spine

"Oh, yes! The boy has graduated! That's right, and not just him but all but one of his friends and she will still graduate at the end of this semester. Dojee started a new Asendor Task Force, and Michael is its head. Things get worse too, he is wise beyond his years and extraordinarily more powerful then we thought. He might have beaten me by sheer instinct, even Dojee underestimates the boy. Gave him an earful for picking a fight with me, but I saw how surprised the boy even was. He has no concept for his power Thive, he...Errrk...! The man shrieked as if he were grabbed by the throat. Michael knew who had been talking now, it was Simein, but at that moment the other man was shushing him like you would a child.

"Shh, shh, shh! I think I heard something like my name come from your mouth! I would kill you now, but then I would have to kill your father as well, and that would just take too much of my time...! Hmm...I hate to say it...but I believe you were followed...I smell someone." Michael felt like ice had just been forced into his veins! There was no way they would reach the stairs before being spotted. Michael looked around frantically for a place to hide. In one instant, Michael looked up and saw a hole in the ceiling of the tunnel, he grabbed Blaze and jumped. He might not have enjoyed the intense training with his abilities—super jumping chief among them, but was very glad he had it. Michael was braced against the walls of the hole with his arms and legs while Blaze was wrapped around his middle. Heavy footsteps echoed right below them, Michael chanced a look down. The head below him came within only twenty feet from the hole they were in, which meant this person had to be nine to ten feet tall. He stood there for a moment looking down the hall, from what Michael could see he was covered in a strange armor and had green glowing eyes.

"Do you see anyone, Thive?" uttered an unnaturally deep voice.

"What did I just get done saying about using names, *Drackiss*? And no, there is no one here..." Thive had deep sarcasm in his voice and made sure to say his name louder than he needed to. Michael wasn't sure if he was just seeing things in the failing light but it looked as though for just a split second, Thive had looked up right at them, but then turned away...

"They must have been quick and ran, or perhaps that kid that you spoke of, either way they are gone," Thive said, going back around the corner.

"In that case you had best get on with your job, if you fail again or bring us anything but good news. You will die, right after you watch all those you know and love burn alive. Thive here will see to it personally. Are we clear?" Drackiss spoke with such evil in his voice that it made Blaze cringe. They heard a heavy door squeak open and closed. A second later Michael saw Simein run passed, however he stayed there for a few minutes just to be sure they were safe to come out. Michael dropped and landed gracefully, considering Blaze was still wrapped around him.

"We need to warn Dojee, Simein is a high-ranked master, he has access to a lot of dangerous stuff!" cried Blaze.

"Right, let's go. It's been long enough Dojee may have started looking for me to give me the list of masters I need to pick from anyway." They bolted up the tunnel and back up the stairs. After a while of huffing and puffing they reached the door and tried to turn the handle…It would not budge.

"Oh well it's a good thing I can phase through stuff or we would be stuck in here!" Blaze said smiling. Her smile faded quickly though as she tried to push her hand through the door and it just hit it instead.

"Ouch! I can't phase through this part of the door!" she said, sounding scared.

"But you went through the other side?" Michael reminded.

"This tunnel must not be a part of the castle, but a way to get in. All the entrances are made so you can't just phase your way in. It's a security system, you can phase outside from in, but not the other way around!" she seemed like she was starting to panic.

"Hey, don't worry. We'll get in if I have to break my way through the rock around the door!" Michael gave her a tap on the shoulder. Thinking he might be able to knock the hinges out of the wall, Michael started ramming into the door. The door didn't seem to be moving even slightly, however it certainly made a lot of noise so someone would certainly hear it. After about twenty minutes though Michael decided that extreme was the only alternative. He brought out his anari over his hands…Which made him realize that he could have been using that to beat the door with, instead of his now very sore shoulder!…He made the anari into spikes and started hitting the rock beside the door. The second he hit the rock the door flew out of the wall. The dust cleared and they could see Pith hunched down looking at them with an odd smile.

"Kinda goin' to extremes to get some alone time, wouldn't you say?" he said, winking awkwardly at Michael, who suddenly found it hard to make eye contact with anyone.

"No time for that kind of joking Pith! What did you two find out? What did you see down there? Don't tell me you found yet another 'shadowy figure'!" Dojee said in a rush.

"Sorry but that's exactly what we found, but we learned who it was this time and who they were working for," Blaze said at once.

"Really? Spill it, quickly!"

"The caped phantom was Simein, and the two he was taking orders from were Thive and Drackiss," Blaze answered, and Dojee turned white as a ghost.

"Do you know them?" Blaze asked.

"You two are lucky to be alive! Thive is Valldiss's right hand man and from what I hear he is even more ruthless then Valldiss himself! He was there when Valldiss killed your parents. I met him that very night. He was fighting Zezz, Warbick, and Kujex at the same time. Drackiss is even worse. Drackiss is responsible for Valldiss turning in the first place. He is more powerful than Valldiss but that won't last long. Still he is among the strongest people alive and one of only ten single individuals that could open our front gate when unlocked! If you had been found, you would be dead! Very foolish of you to go running down yet another mysterious staircase and this time with only one follower! That aside you said Simein took orders from them? I could see him maybe answering to Drackiss but not Thive!"

"Thive got physical with Simein when he let slip his name. He said he would have killed him but that he didn't want to have to kill his father too, only because he didn't have the time."

"He said *that*?" Dojee seemed almost *too* intrigued by this.

"Yeah—and right before they left, Drackiss told Simein if he failed, Thive would kill him right after he watched his family burn alive."

"Wow, I think I know less about Thive than I was aware of—though that would explain why Valldiss gave him his present job. This is bad news and I am going to be taking extra precautions for this trip of yours. You will get three of my staff to come with you, and Pith here will be one of them."

"Is there something bigger going on here? Like some kind of evil plot? I know Michael is important, but for two people like that to be here and so directly involved," Blaze asked, looking at Michael as she spoke.

"I don't know, though it would seem likely. But right now, the only plot I'm concerned with is the one they are most likely planning for you now somewhere on your journey. Simein knew everything, and most likely told them to have someone head you off. I have a few tricks of my own, though."

"But what about Simein?" Michael asked.

"You leave him to me! I have treated that man as a friend, and I do not take betrayal well. Now you go get ready, you're leaving tonight! At midnight, that way it's still *tomorrow* and thus we are sticking to the book's instruction. Go quick you only have a few hours so let's move!" Michael ran to his room and got his sword and anything he could fit onto a tactical rig he was given by Kujex. It was complete with backpack, shoulder and leg holsters, chest rig, and even came with five different knives and a belt attachment for his sword. Ten minutes later Michael left his room and made his way to the armory to get some guns. Rozea was already there getting an assortment of arrows including explosive, and shattering arrows, (those work kinda like hollow point bullets, in that they are designed to break apart as they enter a target. In this case a half inch entry wound leads to a nine inch exit). She also had grapple arrows which were attached to a small winch of high strength cable that could connect to her utility belt. She started strapping knives to her as Cross came over to Michael.

"So you want some firearms for those holsters? Well that is a good idea. I'll get you some grenades as well. My motto is, 'if hitting don't work, cut it. If cutting don't work, shoot it, and if shooting don't work, blow the crap out of it!'" Michael chuckled.

"What if that doesn't work?" Michael asked.

"Ha! That's why they invented running kid!" Both Rozea and Michael cracked up. Rozea's smile quickly faded though, Cross disappeared into the back of the armory and Rozea seemed almost ready to cry.

"Hey what's up with you? Are you nervous about the trip?"

"Hmm? Oh no...I...It's just hard for me. I mean Foeseth and Conshen are love birds. Able's engaged, and you and Blaze at least know that you're in love with each other..."

"Yeah, I guess, Ben just...*wait, what*!?"

"I just don't...I'm afraid that I won't ever get to tell Ben that I love him or how we are going to get married and have dozens of kids!..." KLANG KLANG!! They both spun around to see Ben standing in the door of the armory his shield rolling around at his feet, and a look of dumbfounded amazement on his face.

"You...Love me?" Rozea let out an odd cough like noise while the color left her face. At that moment Blaze, Ryan, Eliza, Alex, Able, and Foeseth all walked in the room and immediately felt the awkwardness.

"Wow it feels awkward in here! Oh, tell me she just farted really loud or something!" Alex said with a huge grin.

"She just said she loves me," Ben said still in a daze.

"Are you saying you didn't know? Dude she did everything but wear a sign man! She's liked you since you met!" Alex said dismissively. Before Ben could respond Cross came back out from the store room with a pile of guns, swords, and bombs that was literally larger than Michael. He stopped dead at the scene studied it for about two seconds then spoke.

"So Rozea said how she felt about Ben, and he overheard it?"

"You got it" Michael said, the rest of the group were all trying not to laugh at this point…well…Alex wasn't, he was hunched over laughing uncontrollably. Zezz, Kujex, Dojee, Warbick, and Pith walked in just then.

"Hmm, this is an odd scene," Warbick said at once, already smiling.

"Secret's out, Rozea loves Ben and now he knows," Alex blurted between gasps for air.

"Oh, very good! It's about time!" said Dojee, exhaling heavily. The other masters all grinned at Ben.

"Wait! Even you guys knew about this?" Ben asked, sounding almost hurt.

"My friend, I dare say you were the only person in the school who didn't know." Informed Zezz.

"Yeah, and as a matter of fact, we masters had a bit of a bet going on how long it would take for you to catch on. Warbick, you owe me six gold by the way!" Kujex added.

Alex was still laughing heartily ten minutes later while Ben tried to convince Rozea to come out of the closet she had locked herself in. The rest of the group was fully armed, and Cross went to Alex to give him some stuff.

"Oh I don't need anything thanks."

"We all know you're a good fighter but you need weapons!" Cross spat. Alex just stood from his chair and opened his trench coat to reveal at least fifty guns strapped all over him. He also had two sets of four throwing knives, eight throwing stars and two short swords.

"Holy crap! Where did those come from!" demanded Ryan.

"My bag of course!"

"That bag couldn't have fit half of that stuff in it!" observed Blaze.

"It would seem you're wrong, wouldn't it?" Alex said indignantly.

While the others continued to discuss this, Michael went over the list Dojee had given him, Dojee had run to the dimensional gate to meet Slim, who had sent word that he was coming. The list had Zezz, Kujex, Biff, Sif, Balo, Slairin, Edgar, Brains, and Ortaiga. Michael found this hard but he knew that he had to choose now so he decided on Balo first. Having been an Argonaut he had an immense amount of experience with such adventures. He had wanted to pick Zezz, but he knew that Kujex had a few dozen quests under his belt as well. Dojee came back with Slim and Slim had them all take off there "Pathetic excuses fer armor." Pith set down a huge chest with a large S on it.

"Al'righ' Michael ya'll get this 'ere piece 'O armor fer yer chest. These bits go on yer shoulders. These are yer leggin's and boots. Now the rest of you lot come 'ere and I'll give ya wha's yers." Everyone got their new armor which was very good because it was all far lighter than what they had—add to that the fact that Slim armor was worth a tidy fortune, they just took it without question.

"Oh...I see ya've managed ter not die yet!" Slim said sounding almost disappointing, looking at Alex for the first time since he arrived..."

"Don't worry there's still time," Alex answered, not missing a beat.

"Do you think you could give them some advice for their trip?" Dojee asked.

"I think so. Let's see 'ere. Okay Ben, yer goin' ta need ter be on yer guard as ya may or may not 'ave somethin' bad happen dependin' on what ya might do. Rozea watch yer step, that is, after wha' *might* happen near the end. Foeseth ya'll do well as long as ya don't do something else...*that* could happen if Able does what he might...if things work out that way O'course. Blaze stick close ter Michael until ya need ter get away from 'im...if he does what he most likely will I mean. Ryan just do whatever ya want ter do, unless ya need ter do somthin' else tha' is! Masters just help Michael unless he doesn't need it, then help the others as they need it...Unless they don't need it either. Michael ya'll be tested most of all, and ya'll decide in the end wha' happens ter them all...That is if tha' is wha' happens anyway. Oh and Pith if all else fails, just punch stuff!" The group just stood there looking confounded. Even Dojee seemed annoyed by this useless gibberish!

"Um…Thank you for…that. I'm sure that *may or may not* come in handy, depending on weather it does or not!" Michael said, irritated. There was a moment of silence then the group broke out into laughter. Slim didn't seem to know what was funny, but just laughed anyway.

"Now let's get you a good meal before you go, you don't know how long it will be until you get to eat again," Dojee said. They all went back to the courtyard that had become their new home for training. Now though the mats were rolled up and the weapon racks were pushed way out of the way behind benches that surrounded the fountain and pond. Now the middle of the courtyard had several tables set up and were piled with food of all kinds—from roasted birds and grilled steak to baked potatoes and pasta. They all ate enough for three people each—since their intense training had started they had all doubled their portions at meals just to keep up with what they burned. Two hours later they were all done with their deserts and Dojee broke the silence.

"Michael, look at that book and see if it will tell you what planet you will need to go to or something like that anyway, so we can point you in the right direction." Michael went over to his satchel and pulled out the book. He turned it to the third page and words appeared immediately.

> *"You wish to know where to go and how to get there too.*
> *One thing you can know, is that I will lead you true.*
> *It isn't as far as you might think, just head west, it'll be a blink.*
> *Three weeks walk and there you'll be, oh how much you're going to need me! Danger fills the night, and you'll be forced to fight, evils unknown.*
> *Stick together friends, for in the dark of the cave you are not alone."*

"I will love it when we have the sword and don't need the blasted book! I know of a pit of lava that would be perfect for it!" spat Kujex. The book said some more in response.

"Watch your mouth dwarf!"

The group was in stunned silence. Not only did this book seem to know who was there but it also seemed to know what was said! Michael put the book away and came back to the group.

"I think I might have an idea where you will be going. There is only one mountain range with deep caves that you could reach in three weeks from this castle. You'll have to go west into the *'Tanglewood Forest',*" explained Dojee. Kujex cursed under his breath while the Warbick let out a sigh "...Who did you want to join you from the list?"

"Balo, Zezz, and if I can Kujex as well," Michael answered.

"Hmm, three as well as Pith, is it? Well I suppose we can make that work. I will just call some friends of mine to fill in. Excellent choices by the way you stand a much better chance with them in your group," Dojee cleared his throat.

"Now I want to make this clear to everyone, Michael is going to be in charge of this group. Not even the masters will contradict what he says—unless he is about to get someone killed. That said, Michael you have over forty thousand years of combined knowledge between Balo, Pith, Zezz, and Kujex. So take their word for what it is. You only have a few hours so I strongly suggest you get as much sleep as possible. You may not have another chance for some time."

They all went to their rooms. Ben walked Rozea to her room. Alex tried to walk Kujex to his room; Kujex started trying to draw his sword as Dojee separated them. Able said something about why they had gotten armed if they were just going to go to bed first, and Foeseth just laughed. Michael dropped into bed, and across the room his satchel started to shake. Michael jumped from his bed and ran to it. The book had started vibrating. Michael opened the book to see what it had to say.

"Before you sleep, I have a word for only you to keep.
You are leading a group of friends, that you love so dear.
Beware of what you want in life, for the price may be severe.
Into the cave your team will go, and follow it so deep.
But only one will leave again, all the rest shall sleep."

Michael felt a chill in the air that wasn't from the snow storm outside. He had a strange feeling. He felt like this book was at least in some measure evil, that it *wanted* him to die on this quest. He threw the book down; he wasn't about to let a book get the best of him! Michael doubted that even this trip would have something that could kill Balo, Zezz, and Kujex, let alone Pith! Still as he got back into bed, he felt another unnatural chill. And just for a second, he thought for sure he heard a malicious laugh coming from the book on the floor.

CHAPTER TEN

"Boy, your face looks weird man!" Alex said as he woke Michael. Michael opened his eyes to see Alex's face not even an inch from his own.

"Maybe it looks odd because you're so close." Michael suggested. Alex popped across to room.

"Nope! Still weird," Alex said at once.

"Well, thanks for that. Could you do me a favor and let me get dressed."

"Are you sure you don't need a hand?" Alex asked in an almost convincing way.

"Get out you creep!" Michael couldn't help but chuckle. Alex was always good for a laugh.

Michael was dressed and fully armed in five minutes—he had been given two 1911 style pistols and a gun called a 'fusion pistol', which fires an energy-based projectile. Slim gave him a pulse blaster that he could sling on in addition to everything else. The rest of the group were making there way down to the main courtyard it was super cold and to make it worse the snow was dropping twice as fast as it had been. Blaze didn't have her usual sword, as it was just too large for her to strap it anywhere and she couldn't just carry the thing. So Slim gave her a pair of swords, exactly the same style as her big one, just much shorter so she could strap them, one on each side. Eliza was given a large machine gun much like a Minigun, but it was pulse based. She was also given a new mace that was basically eight axe heads fixed to a melon-sized metal ball!

"It feels a bit light. I'm used to two ton maces," Eliza said while she swung the ridiculous thing around as though it were weightless.

"Yeah, but ya can swing thatn' three times as fast. Tha' will do ya a favor, plus this one is short enough ya can actually 'ave it on yer back."

Slim gave Rozea a new longbow with elvish writing on it. To go along with it, he gave her what is known as a 'never-ending quiver'. Whatever arrows you put in will be copied as you pull them out thus the number of arrows never changes. These quivers are worth thousands of gold at least. Rozea was speechless. Slim just nodded to her and said, "consider that an early weddin' present." Rozea pulled Slim into what looked to be a bone crushing hug.

Slim didn't bring anything for Ben because he said that Ben's axe was perfect for him …

"After all tha's why his father had me make it fer him when he was born.

Ryan didn't want anything, but Slim said that was dumb and forced two pistols, a dagger, a grenade, and a blaster into his arms.

"Ya'll thank me when ya don't die … If ya survive that is."

Slim had given Able new armor earlier that was blue and white and fit perfectly. This was very good because his old armor was dented up badly from all of their intense practices. To go along with his new armor, Slim gave Able a shield. The shield fit right onto either arm and had a sharp diamond point, and had a bladed edge along the pointed end so he could punch with it just like one of his war blades. It was made of solid trillium and was colored to match his armor; this piece made him look very formidable—more than his large size and build already did. Foeseth was given a great sword—the handle looked like a dragon and the mouth opened to the blade, which looked like its tongue and even ended with a slight fork. With the group all assembled and armed, they were just waiting for Pith, who was still inside getting ready. He finally came out looking … overly ready. Pith was so big all of his weapons seemed like overkill. He had a pistol with a twelve inch wide barrel, a shotgun that slung over his shoulder—its barrel looked like it could have been used on a playground as a tube slide! He had a machete that was nine-feet long and three-inches thick at the spine. Lastly he had a battle axe, each blade was eight-feet wide, seven-feet long, and six-inches thick where they met the handle.

"Um…Do you think it's even fair for you to come along? What would be dumb enough to attack us with you nearby?" Michael chuckled.

"Fair? Not really. But if we're going into mountains and caves, then we may run into trolls. They can get bigger than me and they aren't afraid of anything! Beside that, I haven't left this castle in a while so I'll take any excuse I can get to stretch my legs." Pith slid his shotgun into the enormous holster on his back and went to the front gate and started pulling. The gate swung open with a low groan.

"This is it friends…" Dojee said, "…You are going to be changed by this experience in ways you can not yet understand. You will become family on this trip, and by the end you will have made ties that will never break. But be warned, this will be the hardest thing you have ever done, so dig deep and stick together." Dojee gave them one finale bow then went back into the castle.

"So fearless leader man, which way?" Alex said who was fidgeting with excitement.

"Straight west until the book says what's next," Michael instructed. They marched on in silence through the thick fluffy snow, staying tight together to avoid loosing each other in the storm and dark of night. They had trained outside on the upper courtyard so they thought they were ready for the weather. There used to be a force field covering the courtyard—which was why Michael didn't feel the cold air the first time he was there—but it was turned off for training. Now though, out on the plane they had no huge walls blocking the wind. Out here the air cut through you like a knife, the snow fell almost sideways, their legs sinking deep into it, soon it became too deep for Michael, Ryan, Blaze, Eliza, Alex, and especially Kujex. The others took smaller folks on their backs. Pith—who was leading the way to try and gouge out a path through the snow—had Ryan, Michael, and Alex on his back. Balo carried Blaze and Zezz had Eliza. Kujex however being stubborn said he didn't need carrying. Almost in response to this the ground must have dipped downward because Kujex disappeared out of sight. Still unfazed, Kujex just kept walking under the snow, they could see a small mound of snow moving toward the forest. Able came by and scooped him out of the snow and tucked him under his left arm.

"I'm not a bloody parcel! If I must be carried I'll ride like them!" Kujex swung himself out from under the arm and on Able's back. "I'm not too heavy for ya, am I?" Kujex asked uncertainly.

"Not at all. I could carry Pith for a good long while!" Able said over the wind.

"Is that an invitation?" Pith called back smiling wide. The group shared a quick laugh, then—remembering just how cold it was—the group stopped talking and walked on. An hour went by, then another, it was a long way just to get to the woods and with all the snow they were not making good time. Michael opened the book to see if it would say more now that they were closer to the woods. Words appeared at once...

> "*Wow, you're slow! You are falling way behind.*
> *You need to pick up your pace or you'll wind up in a bind.*
> *Once in the woods follow the path until it ends up dead.*
> *Do not stop to try and make camp or you will die instead.*"

Michael called for everyone's attention and told them what it said. Zezz made a face at the other masters. They obviously would have to stop before they got the sword; the book said it was a three week journey!

"That book is really good at rhyming isn't it?" Alex noted.

"Yes and for the first time it didn't say something clearly. '…until the path ends up dead' is a riddle—an easy one—but still…Obviously the path is going to dead end. However there could be another trick to this. The first riddle may have been that easy as a way of telling us that it is going to start speaking in riddles from now on, or it may just mean that it isn't going to always be straightforward. We must pay closer attention to that now," suggested Zezz. They walked on and on trying to move faster. The sun came up and went down again, and they were about to enter the woods and Pith stopped them at the edge to give instruction.

"I have spent quite a few nights hunting in these woods during off session. It is one of the most dangerous wildernesses you will come across! Watch your footing and *stay on the path!!*" he exclaimed.

"What should we be on the lookout for, in here then?" Michael asked intelligently.

"Do not get close to any body of water! If you see a bright glittering light, shoot it! At all times be ready to run, if ever I should say too. Lastly, as we near the foothills we will be entering troll, hydra, and dragon country. So once there we must make as little noise as possible." Pith stopped talking and the group in unison turned to look at Alex. The snow was thinner in the area so everyone got off the bigger people's backs.

"Hey what are you guys looking at, I can be quiet if I want to! I mean Eliza never even knew I was in her room even once!" Alex said defensively.

"That's true, I never did…Wait, what?" Eliza blurted. The group shared a concerned look and entered the woods. Once in the forest, the scene changed completely. The trees were so thick that the moon, though full and very bright, was blocked out completely. They were all given special lights that Brains created. These lights were powered by mini warp cells, which never ran out of energy. Pith said that there were predators in these woods that were attracted to bright light so everyone set their light to the dimmest setting. Light may have ceased, but sound became an even bigger problem. With every step they took, more sounds seemed to loom over them. This place was a nightmare, distant echoing sounds of beasts waling, crunching underbrush all around them, and occasionally what sounded like the wet ripping and tearing of flesh!

"This place is forsaken!" Kujex groaned, cursing under his breath at the horrid sounds. Balo chuckled and looked back at Kujex.

"If you think the sounds are scary just wait till you meet what's making them." Said Balo playfully, Kujex got a firmer grip on his axe in response.

"Scary! I haven't been scared by something since I was a wee lad..."

"Shhhh!!" Pith hissed, motioning for them to get down. They all looked ahead to see what Pith was looking at. About a thousand yards away a group of trolls were roaming through the woods.

"I've never seen them this far into the woods before! They almost never go this far from their caves, not unless something scared them away," Pith noted, keeping his voice at a whisper.

"You said trolls don't fear anything!" reminded Rozea.

"Yes well, what I meant to say is they don't fear anything until they are given reason to. Family groups usually have ten times this number which means they have lost quite a few. That would mean either there is an angry dragon around, or someone powerful already came through here."

As they sat waiting for the trolls to pass, there came a rustling in the trees not but twenty feet to the group's right. A minute later and a huge beast snaked its way toward the trolls. It was an enormous reptilian creature with three long necks and three diamond shaped heads. If it stood upright it would have been around thirty-five-feet tall, and it was at least ten feet wide at its chest.

"Now *that* is a hydra, and it is stalking them for one of the young ones you see there," Balo stated. Sure enough the hydra was sneaking around the group towards the young trolls. The largest troll sniffed the air and stopped dead in its tracks and put a fist in the air. Michael recognized this as the same gesture used by armies on earth. In a flash, the big troll turned toward the hydra and let out a roar that echoed throughout the forest. The group of trolls walking with him disappeared, and several others wearing full tactical gear and guns just as big as Pith's stood from their hiding places and opened fire on the unsuspecting hydra. It didn't even get to run. In ten seconds the hydra was nothing more than a smoldering carcass. About ten more trolls came walking up from behind some trees to the north of the rest of the group. The troll in the middle of these was in a special armor that looked robotic. He was bigger than the rest, standing over forty feet. In his arms was some type of energy weapon that made Pith's shotgun look like a child's play thing!

"These are not trolls from this land! They have been trained— well trained! They can speak as well! There are few people who have trolls this advanced at their disposal, but they are becoming popular with evil lords. These are most likely Drackiss's troops, if that is the case we are in for more than Dojee even feared!" whispered Pith in a defeated voice.

"How would they even know where to put men? I was the only one who could ever read this book right?"

"That book is not the only thing containing clues to the sword's location. It is just the only thing that was written by Ackatoth himself. Some say no one has returned from going after the sword, but that is not true. Several have gone, some got closer than others. Now for every person who survived this trip hundreds of millions have died; but it just so happens that Drackiss was on the team that got closer than anyone else, he just chose the wrong sword, he would know where the cave is. More important right now though is what we are going to do here. It looks like they are making camp right here which means we have to move. The problem with that is we would have to leave the path entirely. Plus trolls can smell you from a half a mile away, we're down wind of them now but if we or they move, we are blown," Pith answered.

"Let me check the book quickly." Michael opened to the next page from where he left off, and the words appeared in their normal way.

> *You have no choice you must fight before you are found.*
> *Kill them, keep going, use their blood to stain the ground!*
> *You can't go back or they will see, and you might die instead.*
> *So act fast one is coming this way, just do what I said.*

After Michael finished reading, they looked up, and sure enough the second biggest troll was walking toward them sniffing the air. Balo spoke quickly and strong to make sure no one argued at that point.

"You younger lot, follow our lead! Use every bit of strength you have. Hit hard and fast and let Pith and I lead and then Zezz and Kujex. Michael, bring out that anari of yours and shoot off as many of the most powerful energy blasts you can manage! Now or never ... *move!*"

Pith and Balo leaped out from behind the huge fallen tree where they were hiding. Balo was amazingly fast for a twelve foot man: he jumped through the air and struck the troll in the face with his great mace. The troll's head caved in and it fell in a heap. As impressive as this was, it was nothing next to Pith; his speed was nothing short of scary. Before Zezz and Kujex had even moved he had already ripped two trolls in half. Zezz started throwing fireballs at some of the bigger ones while Kujex started making the trolls' guns turn on them and fire.

Michael ran out into the open with his anari out and started generating energy blasts. He pushed it harder and faster than he ever had before. He let off the first shot, and it carved a forty-foot hole through everything in its path including several trolls. Foeseth went to the air firing off electrified balls of fire that were blowing holes through trolls as well as boulders nearby, so there would be no cover in the clearing. Blaze and Rozea double teamed each troll they came across, Blaze would slice them behind their knees, and Rozea would put an arrow in their eyes. Able was taking on three by himself, cutting them down with his war blades. Alex was jumping around teleporting body parts out of nearby trolls while shooting others in the throat. Ryan stuck next to Zezz who was still shooting off fireballs. Ben was zipping through the whole scene so fast that he was only a blur cleaving his axe right through any troll that got in his way. In only a few minutes, the only troll left was the leader who was actually good enough to match Pith blow for blow. Seeing his last man fall though, the troll ran off into the woods. The group gathered together and shared a cheer for their first victory.

"Michael, I can't believe how powerful that blast was! You made a new path through the woods..." There was in fact a huge forty foot walkway that had been carved right through the trees, and a long ways down they could see the body of an enormous creature that was now very dead—from there it was impossible to tell what type of creature it was.

"This heads in the same direction we were walking, but it is more clear. I say we use it! Plus that might be a dragon up there and if it is we will be making camp there!" stated Zezz.

"But the book said we aren't allowed to stop," remembered Kujex.

"Well, we aren't going to make it much farther without sleep. I say we sleep in shifts, that way if anything does come our way we are ready for it, plus all of us get to sleep some," Michael suggested. The others all agreed that this sounded wise and the book had nothing to say. So they looked around the bodies for anything that they could use before leaving. Pith grabbed the big gun that the troll leader had dropped.

"Wow! This is heavier than it looks!" he said looking at the truck sized gun.

"What, you mean it's ten tons instead of eight?" teased Alex.

"No…it's closer to thirteen I would say," Pith replied, oblivious to Alex's sarcasm. Alex just laughed. Other than the gun most of everything else was too big for the others to use, however they did find one other item. Among the body parts was a large devise that resembled an old toaster but instead of two slots for bread it had a screen on the top of it.

"So this is how they did it! The females and cubs we saw with them were holographic projections. This is an advanced model too, they have a lot of different creatures in here, this could prove very useful," Balo informed, "here Pith put that on your belt please. We might just need that later." Pith took it and they pressed on, with a sense of confidence in their group but also more on their guard than before. They traveled to the creature in the distance that Michael's blast hit and sure enough it was a dragon, almost as big as Jake…Just with a forty-foot cavity where most of its rib cage used to be. It had obviously been lying there (probably asleep) after it was hit by Michael's blast. Pith wasted no time. He pulled out his machete, pulled off one of the six-by-ten foot scales and started cutting the meat into steaks the size of cars.

"Pith…Not all of us can eat six tons of meat in a sitting," said Zezz, smiling.

"Dragon meat costs fifty gold per pound! I'm eating two of those steaks myself you all get to share the third," said Pith while hacking at the dragon with excitement. So Michael and Ryan cut out healthy sized steaks for everyone, and even after everyone had their third steak there was still three quarters of the massive steak left. This was the best meat Michael had ever tasted, and he was sure glad to have it, but now he really felt sleepy. Alex stood and looked longingly at the rest of the dragon with a dopy smile on his face. Kujex took notice and nodded at him.

"I know what you're thinking and don't doubt that I haven't tried to think of a way to take it with us. But the one scale alone has got to weigh a few dozen tons. So just let it go." Alex looked at Kujex like he just said the strangest thing ever.

"Why would I want the scale? I was just happy that all this meat isn't going to go to waste…since I'm here anyway."

"You're telling me that you didn't know that dragon scales can be used to make armor worth more than most kingdoms?

"Wait, say what?!"

"And what did you mean by your being here was going to keep it from going to waste?"

Alex didn't answer him instead a huge misty eyed smile spread across his face. He walked up to the dragon, took out a piece of paper from his pocket, made a note, and stuck it on the meat of the dragon with a knife. He then put his hand on the dragon and in a puff of gray smoke it disappeared. He did the same to the scale on the ground. Everyone looked at him in amazement; Ryan was the first to stumble his way to words.

"Did you just…teleport…that dragon?"

"Um…yeah! I didn't eat it! It's out front of Asendor right now, and it has already been spotted in fact…" They all looked at him like he was out of his mind. "…Hey I can hear anyone I think about and I can see through anything! Okay and the cook is very happy. He's saying something about this making up for all the meat disappearing from the cooler!"

Ryan immediately sat back down and tried to act as though he didn't have a clue. He over did it though and Michael, as well as Balo and Zezz noticed, however none of them cared enough to ask him about it just then. Now that they were well fed they took shifts keeping watch. Since Alex didn't sleep he just perched himself in a nearby tree to get a better view, and stayed there all night. Blaze, Michael, Pith, and Balo took first watch, while the rest slept. They traded in three hour shifts, and the fire at the center of the camp was the only warmth to aid them. In the clearing they were in, the sky was clearly visible and was no longer cloudy and with the lack of clouds the temperature fell fast. Still the sky was amazing, Michael was a city boy anyway you sliced it. He wasn't use to a night sky where the stars could be seen so clearly got lost in them and in no time his watch was over. He lay down with his head on his satchel and was about to close his eyes when an arm came across his middle. Blaze had lay down right beside him and put her head on his shoulder. Kujex who had gotten up with Rozea, Ben, and Able gave him an awkward wink and thumbs up. The morning came far too soon, and it was met by the book vibrating much like a large cell phone…

> *Move now, you're doing just fine, get to the mountain and start to climb.*
> *Or try the river and swim across, though that may have a heavy cost.*
> *Either way this won't be fun, but choose one quick or you are done.*

The group raced through the rest of the forest to the base of the mountain. Climbing seemed like a very bad idea as it was a sheer rock face. They looked to their right to see a rocky shoreline covered in snow and a thick mist. Balo waved his hand at the mist and it disappeared revealing a truly grotesque scene. Strewn across the shore of the river were the bodies of tens and thousands of beings of every sort. There were trolls, orcs, gargoyles, dwarfs, elves, and much more. Most of the bodies looked to have been there for a long time, but some still had wet wounds.

"These haven't been here more than a few days," said Kujex, looking over a few bodies.

"Whose men were they?" asked Able, looking at some long dead bodies.

"Um ... I would be more interested in knowing *what* did this to them!" said Blaze, looking at the face of a long dead elf with a look of terror.

"There may be something nasty in the water, I wouldn't know, I've never gone this deep into these woods, no need to if your only hunting," admitted Pith.

Michael was quite sure that trying to climb a sheer mountain would be more dangerous than some angry fish or something! Still he thought he would test the water. He bent down picked up a rock and threw it in ... Nothing happened.

"No offense but if there is something in there, that tiny rock would sooner put it to sleep than get its attention, let me try a different approach," said Pith, grinning. He walked over to a bolder at least twenty-feet taller than he was and twice as wide. He bear-hugged it and started to pull it out of the ground. Once out of the ground Pith put the small mountain over his head as if it were a toy, jumped several hundred feet straight up and hurled the rock at the river. The rest of the team ran away from the shore just barely into the tree line. The huge rock hit the water like a meteor and sank out of sight at once. Pith landed making a crater a hundred-feet wide and twelve-feet deep as watered spilled over the bank ... But, that was not all that spilled onto the banks! Tentacles shot from the water as hundreds of terrible monsters rose from the river's depths. They walked on six crab-like legs, and they had long bodies—around forty-feet—and coming off their faces were ten fifty-foot tentacles. At the center of these tentacles was a mouth that opened into four parts, and each part was covered in hook shaped serrated teeth. Their whole bodies were covered in a gray/blue exoskeleton, and their eyes were milky gray. What most stood out about these things was they had a large cured tail—not too dissimilar from a scorpion—but it could curl under them as well as over.

"*They're Basteels! Get behind us!!*" bellowed Balo.

He, Pith, Zezz, and Kujex all ran forward and started hacking with an intensity that through the others off for a moment. It seemed to Michael that he wasn't the only one who had no idea what a *basteel* was. Then it dawned on him that it didn't matter what they were. Only that they were going to kill him and his friends if they didn't snap out of it. So Michael Jumped forward and started blasting off energy balls as fast and as hard as he could! This turned out to be a good choice; his first two blasts hit two different basteels and turned them into steaming piles of goo. He then tried something new and changed the type of energy he was shooting. What he usually used was some sort of blue pulse energy. But with water all over the ground, he wanted to use electricity to fry them all at once.

"Everyone, get to dry ground!" screamed Michael. The group did not need to ask why as electricity was already pouring off him. Michael bent lower and pushed harder because the basteels were almost on top of him. Michael let loose of the electricity all at once, causing a bit more of a blast than he was attempting. A lightning bolt fifty-foot wide shot out of his hands and hit the closets basteel, turning it to smoldering remains. The bolt of electricity hit the ground and the water greatly amplified, and spread the electric blast around...however it was a bit more extreme than what Michael had planned. Every basteel started shaking then burst apart, as the liquid inside them turned to steam all at once. This didn't stop there, the surge followed the water all the way into the main river and the water started boiling. Hundreds of smaller basteels floated to the surface—boiled to death. The dust and scattering rocks settled, and Michael looked to see how everyone was. Everyone looked just fine—everyone but Kujex that is, he must have been just a bit slow getting away from the wet ground. He stood there as if nothing was wrong while smoke billowed off his head and clothes, and most of his hair was standing on end.

"What? You act as if you never seen me before!" Kujex grumbled as he walked to a nearby puddle to see his face. The second Kujex saw his hair he started cursing his short legs and then scolded Michael for overdoing it.

"All right we have to get back on track, how are we going to get across the river, should we just swim?" asked Ryan.

"I take it you've never heard of a basteel? Well, they are a foul beast as well as a very bad omen! We aren't even in the cave yet, to meet such a creature now…I can only imagine what waits for us. I bring this up to say that if basteels are ever in a body of water, then that water is befouled. Meaning if you were to swim in it that you would be poisoned beyond help," answered Zezz.

"Um…I could just teleport us across you know," Alex said out of nowhere. Everyone in the group just looked at him with a new level of irritation.

"You didn't think to tell us that before we woke the beasts?" roared Kujex.

"Hey, sorry to throw you under the bus Michael, but who was the one who decided the best course of action would be to throw a rock at a dangerous body of water?" Michael had to give it to him, Alex actually had a point!

"Who cares let's just get on with it!" Balo said finally. Alex just pointed his hands at the group and they were instantly teleported to the northern bank of the river. Once there they were suddenly reminded that it was in fact freezing cold.

"Now where do we go?" asked Ben, having to yell over the wind. Michael got the book.

> Its babies are dead, it will be mad, that was not wise to do.
> Now it arose and soon it will know, then it will come for you.
> Move fast go up the path around the peak ahead.
> When you get to the bridge just go across, and into the cave,
> You will be lead.

"I could have done without that first part!" Able spat.

"I know what it meant. I was going to say something anyway. That many basteels that small, would only be part of a nest. We must move fast before the mother comes back, they are *far* more dangerous full grown." Balo said gravely.

They all hurried forward a bit and found the path. They started out very easily because the path was quite wide at first, but as they went on it became more and more narrow. Six hours of climbing later they reached a point where they were holding on to a ledge that had only enough space for Balo and the other big folks to fit their feet on and they had to hug the face of the mountain. Pith had to bring up the rear so he could dig his fingers and feet into the rock. Finally the path widened into a ledge large enough for them to all stand on again. Directly in front of them nestled in the side of the next mountain was the entrance to a cave. Between them and the cave was a thousand foot chasm connected by a huge rope bridge easily wide enough even for Pith. The main supporting ropes were three feet thick and the ropes running the length were even thicker, the boards were actually six foot wide logs just barely sanded flat on the top.

"Well there's no time like the present, let's get on with it," barked Kujex.

"Yes, we must move quickly! It is dangerously cold up here. We have to get into the cave!" added Zezz. They hurried across the bridge and straight into the cave completely unhindered. About a hundred feet inside the cave was a fifty foot tall set of double doors which were swung wide open.

"Is it just me, or should this be harder to get into?" asked Ryan as he walked passed the doors looking back at the bridge they just crossed. He didn't get to look long though, the moment the last of the group came through the doors they slammed shut and you could hear what sounded like locks popping and pounding into place. Pith walked over to the doors and wiped off some of the thick layer of dust and dirt that was on it to reveal the same kind of metal that Asendor Academy's front gates were made of.

"Yep, just as I thought three feet thick of solid trillium! It would seem getting in wasn't what Ackatoth was concerned about!"

"I don't get it! Can't you just break through it?" asked Able. Trillium is unbreakable by anyone, even me! We are not getting out this way, so I guess there is no turning back at this point." It was these words that brought back to Michael's mind what the book had said the night before they left.

> ... *Into the cave your team will go, and follow it so deep*
> *But only one will leave again, all the rest will sleep*

Michael felt immediately guilty that he had not yet told anyone about this, and knew that he had to tell them now in case they were walking into a trap of some sort.

"Um ... I guess you should all know ... the book said something the night before we left ... It ... kinda said that once we went into the cave ... only one of us would come ... back out ..." Michael cringed at the response, which was worse than he expected. Balo swore loudly, Ben, Rozea, Ryan, Eliza, and Able started yelling at him. Pith, Blaze, and Foeseth had their faces buried in their hands' while Kujex took the rope off his back pack and looked to be making it into a noose! Zezz had seen enough in less than a minute of this.

"*That is enough!* Yes he should have told us, but I understand why he didn't! Either way we are here now so we need to figure out how we are going to survive this ...! And Kujex put that away!" Kujex started grumbling and put his rope back. The book started vibrating again and Michael quickly got everyone's attention so they could all hear what it said.

> *So you brought Pith? Who would have guessed?*
> *It seems your team may well be blessed! There is*
> *a door but few can lift that can change their fates.*
> *But to get there you must take the Burning Gate.*
> *That road is dark more than you can ever know.*

Therefore be sure of yourselves or do not go!
Silence is golden among these jagged walls
For in this place your skin is not all that crawls!
Stay close together; don't stray from your own.
You should know that you are not alone!

Even in the icy, stale air of the cave they felt a frigid breeze pass through them. This book seemed to be learning things as if someone were updating it on events, but at other times it seemed presently aware. The more Michael read this book the more he had a feeling that it's author must have been evil. Michael had not told this feeling to anyone because Ackatoth was not only one of the founding members of the Jemini society but also one of their greatest heroes. Alex, had not made a sound when Michael told them about the warning. He spoke slowly, and for what had to be the first time he was completely serious.

"That book is pure evil…" His voice broke just a little as he spoke. "…El'Jay'El was right when he said he felt an evil long since forgotten enter the castle!…" Zezz, Pith, Balo, and Kujex cut Alex off at these words…

"How do you know of him?" demanded Zezz.

"And how did you speak to him and survive?" Pith boomed. Feeling totally out of the loop Michael chimed in.

"Um…what or who is El'Jay'El? And what's the big deal?"

"Do you remember the hall of shadows?" asked Balo.

"How could I forget?" Michael answered.

"Well El'Jay'El is the name of what lives there. He was a "Destroyer of Worlds." They were a group of beings that destroyed planets for some dark force unknown. Even though he turned from evil, he has a power that he can't control—when someone looks upon him they turn to ash, with some few exceptions, Dojee being one of them. But Alex here not only looked at him but spoke to him. This is beyond impossible because his voice is said to be able to shatter *worlds!*" Balo informed him. The group starred at Alex, now in awe, Michael couldn't help but think there was more to Alex than what anyone knew. Alex just smiled a bit.

"Look, I am immune to any power involving looking in someone's eyes or anything like that. My mind can't be read or controlled either, you did notice that my eyes glow red right? Well that could have something to do with it...don't know, but it could. As far as the speaking thing, I can talk to any "Destroyer of Worlds" let's just say I've earned the right! Now we *could* stand here and let me rattle off all of my abilities and my extremely long and drawn out story, however I think we should get back to the matter at hand." The group was still in shock but now just because Alex was acting...normal...responsible even!

"He's right. We need to move on," Michael agreed.

The group started moving on through the cave and none of them were in a talkative mood, even Eliza was quiet! They all had their lights on again because this cave was completely dark without them. It was so dark in fact that it almost seemed unnatural itself, as if the very darkness were against them. They walked and walked with no sign of the tunnel's end in sight, this was getting downright weird. If there was something in this cave with them it either didn't know they were there or didn't care because they were the only thing moving around in this place as far as they could see. They finally had to stop and get some rest.

"Wow! I would have never thought that the biggest threat on this trip would be dieing of boredom! I thought this was supposed to be hard! We're just walking...I'm pretty sure that's easy. I mean, yeah sure we had some trolls at the beginning but that honestly was *way* too easy as well. The book seems to think we are having a rough go at this, but this is not bad, just dull," Rozea blurted all at once. Zezz nodded in agreement.

"Yes, something doesn't feel right to me either! It is almost as if someone was here before us, cleaned the place out or something."

"I would agree with that but this cave doesn't seem to lead anywhere but straight either...unless...A riddle! Just as Zezz said before, the name of the gate may be a clue. The 'Burning Gate,' I bet we need to use fire to find the way out of this tunnel! It might just go on for miles and miles just to drop you off at where you started if you don't work out that a burning gate needs fire!" Michael realized.

"Not a bad thought, but we have been walking now for nine hours straight. We should stop and rest, let's take shifts as before." Stopping in this dark a place, knowing something may be there that would mean them harm made it hard for Michael to rest at all. Still he laid there until it was his turn to keep watch, this time he was partnered with Able, Blaze, Pith, and of course Alex—since he didn't sleep. Pith was holding his shotgun and looking down the tunnel ahead of them as if daring something to move so he could shoot it! Able was doing a similar act facing the way they came, Blaze poked at the fire with a stick they had found, and Michael stared into the flames. Alex decided to go on ahead to see if he could find anything. He turned off his lights since he could see in darkness, he thought maybe their lights had been scaring away what lurked in here and he wanted to know. Michael tried to tell him it was too dangerous but then remembered that Alex was extremely powerful, and can teleport anywhere instantly so the likelihood of something in this cave being able to hurt him seemed slim. So Michael let him go, an hour passed without so much as a sound. Then from deep in the cave, over the silence they could hear a little yelp of pain. Alex appeared with his usual pop still tapping on the end of his sleeve which was smoldering and a blackened.

"Would you like the good news or the bad news first?" Alex asked seemingly proud.

"Ummm…?" Was all Michael could say.

"Good news is I found the burning gate! It's called that because it is really hot, I found it because my coat caught fire the second it touched the thing! …Oh and the bad part is that there was a really big guy with a sword made of fire and he woke up and looked right at me, seemed mad and then he passed through a wall in this direction!"

"*Oh crap!* Everyone up, *now!*" Michael shouted. The others must have had trouble sleeping as well because they were up in a second ready to fight! They crept forward with their lights set to their brightest setting to make as much light as possible. They moved along carefully, Pith and Balo took up the rear and Zezz, Kujex, and Michael lead. After twenty minutes of walking they came up on a gate to their left and found that the tunnel forward had been caved in. It must have happened recently too because dust and small rocks were still settling.

"Well it looks as though the burning gate is the only way now!" muttered Able.

"Okay. So where is this guy you saw?" Blaze asked impatiently.

"He might have friends elsewhere in the cave that he wanted to let know of our presence…or perhaps he's just laying low until we lower our guard some. He may have seen who he was up against and thought better of a frontal assault," Alex suggested.

"Wow! Once again you surprise me by being…well…serious!" stated Balo.

"Hey, I know when things need to be serious. It's just a lot less often than what most people seem to think. Anyway, how do we get through a gate we can't touch?"

"Um…Both Foeseth and Zezz are immune to fire…So that would probably be how!" spat Kujex.

Zezz and Foeseth put a finger on the gate first, They did not know if this was some sort of magically produced heat that they could still be hurt by. But just as Kujex had suggested, they were unaffected and so they grabbed it and started pulling. The gate did not move.

"What's the hold up?" Kujex asked unable to except what seemed to be the obvious answer.

"We can't move it! It is either too heavy, or there is some sort of a trick to it," Foeseth answered. Michael opened the book, there was nothing for a minute then it finally said something forgetting its usual rhyming style.

"You figure it out on your own. I want to see what you do!"

Michael was about to tear that book in half but thought better of it. He thought for a moment as did the others. "Look I'm not afraid to burn my hands a bit. Let me just pull the thing off its hinges!" Pith suggested. Before anyone could say anything he reached out grabbed the gate and gave it a yank. It broke with what seemed like no effort on Pit's part...Problem was—now his hands were on fire!

"Now, would you look at that! I say, that stings a bit!" Pith clapped his hands together and the fire went out—his hands seemed almost unharmed. The book vibrated and Michael opened it quickly.

"That is not possible! You are cheating!
Now your lives are ever fleeting!
He will be more than you can beat, not even Pith can claim this feat!
His army awakes you will all die, unless you get through the Doors of Keri!
These doors can't break, the lock is small, the key a secrete known to you all.
You better run or you won't even get there, then again I don't even care!"

They looked at each other for not even a full second before racing forward. They ran hard through the tunnel which opened to a huge cavern, and large torches lit everything in this part of the cave. A quick look up told them just what the book was talking about. In the roof of this part of the cave were hundreds of holes some around fifty feet wide others a few hundred. Pouring from these holes, were millions of creatures of every kind. It looked as if someone had just broke open a termite mound as they came from these holes like bugs, running down the walls, stalactites and columns all over. There were ghouls, orcs, hobgoblins, goblins, as well as harpies, and worst of all, gargoyles, flying all over.

"By Zeus! Run!" Cried Kujex. They ran all the harder until the ground in front of them came to a sudden stop but for a bridge of rock just barely wide enough for Pith to fit. They went single file as quickly as they could, the army of beasts and brutes bonding after them. Some Cyclopes had joined the army behind them now breaking off large chunks of stalagmites as they passed them swinging them wildly like clubs. Once on the bridge they saw way off in the distance a set of huge doors.

"I don't think we will be able to reach those doors before we are overtaken! Some of us should fight as we go!" Balo called out. Pith and Alex stopped at once as the group ran ahead, a few hundred feet further Balo and Able stopped, then again with Kujex and Foeseth. The rest just ran hard until they reached the door. Michael turned to see where his team was and how they were doing, and had just enough time to dodge a sword from a gargoyle that had caught up to them. It was nine feet tall and had thick armor, in it's hands was a sword kinda like a claymore but with a much wider blade. His golden yellow eyes shined dangerously. Michael responded with an energy blast, but it missed; the gargoyle jumped to one side and lounged with it's sword. Michael blocked it with his sword, then used his free hand to shoot off another energy blast. This one tore a hole through the gargoyle's chest and through several others behind him including one who was fighting Ben who gave him a nod of thanks and went on with killing stuff. Blaze and Eliza where back to back, Eliza was shooting her huge gun into the crowd of rushing monsters while Blaze sliced down anything that got close enough. Rozea was deeply enjoying her new quiver and bow as she fired arrows two at a time into the crowd as well.

Ryan was using the spear he had bought from Slim back at his shop and was taking on three gargoyles at a time. Zezz had his big axe out and chopped through every extra thing that came by. Way down the bridge Michael could see huge sums of creatures being thrown over the edge of the bridge. It was at this point that Michael finally noticed what was down under the bridge. Over a thousand feet below, there were millions of sharp-toothed beasts covered in fur and several eyes, other details were impossible to see from this distance. They would pounce on the falling creatures and tear them apart savagely. Pith and Alex were charging forward as were Able and Balo. Alex was teleporting twenty or more creatures over the edge with a wave of his hand—not being careful to teleport their *entire* bodies. Able was flipping through the air slicing through dozens at a time. Pith was just moving forwards, he was so big he would just push everything near him over the edge. Balo was swinging his huge mace knocking ten or more apart with each blow. Foeseth was flying overhead his whole body engulfed in flames as he would swoop down and plow thirty or forty at a time over the edge, or just cut them in half with his great sword. Kujex was jumping around much like Able but using his control over metal to crush enemies with their own armor, as well as throw their own weapons into their faces and so on. He was also shooting off lightning bolts at some of the Cyclops that caught up to them blowing holes through their chests. Ben moved toward them handling ten at a time with not much problem. He was slashing through them so fast it was almost scary. Rozea seemed quite pleased by her man's display. She moved right beside him and drew her great sword, and started hacking along with him. A moment later the army seemed to thin, but off in the distance you could see a wall of creatures larger than the first storming toward the bridge. There were far more Cyclops in this group but now to add to it there were now many trolls in this group too. Michael called his team to quickly gather while there was a break in the onslaught of enemies.

"Hate to be a downer but we only took out a fraction of them, we can't keep this up for as long as they can!" Zezz said quickly, "you have to find that key and lock, you figure out the riddle we will take care of them.".

No sooner had he finished talking when the next wave had just about reached them. Balo, Foeseth, and Pith took the point this time powering their way through the crowd smashing and tossing everything in sight. Alex just stayed back and with a bit more effort than before started throwing hundreds of them off the bridge with each wave of his hand. The others had gone back to doing as they were, Michael turned to the door. He could tell by looking at it that it was solid mallieum and thus was in fact not going to be broken, even by Pith. He had to find this lock and fast, so he just started pouring over the door feeling it with his hands as there was no visible markings on the door at all. Michael knew this could take a long time, these doors were huge, nearly the size of the main gate of Asendor. But Michael all at once lost a large sum of time to be able to look when a roar unlike anything he had ever heard rang through the cave.

He looked back to see what made it to see another horrible sight! A being just as tall as Pith came walking behind the army. He had bull-like horns and red skin and a tail. His arms were nearly as big as Pith's and as he got closer to them his skin seemed to turn into red hot rock! He had a sword of fire in one hand and a shield in the other, he was smiling evilly and at that moment was looking at Pith like he wanted to fight. Pith wasn't the type to back down from a fight and drew his machete along with his axe and ran at the fiery being. Zezz chanced a look at Michael and hurried over to him when he saw that Michael was watching the fight.

"That is Kronos! Pith is much stronger but less than half his power! Kronos is just as powerful as Zeus himself! You must get that door open, *now!!*" Michael moved faster and then got an idea.

"Alex get over here!" Alex popped over in an instant. "...You can look *through* stuff but can you look inside something? In this case to see how the lock works?" Alex just smiled and looked at the door. His eyes looked up and went down and stopped.

"There it is!" Alex walked up to the door and pushed on what looked to be a perfectly solid part of the door and it pushed in as though spring loaded. He stepped aside and Michael looked at the slot, it was around nine inches long and a little over an inch tall ... Michael had a crazy idea. He took the book from his satchel and stuck it into the slot—it fit perfectly. The book was instantly sucked into the door and out of sight, loud pops, and grinding metal from the tumblers told them the doors were opening. The doors opened oddly lifting up and then swinging apart.

"Quickly! Through the doors!" cried Kujex. Pith didn't waste time he gave Kronos a hard kick and sent him through the rock wall beside them and out of sight. He then ran full out toward them, he looked back at the army of monsters which now had several hundred trolls, including the one that Pith had fought earlier. Pith waited until everyone else was through the doors, when they were he pushed off from the ground in an amazing jump and landed hard just in front of the doors which were now starting to closing. He turned and gave the bridge one huge stomp. It cracked and started breaking, the still-approaching army started falling as the bridge fell apart.

"Get in here man you're not small and the doors are closing!" cried Zezz. Pith sprang through the doors but a little late. Pith's left arm had not made it in before the doors slammed shut. He let out a low growl of pain, but didn't seem to be worried near as much as the others who were all acting as if he should be dying. Pith just looked down at his shoulder and a new arm started growing out, even Zezz and Balo didn't know he could do this and they were straight up amazed.

"You have some secrets there my boy!" Balo exclaimed.

"Yeah, Dojee said that I have some secrets that even I don't know about! But my having 'regen' wasn't that much of a secret, I never get sick, and I don't have scares, yet consider my past ..."

Pith looked at Balo, Zezz, and Kujex who all had a look of you-said-too-much on their faces. "Oh…right…well anyway let's get going."

Michael checked the back of the door with the keyhole, and sure enough the book was sitting in a chute, sticking out from the door. Michael grabbed it and went to the next page. The writing was already on the page as if the book could not wait to say what came next.

> *'WOW! How exciting! You got this far now only two chambers to go.*
> *What lies ahead may seem easy but he is quite a foe.*
> *You must beat him! Get the key that swings from his neck.*
> *Be warned it won't be easy, he's the hardest foe you ever met!*
> *He's as fast as light, has more power than a star,*
> *So work together or die where you are."*

"This is something Dojee never would have thought! It is only because Kronos never fought me before that he did not just start killing you all, he wanted to see how good I am. He is a foe beyond any of us, but if we are to take that book literally than there is another super power down here greater than he. I find that almost hard to believe, Kronos is tied with Hercules and Hemdallr as the second strongest person alive after me. To add to that he has over fourteen thousand years of battles under his belt and a huge number of powers, plus magic! Who would be down here greater than that?" Pith asked.

"Well, there are those who have beaten Kronos, through fighting skill and intellect. Plus Kronos is full of himself and that is a weakness too, though it would seem odd that someone so powerful would even be down here just to guard a sword. Kronos wouldn't take orders from Valldiss or any other living person I could think of. It would seem likely he just stayed down here to keep people from what he could not have. Regardless who is down here we have no choice but to go on, even if we could get this door open again you took down the bridge." Balo answered thoughtfully.

They walked along another tunnel, this tunnel was not straight though and in a few places rock jutted out so that Pith had to ... make room ... for this reason he stayed in the back. Michael was ready to fight, having all but sat out of the last fight made him feel as though he owed the others, so he lead the group. After several minutes of walking they came to a sharp left turn. Alex looked ahead to see what was coming and said that a few hundred feet down there was a right turn and that he could see the light from a fire. They slowly went around the left turn and came to a halt about fifty yards from the edge of the next turn to see if they could hear anything.

"I tell ya I heard them orcs squawking like they do when somebody is in their cave!" said one voice.

"Well then take Bib and Soaf and check to see if they got through." This voice was intelligent and somewhat off, it was hard to tell why it seemed off with the echo of the cave, but Michael was certain that something wasn't right about it. The group got ready; most of them went back around the corner out of sight, while Michael and Alex stayed up where they would be able to take them by surprise.

The three men rounded the corner, one was an ogre and bigger than Balo or Able, who were both over twelve feet, and he had green glowing eyes. He carried a spike club in one hand and a lantern in the other; the other two were triclopsian,—big pink, green, or blue skinned people with three eyes, and two just like a human and one in the middle of their large foreheads. They each had large guns with blades attached to the front of them. Michael and Alex jumped out at the last second to take them out but the ogre was not a fool. He saw them coming and very quickly dogged them both. Michael managed to plant his sword through one of the triclopsian's faces, the other backed away and started shooting. The ogre ran back yelling in some odd language.

They're surprise attack ruined Michael just shot of a blast turning the remaining triclopsian into a pile of goo. The rest of the group ran from cover and they all went around the next turn together. The ogre was waiting for them, now armed with a much bigger spike club and covered in body armor. Fifty feet behind him was a man standing with his back to them and his arms crossed behind him. The ogre was fast for his size and quite strong, he swung his club at Michael,—who dodged it just barely. His club hit the nearby wall knocking a huge chunk of rock loose which would have fallen on Eliza had Rozea not yanked her out of the way. Balo ran forward and met the ogre's club with his mace. To everyone's shock the ogre threw Balo off without difficulty, Zezz answered and by charging with his arms and axe covered in fire. The ogre side stepped him and a gem at the top of the club that none of them had noticed shot a pink blast at Zezz hitting him in the chest and throwing him into the wall behind him. Michael had seen enough, this ogre was obviously more than just a brute but Michael was also quite sure the man by the fire was the one the book was talking about. Michael brought out his anari, charged his hands with energy, and walked up to the ogre. The ogre swung his club at Michael. Michael caught the club with his left hand and punched the ogre hard with his right. While the ogre staggered Michael planted a hard kick to his stomach and sent him across the chamber that the tunnel opened up to. He hit a wall hard but was back on his feet in a second but now he was shaking his head seemingly a little dizzy, his eyes were no longer glowing green.

"What…? What happened…? Where am I…? My team!! Have you lot seen my friends, they…" The ogre didn't finish speaking before the man by the fire hit him hard enough to send him into yet another wall. The punch was so fast. It was a blur. This time he did not get up, he appeared to be breathing but unconscious. The man from the fire looked at Michael; his eyes were glowing green as well. He was about nine-feet tall and had slightly tan skin. He had pure white hair pulled back in a tight pony tail. His hands and forearms were rapped like that of a kickboxer, over that he had fingerless gloves with metal plates on them and armor on his fore arms as well. His chest had some sort of leather armor, and his legs had plates covering his thighs and boots with metal covering his shins and coming to a sharp point to cover his knees. He was unarmed but for a single bo staff he had strapped to his back.

Michael looked at this man for just a second and one of his feelings came, telling him that this guy was *way* out of his league. Still, if he should fight this guy he felt that he needed to knock *him* on the head just as the ogre. Michael had spent too much time *thinking* and this man got tired of waiting. Before Michael even knew what was happening he had been hit what felt like several hundred times around the stomach! What was worse was that this guy was the strongest person Michael had ever fought. After a few minutes Michael pulled himself out of the hole his body had made in the rock wall. By the time it took Michael to regroup, Alex was on the ground just starting to stir from his own pummeling. Rozea was on the ground still knocked out as was Eliza. Zezz was getting off the ground and Pith was climbing out of a hole of his own!. At the moment Able, Ben, Balo, Blaze, and Foeseth were all fighting this man in a flurry of martial arts unlike anything Michael had ever seen, Zezz then adding to it was just crazy.

Who was this guy? How could he be able to fight six amazing hand-to-hand fighters at once, two of whom were some of the greatest warriors of the age and do so with hardly breaking a sweat? The man went seamlessly from one martial art to another, each time deflecting their blows as well as landing a few in return. Watching this Michael had no idea how to beat such a foe, he was just too good a fighter. Zezz even tried to use his fire and threw a fire ball at him but he simply caught it and threw it back. All at once an idea came to him, he needed to know more about fighting, he needed to be nearer to this guy's level and Michael just so happened to be able to absorb others powers. This guy was very powerful so Michael knew this was kind of crazy to do, but if he didn't try someone was going to die soon!

"Hey! White head! Fight me, like a man! No powers, just skill against skill!" Michael challenged. The man jerked his head at Michael in shock, then a grin spread across his face, it was enough to make them cringe because the smile looked nothing like the face it was on. Michael could see what looked like someone else's face coming through this man's. Whoever was controlling this man was quote powerful obviously but they must have had their hands full keeping the control over him; this thought gave Michael an idea. The man was laughing looking at Michael's friends who were all nursing their very sore bodies.

"You would challenge me, boy? I am Akuma, god of wondering warriors and the greatest fighter alive!"

"In body maybe, but I know that the one talking is someone else controlling him. And I'm guessing he is fighting you tooth and nail. I doubt you'll be able to keep his mind under control while dealing with what I have in mind!" Michael took off his gloves and at once Kujex—having helped Dojee train Michael to control his power—knew what Michael was up to.

"Everyone back, *now!*" He screamed. They didn't argue and they all ducked back into the tunnel. Akuma was on Michael in a split second; Michael had no notion to actually fight him. Akuma got one hit in but instead of striking back Michael just grabbed the bare part of Akuma's arm and started absorbing his powers. This was…well…*painful!* Michael was in no way ready for what this felt like. It was like a white-hot knife was being stabbed into him all over his body, while he was being electrocuted. Akuma was in just as much pain if not more, as he was writhing and screaming. At times the screams sounded like they were coming from the one controlling Akuma instead. Michael was starting to gain powers now, Akuma was very strong, more so than Warbick as a matter of fact! He also had a very high level of invulnerability and could also create force fields around himself. This was why they couldn't seem to hurt him. Michael was starting to feel like he might fall unconscious from the pain when a sharp thud came from the back of Akuma's head. The ogre that had been lying to the side unconscious for most of this had come to, and struck Akuma on the head with his smaller club. Akuma was back on his feet in seconds but with kind normal looking blue eyes. Michael had gained a lot of Akuma's thoughts and knowledge, including decade's worth of martial arts training, some Michael already had studied himself, others he never even heard of. Michael learned that Akuma and Bolen were leading a group through here not but a few weeks earlier, they had come in a different entrance and Michael was thinking of having his team go out that way and let him go it alone or maybe just one other person. It was time to change things so this book and this trip didn't claim his team's lives. But it turned out that this entrance was on the wrong side of the mountain; and there was a cave-in anyway so it wasn't an option. Michael was stronger now by a fair margin having gained much of Akuma's strength, and he could even feel his own muscles grow a bit under his clothes. Of course at this point, his ability to absorb powers by itself, had proven more effective than what Michael's newfound abilities would have been against Akuma anyway … but it worked at least. Bolen looked at Michael fearfully …

"What manner of man are you? How is it that you could hurt someone as mighty as Akuma with nothing more than a touch?" asked Bolen.

"It's a long story—more important now is finding the next step," Michael opened the book.

Wow, you beat a man who was the very best, now I'm impressed!
That was going to be your hardest test.
You are too good you little pest!

This must get harder so you can know just what it is you are going to have.
For the sword must be earned if you wish to learn it's secrets I've hidden away.
You must choose one friend to go with you, all the rest must stay.
Even the one that comes with you now will not leave with you this day.
For to leave this cave with the sword, a high price you must to pay!"

Michael had come to his end with this book and shoved it in his satchel; he looked to the others who had heard him read. They all looked worried and Michael felt annoyed. What had they been doing here? Feeble acts that anyone could do? Were these simple feats of skill that anyone could match? *No!* They had gotten through several obstacles that had claimed countless lives before them! So many people had tried to get the sword for so long the number that had been claimed was estimated in the *trillions*; and they all knew that because *they* were the ones who told him that!

"Are you guys kidding me? Are you still afraid of this book and its stupid rhyming bull crap? We have done what few have ever done and the only others who got this far ended up as slaves! Except Drackiss and his team but they chose the wrong sword! We are going to make a healthy few stands after this and I don't give a rip what the book says! I'm done listening to that thing and I say it's time we take this into our own hands. We are going to split up. Pith, you, and the rest of the big guys use your beef to carve your own way out of here…"

"Hold on here. Who is going, and who is staying? And just witch way should we go?" Zezz interrupted.

"Alex and I are going on, the rest of you are leaving. As far as which direction…Alex could you please take a peak and see which way the academy is from here?" Alex looked for less than a second before pointing at the wall behind them and to the right.

"If you don't mind me asking why would you choose Alex over the rest of us? And why only you two, why not take one more at least?"

"Alex just makes sense. He can see through anything, hear anything, and he can teleport. That way if all else fails we can just pop back to the academy."

"Hmm...I see your point. But, just the two of you? What if you run into another army or something?"

"Well, don't take this the wrong way but I had to hold back a lot with my energy blasts so I didn't hurt any of *you*! I could have taken out a fair number of that army with just one blast! With only two of us there are less people to keep track of and thus less that could get hurt."

"I see...I know Dojee will be very unhappy about this...And I don't know that I agree with you...But, you have displayed great poise and sound judgment well beyond your years. Plus it does seem that if we are all to survive this, then we need to stop doing just as the book says. I have no doubt you will find your sword, but you should go now. We'll seal this tunnel before we leave so nothing can sneak up behind you."

"Could you do me a favor? One of our group managed to go farther than we did. He was once Grand Master at Asendor...before Dojee that is. Former master Idoe." asked Bolen. Michael recognized the name at once. There was a huge painting in the dining hall with his name on it...though he didn't look much like a warrior.

"Master Idoe is down here?" breathed Zezz.

"Yes. I fear the worst, but if you can, would you see if you could find him?"

"We will do what we can, should we find him," Michael answered. Bolen nodded in appreciation and the group turned to the wall Alex had said was in the direction of home. Akuma walked up to Michael and gave him a bow.

"You will need this. I have no idea what for...anyway good luck to you, and thank you for not killing me," Akuma spoke in a quiet peaceful voice. Michael and Alex gave one final goodbye as they walked into the next tunnel. Pith waved back then gave the roof at the mouth of the tunnel a quick punch. The roof collapsed and Michael could no longer hear the others; Alex and Michael were now on their own.

Chapter Eleven

Alex looked like he was quite happy and practically skipped along as they went down the tunnel. They walked for near an hour once again with now sign of life. Though this tunnel had torches they only lit up the space right by them. So Michael and Alex turned their lights back on to make it easier to see. They were now coming up on a set of heavy metal doors and Michael picked up the pace, just ten feet away Michael felt Alex grab his shoulder with more strength than Michael knew he had! Just as Alex did a HUGE double bladed axe swung down in front of them like a pendulum missing Michael's nose by less than an inch.

"Thanks...That could have been bad!"

"Anytime, just try to watch your step, the next tunnel through this door is filled with traps." Alex grabbed Michael and popped on the other side of the axe...

"That really is a handy power!" Michael said.

"Yeah, we'll have to shake hands some time so you can copy it. Now this door is a booby trap all on its own. We need to get it open fast and um...don't stand there or anywhere by that wall...in fact, we should go back to right by the axe." Alex said, looking through all the traps. They both stepped carefully back to just in front of the axe. Michael thought for a moment as did Alex. Michael could think of nothing else but to shoot a powerful blast at the door in hopes that it would break through the door all at once and break the traps too. The doors were large—around sixty-feet tall—so Michael was going to need a blast like the one he used against the trolls that ripped a forty-foot hole through a dragon! Michael brought out his anari and caught hold of the shaft of the axe behind him. He pushed hard as he could and the shaft snapped. Michael turned and chucked it at the doors. The blood-stained axe sunk into the door and made it buckle some as it did a trapdoor above the double doors sprang open and about a hundred three foot metal spikes shot out with force enough to stab into the rock floor!

"Wow! It would have really sucked to get hit by those!" Alex said in a "matter of fact" voice. Michael bent low and started generating as much energy as he could and made it into a huge ball at least fifty-feet wide!

"Umm…I think it might be big enough dude!" Alex said, sounding a little concerned. Michael decided Alex was right and shot off the blast, pushing it harder than he had before. The blast tore off toward the door at speeds enough to break the sound barrier. The blast hit the door and turned it into a molten puddle and kept right on going. It blasted through rock walls, and traps—some of which would spring a bit, then fall apart. The blast just kept going and every so often you would hear another bang which was the blast going through yet another wall or something. Right in front of them a spear shot out from beside the door with enough force to sink ten inches into solid rock. To the right side of the doors, a horrible set of five-finger-like blades folded up out of the ground and clapped together hard enough to make sparks.

"*Wow!* Am I glad I had us move back here!!" exclaimed Alex.

They walked carefully on through the smoldering ruin of a door and crept slowly at first, just in case there were yet traps that had not been tripped. Michael brought his anari back in since it made him nine-feet tall, he might trip a trap, designed for big people or something.

"Good thinking dude!" Alex said seeming impressed at Michael's good idea.

They walked on for a while, the blast had made several shortcuts for them cutting down their time quite a bit, looking down each hall that they were able to skip they saw bodies by the millions. These hallways snaked around all over the place, so they were very glad for the short cuts they now had. One hall they were passing made them stop and stare a bit. A little ways down the hall they could see bodies that had been cut in half…and some a bit more than that. There were so many bodies here that the smell made them want to vomit! Michael wanted to know what was down this tunnel, so he picked up a shield from a fallen warrior and chucked it down the hallway. Right before the shield hit the ground the wall opened up and a nine foot wide saw blade shot out from the wall and sliced the shield apart. The two halves flew off and caused other blades to pop out all over the hall.

"Wow! I'm glad we don't have a bunch of people with us in here to have to worry about!" Alex said, patting Michael on the shoulder. Michael just nodded as they started moving again.

They made their way through yet another wall and heard a voice come from their left that made both of them jump! Having had no sign of life for so long hearing a voice spooked them pretty badly. They looked in the direction of the voice to see a small wing off to the left. On the right side of the wing were six prison-type cells. One of the cells had a man who was pinned to the floor by more than thirty spears and other pointy things stuck through the bars. The cell closest to them housed a large Minotaur—around twelve-feet tall and at least eight-feet wide at the shoulders. His left horn had obviously been lost in a battle or something because it had been replaced with a metal one. His left eye had also been lost as the entire upper left corner of his head was now a metal plate, and his eye was glowing yellow with cross hairs over the front of it like on a scope for a rifle. He stood near the gate of his cell looking at them as if they were the most beautiful sight he had ever seen.

"Thank Zeus! You two must be quite something, being so young yet making it this far! My friend and I have been here for quite a long time and we were beginning to think we were going to die of old age before some one came by." Michael wasn't sure at first, but it seemed as though the Minotaur meant that the man pinned to the floor was the friend he was talking about. Michael was quite sure he must be mistaken because that man seemed to be as dead as a person could get!

"Who are you two? What happened to your team?" Alex asked.

"Oh, my name is Blithden. This is Baldr, one of the guardians of Asgard. We are all that is left of our team. When we got here these traps weren't even installed yet, this was where the army of brutes had their barracks. We got to watch them put the traps in place. The main barracks is just ahead, we met a very powerful warlock there, he got the drop on us and managed to put some kind of bind on us, we couldn't break free. He put us into these cells and hit that blasted thing on the wall and thus turned on the force fields. They are pretty powerful; if you touch them, they take off what you touch them with! I lost two inches on my tail because of these things! Baldr's cell field shorted so the warlock and several men with him just pinned him to the ground. Savage wouldn't you say?"

"Okay…I'm sorry to have to tell you this but…your friend is dead," Michael said finally having had enough of the man speaking of his friend as if he were still alive. Blithden just looked at Michael then at Baldr's body and back. After a few awkward moments Blithden just started laughing, he would then look as though he was going to straighten up but then gained a new fit of laughter. Michael was getting annoyed and it must have shown on his face because Blithden stopped laughing at once and looked at him now as if he were crazy.

"You…You don't actually think Baldr is dead do you?" he asked in a skeptical tone.

"Umm…He has at least thirty spears stuck in him! So yeah, I do!"

"Well, you made a good guess. I have thirty-*six* spears in me, but you missed the eleven swords and that throwing axe in my left butt cheek!" Baldr talking was not something Michael was prepared for. He knew there were powerful people out there and some pretty outlandish powers as well. But a man who was now more or less a living pin cushion was just not on his radar! He let out a yell something between a scream and a girlish shriek, while jumping a few feet in the air! Alex turned to him rather slowly with a surprised on his face.

"Are you flipping kidding me?"

"He…How can he be alive?"

"I could have told you his heart was beating! Man, do yourself a favor and lose the ability to make that noise again, or it will really effect my ability to hang out with you…You lost like fifty man points right there! Anyway I'm Alex and this is my…fearless…leader Michael Rains." Michael just nodded his head sheepishly. Alex went over to the wall with the controls for the force fields, but there was a slimy green corrosion all over it.

"These things aren't going to work anymore. How long have you two been down here?"

"You would be surprised by just how aware of time you become when your body keeps on trying to heal from spear wounds while the spears are still in them! It has been 387 years, nine months, twelve days, and fifteen hours since we got trapped here."

"How have you survived without food?" Alex asked.

"Oh I don't need to eat…though I would kill to get even a bite of a roasted game hen, or a fatted calf, Or maybe some honeyed ham!…" Baldr paused for a moment. "…Blithden here has taken to eating the rats that wonder into his cage, he can generate fire so he just catches them and roasts them."

"Yep, it's a little gamy, but if you roast them on a spit so their fat drips off, they aren't that bad in truth."

"Okay, well let me get these spears out."

"Don't take it personal if I curse at you. It might hurt a bit!" Baldr said through gritted teeth.

"Hmm...I'll just pull them all at once, like taking off a bandage." Baldr sounded as if he was going to tell Alex to wait. Before he could though, Alex waved at the spears and instantly they were out of his back and across the room. Baldr let out a yell that rang through the cave a fair bit louder than Michael would have liked. Baldr slowly got to his feet as the last of his holes healed, he was just as tall as Blithden and though he didn't have quite as much muscle, he still had a heavy build. He wiped dirt from his huge chest and bulging arms then stretched out his hand toward the back wall of his cell, Michael nearly asked him what he was doing when he started hearing an odd pounding sound. A moment later the wall of his cell split open and a hammer slammed into his hand. It was nine feet tall and the handle was four inches thick. The head of the hammer was double sided. The face was round and about two and a half feet across. The back of the head was a slightly curved round spike. At the end of the handle was a counterweight that ended in a sharp round spike. Baldr stepped forward to the corroded control panel and put his hammer through it like it was made of play dough. The force field for Blithden's cage fell. Blithden put his hands on the bars of his cell door and squeezed. With what seemed like no effort the door folded like foil. Blithden stepped out of his cell and straightened up. As it turned out his cell was a little small for him, he wasn't twelve foot, but a little over thirteen, and now out in the open he seemed to be wider too. He didn't have a weapon so he grabbed the cell door and twisted it into a makeshift club.

"Now which of you two is the leader?" Blithden asked.

"I am. As it turns out I am the new Guardian, and to prove that *I have The Book Of Ackatoth* it was also my idea to go after the sword, so I got the joy of leading," answered Michael, it actually felt good now, claiming that title, it gave him new purpose and he felt it was about time he start taking it all more seriously. After all just as Warbick had told him his first night in this dimension, it wasn't like he had a choice, so embracing it seemed better than another option.

"I was wondering how two people as young as you could make it this far! It is an honor to make your acquaintance! Now how did you lot make that energy blast? Never saw a thing like it in my life!" Baldr exclaimed.

"It was Michael here! And he was hardly even trying either!" said Alex, slapping Michael on the back.

"That is very impressive I must say. It would seem that you don't need it, but would you two want any help then, or should we be on our way?" Blithden continued.

"I would be honored if you would join us! We helped two others who had been trapped down here. They said there man made it further and if we could they asked us to keep an eye open for him, you two would make it easier to help him if we find him. Plus, you really shouldn't just go running off by your selves. Even if you have been getting rats on a regular basis, I doubt you are at a hundred percent! We are lacking a bit of sleep but are otherwise at peak health. Add to that, if you come with us you'll get to see what you came down here for in the first place!"

"I would say we are the ones who should feel honored! Most would not have risked their lives to stay here and get us out of our predicament. You have a good heart, and you are right, we would most likely not fair very well on our own at the moment. As far as another man getting this far, I didn't see him come by, but that doesn't mean he didn't. So in any case are you just following the path you made or…Did you hear something?" Blithden interrupted himself when the muffled sound of distant voices caught his ear.

"Someone must have heard his scream." Michael whispered.

"…I think someone may have let them loose after all this time. We should be careful. Not many could get this far, even the two I trapped; I was only able to catch because I surprised them. So keep a watchful eye!"

Michael motioned for the other three to get back out of sight. Several men came around a corner about a hundred feet down the hall that Michael's blast had made. They didn't see him at first because they were too busy looking at the immense tunnel that was not there an hour ago! Michael used the time this distraction made to his advantage and shot off three heavy blasts each of which at least ten feet wide. He made sure they were concentrated and powerful and he shot them off as hard as he dared. The shots sped down the tunnel at speeds no less than twice his last blast. The men down range didn't even have time to think, they were all turned into smoldering remains in a fraction of a second. There was a loud curse followed by a rather normal looking man rounding the corner. He wore oddly styled robes of black, gold, and purple; he had a broad sword at his side and a strange staff in his right hand. His cheeks were sunken in a bit, and his eyes had an unnatural look to them, but they were not green like Bolen or Akuma. His hands were blackened and his fingers somewhat longer than normal. His nails seemed to be more like claws, and he gave Michael an odd smile that made his face look inhuman and vile.

"Michael, step aside please. I have no doubt you could just blast him to goo, but Baldr and I have some choice words for this man!" Blithden and Baldr stepped out into the tunnel, and the man immediately started shooting green bolts of energy from his staff at them. Michael and Alex stayed back and watched, ready to help at a moment's notice. Baldr kept the man jumping around by swinging his hammer like a madman. Blithden just made sure to keep out of the way of the warlock's energy bolts waiting for his moment to strike. Alex watched this with great interest, and Michael noticed he wasn't watching Blithden or Baldr but the warlock.

"What are you thinking?" Michael asked hesitantly.

"I was wondering what he would do if his staff was no longer in his hand…well, I want to see." With that Alex snapped his fingers and the warlock's staff disappeared in a puff of smoke and reappeared in Alex's hand. This was way more than what would have been needed to distract the warlock. He was suddenly just waving his hand, (to no effect at all) at Blithden just as Baldr's hammer came down on him like a meteor. The warlock vanished from sight into the large crater in the floor that Baldr's hammer had made. This was good in Michael's mind because he was fair sure he did not want to see what was left of that man! Blithden was laughing no doubt still considering what must have been going through the warlock's mind the moment his staff was gone and the shadow of Baldr's hammer appeared!

"Great style my friend! What do you plan to do with that staff now?" Baldr chuckled.

"Oh, I don't want the staff. It's a pretty dark thing…but I will take the large emerald out of it though. He put his hand over the stone on the end of the staff and it popped out into his palm. He then carelessly chucked the staff down and shoved the tennis ball size stone in his army green bag.

"All right let's keep moving. I feel as though we are quite close, but let's move quietly as possible." suggested Michael. The others just nodded and they moved on in silence.

⁂

The cave was starting to get warmer as they moved along and up ahead an orangey red glow told them why. They had walked for hours and were ready for action of some kind just to keep them awake at this point. They came to a hard, right-hand turn and could hear bubbling and sizzling noises coming from around the bend. They finally made it around the corner to another cavern; this cavern was the biggest they had yet seen. They were standing on a ledge maybe twenty feet by fifty feet. Straight in front of them was a very narrow path of rock in some places five-feet wide but in others barely over a foot. Several hundred feet down was a swirling, bubbling pool of lava!

"I am not going on that path!" stated Baldr sharply; he seemed on the verge of hysterics.

"Well there are points where the path looks weak anyway. I wouldn't trust it to hold us even if it were wide enough!" mentioned Michael, looking ahead to parts of the path were deep cracks were plainly visible.

"So how do we get across this, fly?" scuffed Blithden, Alex smiled at these words and looked at Michael as if he had the answer.

"What are you staring at me for?" Michael asked indignantly.

"For crying out loud, your anari has wings dummy! Now bring it out and fly us over to the other side!" Blithden and Baldr looked at Michael with new interest as he brought out his anari.

"I have to say, I didn't see this coming!" said Blithden.

Michael had not yet used his wings and was not even sure he could carry their weight so before trying to take them, he flapped his wings a few times to get the hang of how they worked. He was very surprised at their power, because with the first flap he lifted twenty feet in the air. It took him a few minutes to get control, enough to hover low enough for them to grab onto him. Blithden took one foot and Baldr the other. Alex just wrapped himself around Baldr's leg, Michael was surprised by how easy it was to fly with what had to be four thousand pounds of meat between the two big guys not to mention Baldr's hammer! He flew as fast as he dared and kept and eye for the other side, the cavern bent to the right a bit keeping the other side from view. Then after a few minutes they could see way off in the distance a large ledge with a golden cage of some sort on it. Ten minutes later, they landed on the ledge and something dawned on Michael.

"Hey! Why didn't you just teleport us over here? That could have been much farther, I could have gotten tired, who knows what could have happened!" Michael said feeling annoyed.

"I haven't been able to teleport since we entered this part of the cave. I think the sword is in this cage here and Ackatoth wanted this last part of the trip to be harder so he put up some kind of field that inhibits certain powers. Like if you're being able to fly were a power I bet it wouldn't have worked either! Besides that if I don't know where I going when I teleport it is very dangerous, I could end up having a leg stuck in a wall or something." At that moment the book shot out of Michael's satchel and started vibrating so much that he felt it would be unwise to ignore it—even though he wanted to.

> *"You made it! Holy crap!! You even got through all my traps!*
> *No doubt you earned unknown, armor, swords, axes and more!*
> *Take it all if you can, I'll even let you give some to your men!*
> *Now I can not tell you which sword is the one, but you will*
> *Know when you find it, now go have some fun!"*

"Is it just me or is that book being way to nice?" Alex asked in a completely serious voice.

"Yeah, I don't trust this book for as much as I would a hungry dragon! Let me find *the* sword first then you lot can pick stuff out. There may be traps or something if I pick the wrong sword first or whatever! Keep a sharp eye, okay?"

"That sounds wise to me," answered Blithden

Michael walked into the cage. The ledge they were on was perfectly flat as was the wall of rock it jutted out from making a perfect right angle. The cage went from the ground up about forty feet to meet the wall, forming a quarter dome shaped cage. The cage was big, nearly two hundred feet long from end to end, and in the cage there were so many swords, axes, and other deadly objects that were hard to keep track of. Michael walked around for quite a while unsure of what to even be looking for. It was as he thought this that a random barrel off to the right corner of the cage caught his eye. There had to be a hundred barrels filled with swords in here but this one stood out, not because of some ornate, kingly sword adorned with gold and jewels, no this barrel stood out because of one item. Nestled in the back of several dozen swords, was a sword barley visible rapped in burlap cloth. Michael reached past all the others and pulled out this sword. He was almost shaking at this point; he took off the burlap to reveal a very ordinary looking samurai katana, with steel-colored guard and pummel. Its sheath had a simple mat black finish and the same steel-colored metal fixtures. But what caught Michael's eye was a simple letter A on the pummel, as well as on the sheath just above the hilt. This A had to be the mark for Ackatoth … *This was it!! He had found it!* After all they had gone through, he had the sword! He had to admit he was somewhat disappointed by just how simple it was. It didn't look special in the least. But who cares about that he had no doubt that this thing had some kind of secret. Come to think of it the book even said as much!

"Here … here it is!" He said finally. The others, who had waited outside until the sword was found, came hurrying in.

"Are you sure *that* is it?" Alex asked obviously having expected more as well.

"Yep, but just to prove it lets test it on something … How about Baldr's hammer?"

"That would certainly settle it! If it can handle such a blow than it would have to be Ackatoth's sword!" Blithden stated.

So Michael drew the sword and at once there was an odd noise followed by loud popping noises all over the cavern. It did not take long for them to figure out what was happening … The lava was starting to rise!

"Okay, time to go!" shouted Baldr.

"Wait let's not get crazy here, look the lava is rising quite slowly and the popping I think might have been those notches in the wall there that weren't there before. They are big enough that it should slow down the lava quite a bit as it reaches them. Still I think we should take what we can quickly all the same," observed Alex. Sure enough Alex was quite right, the lava was rising but very slowly; still as it inched closer, the heat in the cavern rose much faster than the lava did.

"Quickly grab what you want and let's leave," Michael said.

Blithden rummaged around and all at once bolted for the largest weapon in the cage. It was a hammer much like Baldr's just two feet longer and with a head twice the size!

"I thought I would never see it again! It's no wonder I couldn't draw it to my hand, the same power that stopped Alex from teleporting must have blocked my ability to do so! He grabbed belts and strapped them on then slung his hammer, he then caught up four different axes and a mace. Baldr had put on several belts as well and strapped on four swords plus one in his hand and a shield in the other he had also already put on a suit of full body armor with a helmet that made him look scary. Blithden made his way to the armor as Alex tried teleporting again and found that the barrier had been lifted he said very quickly, "All right finish putting stuff on and let's get out of here, I got my teleporting back! I'll just teleport what we don't want to carry." They finished in a few seconds and Alex sent the rest of the stuff to Asendor.

They left the cage to an unwelcome sight. The lava had sped up and was now only fifty feet below them!

"Blast! We took too long!" Baldr exclaimed.

"Look there! A door opened over here!" Michael pointed to a twenty foot tall door way that opened to the left of the cage. They didn't waste time as the lava had already gained another ten feet so they bolted through the door and up a set of stone stairs. The stairs went up for a long ways they lead to a landing then about fifty feet ahead started going back down. As they neared the other side the roof above the fifty foot landing started to lower…as you can imagine this made them speed up. They ran down the stairs as fast as they could, Michael chanced a look up at this ceiling to see that it was shaped just like the stairs.

"Um…Faster please!" Cried Blithden as his head was now far too close to the ceiling for comfort.

They reached the bottom and all dove out and just in time as the last twelve feet of the ceiling dropped all at once! Michael stood up brushing off a large amount of dirt from his front. The floor of this room was very dusty, a quick look around showed that there were super old pieces of furniture in here set up like a personal quarters. There was a table and some chairs, a squashy armchair set next to an ancient fire place both covered with centuries of dust. Over in the far corner was a very large bed with an old quilt over it. Beside the bed was a desk and chair and sitting on the desk was a stack of gold bars that had just sat there in the same spot of the wooden desk for so long that they had sunken almost a whole inch into the top of the desk. Alex took one look at the bars, pointed his hand at them and they disappeared.

"Okay. Now this trip is getting good!" said Alex.

Michael walked over to the desk and looked it over, and then opened the drawers. Most of them were just filled with dust, but the largest wasn't—it contained another book similar in looks to his but much bigger. Michael took it from the drawer and carefully put it on the desk. Baldr had just finished scooping most of the dust from the fire place and threw some of the wood that was stacked next in to it and Blithden lit it. The room filled with light and Baldr tested out one of the chairs to see if it could hold him … It could not. Michael opened the book and instead of being some mystical thing with letters rising through the pages, it turned out to be a very normal book that had been written a very long time ago by now the ink was very faded, it was even hard to read in places. This made the first line all the more chilling as Michael read it aloud. *"Hello, Michael my friend…!"*

"How could Ackatoth have known that I would be the one to get the sword? I mean my life didn't even go the way it was meant to! My parents were killed, and I grew up in a dimension that knows nothing of Jemini or our world! That's how I got my name. I doubt my name was the same with my birth parents!"

"Well I don't think it is too much strain on one's mind to believe that Ackatoth was an oracle. He may have seen what was coming. He was a man of many talents after all," suggested Blithden. Alex went over to a door in the left corner of the room that the others had not noticed until then.

"There is something shiny down the steps on the other side of this door! Can we go look?" Michael closed the book and put it in his satchel. He also pulled out the guide, no one would need this thing again, and he had wanted to do this for a long time anyway. Michael walked over to the fire and threw the book into the flames. Instantly there was an ear piercing scream that filled the air the book melted into the flames which started to grow. The room started to shake too, and they all decided to leave! Baldr turned the door to splinters with a kick, and they all ran down a small staircase into a large square room filled with gold! Alex was speechless for a split second, but with a happy wave the gold was gone. They didn't stop moving though because the shaking was getting worse. On the other side of the room of gold was another tunnel and they rushed into it. It sloped downward at nearly forty-five degrees, and it became hard to run because the floor here was flat and still very dusty. At last Blithden's hooves became too dusty to grip the ground, and he slid forward knocking Baldr and Michael over, and they all slide down in one big jumbled mess. Alex, who was bringing up the rear, saw this and mistook it as intentional and quite purposefully dropped to his butt and slide down after them acting like a child at a playground. After a while, they landed at a three-way passage that looked terribly familiar: there was a tunnel to the left, one to the right, and one straight ahead. The tunnel to the left had caved in at some point about a hundred yards down and nothing else was visible down there. The right was dark at about twenty feet in, and smelled bad. Down the passage in front of them they could see flickering light of torches and hear what sounded like heavy pounding. Out of the options going straight was the one that seemed best so they went forward. This tunnel opened to some sort of antechamber, down some steps and ahead was a two-hundred-foot wide circular door covered in strange markings. The walls of this room were made of huge gray bricks; and to the left there was a fountain of water that looked quite good; they all at once realized just how long it had been since their last drink. But at the moment what was more on their minds was what was behind the wall to the right. The pounding and the shaking of the cave was coming from something behind this wall. With each pound the wall buckled more and more until it finally broke open! Michael, Alex, Blithden, and Baldr were all ready for the worst—Blithden had his two biggest axes in hand Baldr had swapped his sword for his hammer, and Alex had a sword that he made pop into his hands as they stood there waiting for what came. The dust settled to reveal Pith and Balo knocking away some still hanging loose bricks as was Bolen and Able. They looked up with a start apparently not expecting to see Michael here.

"I told you weren't digging straight! But who wants to listen to the dwarf?!" Kujex said acting angry and hurt.

"*No one!*" retorted Able, Ryan, Blaze, and Zezz all in unison.

"What happened to you guys? How did you get here?" Michael asked.

"Well, about twenty minutes after we started tunneling our way out of here we ended up tunneling right into a barracks for the portion of the army we didn't manage to kill. As you can imagine we had to fight our way out of there pretty fiercely. Well by the time they were all dead we were nearly the same only from exhaustion! We followed an already existing tunnel that I thought lead in the same direction as we were headed anyway and got away from the smell of the bodies and we took a rest. Once we woke we started walking, and walking, and walking. There is an endless labyrinth of tunnels down here. We came to the same spot twice before I started tunneling my own way again..." Explained Pith sounding oddly like Eliza talking fast and without a breath ... "It would appear I took us in the wrong direction. But at least we found some friendly faces!"

"Yeah, and what are the odds that you come to the place we do at almost exactly the same time?" Michael added.

"Is that Blithden and Baldr with you?" blurted Balo, who had just gotten done wiping dust from his face.

"*Balo?* ... Why it's been quite a long time!" Blithden walked forward and gave Balo a brotherly hug as did Baldr. Zezz and Pith joined as well also having known them from long ago, even Kujex had a dopey smile. After this Michael told them all how *they* got there and showed them the sword of Ackatoth. They all let out a cheer when he told them this, they were all overjoyed that Michael had gotten what they had set out for, even Bolen and Akuma said that the right man got the word and patted him on the back.

"All right, now I guess we need to get through this door. The question is how?" Zezz said looking at the colossal door. Pith walked up to him looking somewhat puzzled.

"You do remember I'm here right? Plus even if I wasn't between Blithden, Baldr, Balo, Bolen, Akuma, Able, and Foeseth I think you might have enough strength there to open it." Pith looked at him with a grin.

"Yes well ... I just ... Oh, I guess you're right!" Zezz chuckled. Pith walked up to the door put his hands on it and pulled. This door was no match for Pith though, It moaned for less than a second before he tore it right off the hinges. He took a step back and set the door down beside the doorway ... or ... well he kind of dropped it. But that was do to the fact that they now could see inside the next room, a room big enough to put any at Asendor to shame!

It was so big none of them could see the end to the left or the right. The ceiling was so high that even Pith could barely make it out! Filling this room was a sight not a one of them had thought of, rolling dunes of gold! Gold coins, gold nibs, gold bars of every size. And not just gold but gems of every kind—rubies the size of cars, sapphires larger than a school bus, and diamonds the size of a house and so much more. As they walked in, Their jaws hang low and their eyes bulged in awe, Kujex swore, Able let out a whistle, and Alex started crying. They all walked forward a few paces when a huge forty-foot troll came running around the mountain high pile of gold to their left. He was decked out in trillium armor and had a sword that Pith would have loved to own.

Michael walked forward to meet this troll with his new sword drawn. He had gone through so much to be scared by one troll. The troll charged towards him. Michael jumped into the air and in one smooth motion he brought out his anari and using his wings flew right at the troll's sword and hit it with his. "*KLANG, KLANG!*" The top half of the troll's sword was sliced off clean as if by some sort of laser. The troll stopped dead, he took his helmet off, and brought his sword up to his face to look at the cut. His eyes went wide, and he dropped the rest of his sword got down on his hands and knees and brought his face very close to Michael's. The others were ready to strike at a moment's notice but Michael waved them off. The troll was scratching his head as he looked at Michael and then he finally spoke.

"Duh…How did you do dat?" The troll asked in a simpleton sort of voice.

"Um…I have the sword of Ackatoth. I guess *it* can do that." The troll let out a gasp, then smiled wide, his two large tusks sticking out oddly.

"Oh joy! Dat mean you troll's new master, it does!" The group let down their guard some, seeing that the threat was gone.

"I'm your new master huh? So what does that mean?" Michael asked him. The troll stood up very quickly and saluted him like a soldier.

"Troll do as you ask anything you need, troll do!"

"Hmm…well first what is your name then, so I don't have to call you 'troll' I mean." The troll thought for a minute then smiled…

"My old master used to call me 'stupid troll,' or sometimes 'I should kill you!'" He boomed happily. Eliza giggled at this and Alex finally stopped crying, and looked up at the troll and at once popped in front of Michael.

"What's going on with the troll? And can I swim in the gold now?" Alex seemed about to start crying again.

"Oh snap out of it! We have got to find the way out of here before we can think about taking anything out of here. Here, you can help me out. This troll here is bound to me now because of the sword but he doesn't have a name. How about you pick one out for him."

"Bob," Said Alex instantly.

"Wait don't you want to …"

"…Nope, he looks like a Bob." Alex interrupted, "how would you like the name Bob?" Alex asked. The troll started getting misty eyed and couldn't seem to answer but just nodded his head.

"See, he loves it! Now, you find the way out, I'm going to go hug that diamond!" Alex wasn't kidding either—he immediately walked over to the nearest diamond and just started hugging it. Michael slapped his hand over his face shaking his head. "Okay Bob, do you know how to get out of these caves and back onto the planes?"

Bob looked concerned. "Oh master, ice been falling three days, very dangerous out side! But there is a way my old master would take to leave the cave in bad weather! Come I show you!"

Bob lead Michael, Pith, Zezz, and Blithden to a very large circular trapdoor on the floor at the center of the room.

"You lift dat, and there is a tunnel. Don't know where it goes me born in cave!"

"Well then, you should be happy to know you're coming with us! Zezz said happily. Bob got misty eyed again.

"Alright Bob, is there anything bad that happens if we open this?" Michael was doubtful that leaving here could be quite so easy.

"Not bad. just cute little snakey come out!" Bob said. Michael, Zezz, Pith, and Blithden all exchanged glances. It seemed quite possible that what Bob might consider a cute little 'snakey' others might consider a horrible man eating monster!

"Where does this snake come from?" Zezz asked.

"Those doors!" Bob pointed to a set of double doors about three hundred feet away from them.

"Well Bob, do you think you can put some big heavy stuff in front of those doors so they can't open?" Blithden asked.

Bob seemed to be thinking hard on this as though it were a difficult question, then he finally just nodded and ran over to the doors and started stacking large stone statues that were around the walls of the place in front of the doors. Michael, Zezz, Pith, and Blithden went back to the others just in time to catch the end of an argument between Kujex and Alex.

"...There's a limit! Now stop being a blasted fool!"

"I can do it and I'll show you!" Without another word Alex walked over to the closest pile of gold and put his hands on it. Kujex just started scuffing, but it was short lived because after about a minute the entire pile of gold disappeared!

"*How the...*?! Why, it's not possible!!" Kujex was beside himself and Alex was not ready to stop. He started popping form pile to pile making them all disappear. Every coin, bar and gem. In what seemed like no time the entire room was empty, and Alex was lying on the ground catching his breath. Bob had come bounding over when the first pile vanished and was staring at Alex in wide eyed amazement scratching his head. But now that *all* the gold was gone Bob couldn't handle it anymore. He reached out and grabbed Alex around the middle, and turned him upside down and started shaking him.

"Where you put gold? How you do dat? Why you do dat? Now they going to come! They be mad!" At these words hisses and pops starts sounding around the room just as they had in the lava filled cavern.

"I remember this music! It is time to go, *now!*" Baldr roared. Baldr was right to yell as it turned out. Doors started opening all over the room and yet more of the army of brutes came flooding into the room. Pith pulled out his axe and readied himself for the cyclops and trolls running toward them. Bob ran to Pith's side his helmet back on. Pith handed him his machete. Zezz ran to the trap door followed closely by the others and started to try and pull it open. Many of the approaching men and beasts started crying for him to stop, but not before Blithden reached over and gave the door a yank, pulling it out of the floor entirely. He tossed the door deep into the army and looked in the hole. Zezz showing no fear jumped in the hole with his arms ablaze.

"Come on get down here, It's a long ways so be careful!" he called. *Boom! Boom!* A banging was coming from the doors behind them and now the army stopped fighting. The doors they had come through just snapped shut and they were now frantically trying to escape. Pith and Bob came running over to the hole and Pith jumped in followed by Ryan, Eliza, and Blaze...*Boom! Boom!* The doors broke and the largest snake Michael had ever seen came bursting through them. It was fifty-feet wide and would have been hundreds long. It slithered right for them, and they scrambled into the hole. Michael was the last in the hole, and they didn't bother to see if the snake was following them or eating the army they just ran. They moved on for a while then were forced to stop for a rest, in the distance they could hear horrible screams, and also yelling getting closer. Some of the army must have jumped in the hole too.

"You lot go, I'm going to close up this tunnel" Pith Commanded. They all started running again as Pith started breaking the tunnel roof. They ran a little farther and the tunnel changed again, and once again Michael felt like this was familiar as if he had been down here before. Michael wasn't sure yet why or how but he knew they had to keep going. This tunnel was old and by the dust and cob weds it hadn't seen use in a while. Pith caught up to them and they walked for a long time. Michael didn't know just how many miles they had gone but it felt like at least twenty! This tunnel was not carved out of raw rock but was lined with the same bricks as before. The walls in here were damp and there was a smell of mildew in the air. They could hear the sound of running water and a shimmering blue glow coming from up ahead. They slowed down as they came around a left hand curve in the tunnel that ended at the mouth of a chamber that looked like it was once some sort of great hall. Not one of them had any time to look around though, no sooner had they entered the hall then they all thought of running right back out of it! Lying not but a hundred feet in front of them was a very large dragon. It was sleeping when they walked in, but it smelled them at once and woke with a powerful roar. This dragon was twice the size of Jake, standing on all fours it was at least five hundred feet tall and a good twelve hundred feet long with his tail! It's head was larger than a city bus with ten foot long teeth! Enraged at their presents, the dragon started trying to stomp on them while breathing fire all over.

"Find cover!" screamed Kujex. They all ran to the far walls of the hall where bits of the roof had caved in long before. Everyone scattering mad, the dragon was unsure who it wanted to kill first. It looked around and locked eyes on Bob. It ran toward Bob and Michael was afraid Bob wouldn't be able to get out of the way soon enough! Michael shot a ball of energy at the dragon's face to try to distract it far long enough for Bob to take cover. It worked but as with many other times it worked too well! The blast hit the dragon right in the cheek; but instead of hurting it, the dragon just looked ticked off! This was a far different dragon than the one he killed at the beginning of this trip, that one was a standard red. This dragon was jet black, and it was covered in spikes. Every single scale had three spikes sticking out at least six feet, the tail ended in one huge twenty-foot spike. Even the head had two horns that curved forward toward his snout which was wider than it was long—like an arrowhead.

The now angry dragon was much more interested in Michael, and he felt moving quickly was a great idea. So in a flash Michael's anari was out and he was airborne. Once flying the dragon became less interested in him and looked back to the ground everyone had managed to take cover except for Alex. He stood there staring the dragon down completely free of fear. The dragon sniffed at him and Alex shot a blast of red energy at its face. Michael didn't know that Alex could shoot energy blasts, but at this rate he was just willing to assume that nothing was off the table when it came to Alex! Alex's shot missed but the dragon was quite annoyed and tried to stomp on him with both front feet. Alex simply teleported out of the way, the dragon shot its head toward him in shock and tried to pounce on him once again. Alex just started popping here and there as the dragon chased him exactly like a cat chasing a mouse! From where Michael was, it was honestly funny to watch and what added to it, every time the dragon missed Alex it got more and more agitated growling in anger. Finally getting tired of this game, the dragon took a deep breath and started breathing fire again. This time however it was not just straight fire, but fire balls with some sort of pulse energy in them. Alex was still keeping out of harm, but it was clear he couldn't keep it up forever. Meanwhile as this was going on Pith and Balo were able to sneak over to the rest of the group who were all hiding behind a huge fallen pillar. They had been talking and came up with a plan. A few minutes later Foeseth flew up to meat Michael to tell him of the plan.

"It would seem this is an unknown breed of dragon! The others have no idea how your blast didn't kill it! We looked at the tunnel out of here and we aren't going to be able to move into it quickly because there is a lot of debris in the way. So we are going to need to work in groups, Bob and Pith are going to work at getting the tunnel clear while you, Alex, and myself keep the dragon occupied. Meanwhile Blithden, Bolen, Balo, and Baldr are going to work on bringing that biggest pillar down…" Foeseth pointed to a huge pillar that was at the far left side of the room—there was one identical to it on the right side of the hall. "…The others feel that should be more than enough to at least pin the beast so we can leave," Foeseth continued, "but it will almost certainly make the roof cave in so we will need to be very quick!" Michael gave Foeseth a nod, this plan was risky not to mention completely crazy, but they had to do something because the dragon wouldn't just let them leave! Michael swooped in first to give Alex a break; he tried fire this time instead of energy and found out that fire was a bad idea. As the fire ball reached the dragon it just sucked it in and then blew it right back at Michael!

Foeseth flew right at it and shot a lightning bolt from his hand right at its face. The dragon staggered back a few steps and tried vainly to wipe the lightning from his face. Alex then popped right onto the dragon's face and punched it in the eye. The dragon got mad and swore!!! Everyone in the room stopped for a second. It was common knowledge to most that only small dragons could talk and that dragon's this size were just beasts! But this one just used an English word! Alex left his face quickly and the dragon reared up on his hind legs so that his head nearly touch the thousand foot ceiling. He then put all doubt of what they heard to rest by speaking out right…!

"That was a mistake you little fool! Now I will kill you all slowly!" The dragon's voice was a deep growling thing that boomed like thunder through the hall. The dragon then started to shrink in size! Its hind legs became proportional to his body, and his front legs morphed into arms! Even once he finished shrinking he was still a hundred feet tall, and his arms were a good twenty-five feet wide!

"Now you will taste the wrath of Gondra, lord of the dragons!"

Things from this point became so chaotic it was hard for them to know what was happening at the moment. Pith and Balo tried to get the attention of the others who all the while had been hacking at the pillar. Regrettably they were too late. The dragon had taken notice to Pith at last and seemed to change in countenance at once but that was when the pillar came down. Gondra move out of the way but the roof started to fall and faster than any had imagined. The group moved as fast as they could through the tunnel ahead but the cave in was spreading. The tunnel started to break apart.

Alex had picked up Eliza and was carrying her as he could run five times as fast as she could. Foeseth grabbed Kujex just as a rock the size of a dump truck landed where he was. Blaze was keeping up just fine, and Rozea was right beside her when a large rock fell on Rozea pinning her leg. She let out a cry and everyone turned back but only in time to see the rest of the roof cave in … Rozea was gone! Ben let out a scream and ran to the rock wall to try to dig her out but the cave in was not finish. Blithden had to literally carry Ben away as he screamed and cried Rozea's name. The group ran hard and all at once the tunnel turned hard right. They jumped around the corner kept going. Blaze was crying, and she started to slow down. Michael picked her up in his arms and kept running. This tunnel look *very* familiar again and he knew he had been there before! That's when it dawned on Michael where he had seen this tunnel before.

He and Blaze had been down here in fact … A minute more of running and they came to a large metal door. Able slammed into it, throwing it into to wall of an adjacent tunnel. They came out into an antechamber which leads to a tunnel that even the master's knew! They hurried forward and turned right into the tunnel. A short ways into the tunnel Michael looked up and sure enough there was the hole he had jumped into with Blaze to keep them from getting caught by Drackiss and Thive! Blaze saw it too and climbed out of Michael's arms ready to run again. They had outrun the cave in and didn't need to be moving so fast, but all of them were ready to never see another dark tunnel as long as they lived! They got to the staircase and Blithden put Ben down and took the lead. They reached the top in ten minutes flat and Blithden didn't even slow down. He took his hammer off his back and hit the door once. It flew out of the wall and across the hall. They all rushed out of the hole and bolted toward the main entrance hall. As they got close they could hear the voices of Dojee and Warbick shouting orders to apprentices as well as other masters. When the group broke out of the hallway into the Great Hall they were met by two thousand battle droids all pointing blasters at them. The second Dojee saw who they were he gave the order the lower they're weapons.

"By Zeus! You made it!" he exclaimed. Zezz walked up to him almost ready to cry.

"Not *all* of us ..."

CHAPTER TWELVE

M ichael was so exhausted he stayed in bed for two entire days. He finally decided he needed to get out of bed, but even though it had been days since he had any food he didn't think he could eat. He took Rozea's death very hard and being the leader of the group, she was his responsibility and he failed her. He got out of bed and started walking the halls. He didn't notice all the people saying "Hi" to him as he went by, nor did he pay attention to where he was going. After an hour of walking he found himself outside the upper courtyard that had become the training grounds for his team.

He looked at the doors and saw that the label had been changed. It used to say Northwest Private Courtyard now it read, "Asendor Special Task Force Headquarters." Michael had forgotten about his new job a while ago. And after losing someone on his very first mission, he was sure he wouldn't be the leader of this group anymore. Michael opened the door and found that the courtyard was gone. It was replaced with a fully enclosed room much larger than the courtyard was. To the right, there was a computer room filled with monitors and server towers, in front of which sat several desks each with their own computers. At the other end of the room was a large matted training area where several people were being trained just as Michael had been before his trip. Ahead of him was a hallway that read 'Barracks'. Michael walked down this hall; there were rooms for all the members of his team. He came to the room marked Rozea and stopped dead.

It was adorned with a picture of her smiling happily. There were flowers all over the door and floor around it. Michael had taken it hard, but he had not yet cried, seeing the smiling picture though was more than enough. He fell to his knees and wept bitterly. He didn't see the door to his right open nor did he see who it was who took him into their arms. He didn't care either, a true friend was dead, and he felt responsible for it, it was just too much to bear. He was lead into the room and into a chair. He felt a hand go into his and knew it was Blaze's. He wiped the tears from his eyes and looked up. His whole team was there, and all of them seemed to have red eyes. Even Kujex had been crying and his eyes still looked wet! Even Dojee's eyes were red but he managed a gentle smile as Michael looked at him.

"I …I'm sorry …I'm sorry for failing as a leader, I …" Michael was cut off by almost everyone wanting to say something, but they all let Dojee set him right.

"My dear, dear boy! That is not a burden for you to bear. Everyone in this group knew the potential costs of going on this trip. Rozea made her choice and that has nothing to do with you! To be honest, I was beginning to hate *myself* for letting you go! I feared none of you would return after a while! You took two whole weeks longer than you were supposed to according to the book! But I too had taken a burden I did not need to bear. You said you were going even if you had to go alone, of course I'm glade you didn't go alone or you would have certainly died! You did not fail anyone! You made it through something very few ever did before you …and you got *the sword!* You got your prize …"

"And I would trade it in a second to get Rozea back!" Michael said fighting off more tears. Blaze gave his hand a squeeze.

"Hmm …I think we all feel that way. It is a sad thing to lose a friend, even more in that way. But know that she did not die in vain! She died doing what she felt she needed to do, and she died with honor! Remember her for her bravery and her strength. Not as a way you failed."

That afternoon the entire academy body and staff met outside in the arena at the far right of the main courtyard. They held an elegy, and for the first time in several hundred years a monument was built in Rozea's memory. They would be putting it in the Great Hall right beside the statues of the greatest warriors Asendor Academy ever had. Rozea's father Crozoe Mimff was given Rozea's graduation plaque as well as a medal she was meant to receive for being the greatest archer the academy ever had! He seemed to be in a bit of shock but took them and turned to Ben. He walked to Ben and with a tear in his eye he said, "She would have wanted you to have this, my son! Thank you for being good to my daughter…and letting her experience love…if only for a short while…!" Overcome with grief Crozoe had to walk away and Ben was brought to tears again.

The entire academy was quiet for two days. But it was time for Dojee to debrief everyone on what happened. Ben was excused from this as he was still coping with the loss. All the rest were there though, even Blithden, Baldr, Bolen, and Akuma were there—all of whom had joined the task force. Michael had found out that several other people had joined too. Balo, Zezz, and even Kujex had all stepped down from their positions as masters to join as well. Pith was made a master and took Balo's spot as forth in command. Sif took Zezz's third spot. Brains and Ortaiga were also a part of the task force now, and Dojee was going to be interviewing a few hundred people to fill the Master slots later that day. Dojee waited until they had all taken their seats before he began.

"So let's just make this simple. Just start from the beginning, and give me the important details."

Michael started off with their meeting the battalion of trolls, then the basteels and at that instant realized that they never did see the mother!

"It is just as well. They are very hard to kill when full grown!" Dojee stated.

Pith picked it up from here telling the story in great detail. He got to their meeting Kronos and his army at this Dojee nearly fell out of his chair! Alex then chimed in for how they met Akuma and then their splitting up. Dojee was not happy to hear that they split up at all but found it more than interesting that they wound up back together. It did seem more than unlikely and Michael found himself wondering if there wasn't more to that than they even knew. Alex continued telling the story and really got into it when he got to tell Dojee about the room of gold.

"Yes, I was going to ask if you all knew where all that came from…By the way how did you know about the vault you put it in?" Dojee seemed more amused than anything.

"I can see through anything, even a shielded vault!" Alex answered.

Zezz took over with the story from there and spoke very deliberately as if trying to tip off Dojee to something without saying it. He spoke of the grand hall in which they met the dragon and Dojee's mouth dropped.

"That was the remains of the old Academy! Why no one has seen that since the Great War!" he exclaimed.

"Yes but that is not all! Gondra was there! He is still alive! Do not ask me how because I don't understand it myself, but it was him!" Zezz cried. Dojee was beside himself.

"Did he make it out?"

"Don't know, he certainly didn't come our way, and the cave in was pretty violent. That said, if he managed to live that long down there then I would say he might have made it out!" Michael and the other younger folks in the room didn't have a clue what they were talking about so Pith explained it.

"Gondra was the leader of the dragon's and their king. He was the only dragon ever recorded to be a Jemini. Not only was he a Jemini he was a very powerful one. He was one of the leaders during the great war and also a good friend." Pith made a sad face.

"What do you mean a *good friend?* Do you mean you were alive during the Great War?" blurted Able.

"As a matter of fact I was! I was only twenty-two years old when it started. You have never seen such carnage …!"

"But you all said that Kronos had more experience than Pith and that he was beyond him." pointed out Ryan.

"Yes well that is because, no one outside this room, save a few select souls, knows what you just learned. Pith here is a special case, I don't even know just how much yet, but I do know this. He has lived for over sixteen thousand years and is still only about thirty years old in body. I don't know how powerful he is and he is of no known race. If the wrong people knew just how strange his case is they would want to lock him in a cage and use him as a test dummy in some lab! People must not know his true story for this reason, most of all. The GUF and The High Counsel do not like people being … well … strange. They made *magic* illegal, and they openly call any being with natural powers an evil beast and they hate anything they don't understand. If they knew that Pith was such a mystery they would do whatever they could to catch him. They already don't like him because he is 'too strong' for the same reason they didn't like Ackatoth for being so powerful. They want to feel like they are in total control, and if they don't they will act violently to get the feeling back. All that being said you are all sworn to secrecy! They all agreed to this and Michael finished the story. He told of the tunnel they found themselves in being the same one that he and Blaze were in before. Dojee was very troubled by this.

"I wonder if it is possible that they knew just how close they were."

"Well that brings me to a question that has been bothering me." Michael admitted.

"Really, what's that?"

"The entire trip felt almost as if it were being manipulated, as if someone were controlling what happened in that cave. I know someone was linked to the book in some way because when I threw it into the fire it let out a scream!"

"A scream? That...that's not possible..." Dojee trailed off again lost in thought just like when he failed to tell Michael how he was having visions. For some reason Michael was beginning to feel as if they were somehow connected. After a minute Dojee snapped back to reality, he said that he had heard enough for now and that Michael and he needed to talk alone. The others left and Michael moved to the chair next to Dojee.

"What I'm about to tell you cannot leave this room. I fear it making its way to the wrong ears. I believe there are still more traitors in the staff of Asendor so I don't know who to trust beyond a few. Now...you said that when you first picked up the book, it knew you by name correct?"

"Yeah..."

"And, the night before you left, when it told you your team would have to die for you to get the sword. You said you heard a laugh coming from the book?"

"Yes, it was not pleasant either."

"Hmm...If it did that, then let out a scream when you destroyed it then that means someone was writing the book as you went. The book had to have some sort of property that allowed the one writing it to know who held it, and even who was speaking around the one holding it. Remember that time with Kujex?"

"But, I thought that the guide was made by Ackatoth. Wouldn't he be the only one who could write it?"

"Oh, it was, and he did! That is what I am getting at. It would seem that Ackatoth is still alive!" Only he could write in that book and only he knew where the sword was precisely. I fear that this is by no means good though, as you said yourself the book felt evil. You have a sixth sense, you get feelings that always turnout right. Put the two together and that would mean that Ackatoth turned evil!" Michael's head was hurting...

"What does this all mean?"

"It means life is going to get a lot more dangerous for you if I am right. You are his heir, but if he isn't dead than that means two people will be able to operate the main gate. What that will mean is impossible to know but if he is evil I would say it could be very bad! It is also worth noting that if Ackatoth is evil he may either try to turn you...at some point...or he may just find a new heir."

"How could he do that? I thought once a gate keeper sets the rules for their heir they can't be changed again? Eliza had explained this once before."

"Well to be frank I am sort of surprised you would have to ask that! Ackatoth was a very special case in every way. I for one, I don't know that anyone could actually know what he was or was not able to do. For a while there, it seemed like he was finding new powers he already had and just didn't know about, at least that is what he told people...That was before he even learned he could absorb powers. By what was *thought* to be the end of his life there is no telling what powers he had. And now if he *is* still alive after hiding for more than fifteen thousand years, his power could know no bounds. All this is more or less speculation though at the moment. We know too little right now to be sure." Michael sat thinking for a minute. He wanted to ask Dojee about some other things but he didn't know where to start and Dojee let out a laugh.

"Remember how I said you need to keep your thoughts in check? The more chaotic you let your mind become the less safe any knowledge you have becomes. You need to control that so people can't just jump in your mind so easily. I know some of what you want to ask me, but out of respect I will let you ask it."

"Okay...well...What do you know about Alex and Ryan, I mean from before they came here?"

"Hmm...in Ryan I do know some about. I figured out his little secret the night I came back from meeting with the board to approve your graduating. He had been walking the halls at around two in the morning! Now that was the same night you caught the

Russian sneaking about and he caught the assassin. But an event that I let slip passed me at the time was the disappearance of about three hundred pounds of pork. I later went to the chief to ask him exactly what it looked like ... he showed me the carcasses of several pigs striped down to the bone completely. I knew at once what this was, and soon realized that Ryan was the culprit. I pulled him aside a week before you all left to let him know that I knew what he was and that I was going to help him. In only a week, he managed to learn to control it and as it would seem quite well or you wouldn't have needed to ask me about this ..." Michael was lost. Dojee could have been speaking ancient Elvish for as much as Michael understood what he was saying, his confusion shown on his face.

"...Ha, ha! You don't get it yet, huh? Ryan is a werewolf..." Michael just stared. "...That's right, and quite a powerful one. He isn't even fully aware of what he can do. See, normally it takes at least a decade to learn to control the craving for raw flesh. From there it takes another ten to gain control over when your body changes. After about a hundred years your average werewolf will finally learn how to take their beast form. Ryan is only twenty-eight years old, and yet he can now go into beast form at will! He isn't willing to tell me who his parents are or were so my guess is he is either ashamed of them, or afraid of losing friends due to his blood line. Quite a few people hate weir creature of all kinds with a hungry passion, so that would be understandable ...!" Michael sighed heavily. He had not considered one of his best friends would be a monster of some sort. But then again something Dojee said came to his mind, it is not as important *what* he is but *who* he is.

"Okay, so what about Alex?"

"Now he is another case entirely! I thought we knew who he was ... at least somewhat ... But it would appear we were wrong! First off he has more powers than what he is willing to share, which makes me wonder what it is he is hiding ..."

"He spoke to El'Jay'El did you hear about that?" Michael blurted. Dojee smiled at Michael and took a sip from his tea then answered.

"Yes, I know. El'Jay'El told me the first night…" Michael didn't get it. Balo and Zezz both seemed to think that was more or less not something people could do. They said Dojee could look at him but not speak to him…

"I know that the masters told you no one could speak to him and that is because they actually believe that! You are the first person, after Alex, to ever hear this that was not a grand master here! El'Jay'El is not quite as dangerous as people think…That is to say he doesn't lack control over his powers anyway. The rumor that no one can look at him came from long ago and no one is sure of the details but him and he will not discuss it. The point though, he isn't a villain nor would he kill someone for no reason. Now as far as Alex having private talks with him out of nowhere I am not sure how that happened. El'Jay'El acted as if he knew Alex already…called him by a different name…Al'Nex'Al…I am not going to tell you who that name belonged to because it has no bearing on Alex. I explained to El'Jay'El that he was mistaken and showed him how. So it may have just been a case of mistaken identity…" Dojee's voice had changed during this last statement, almost as if he didn't fully believe his own words…Michael knew he was hiding a lot from him, but he also knew that Dojee had his reasons.

"Um…What ever happened to Simein?" Michael asked having nearly forgotten his treason.

"Oh well…Let's just say…I forgot *my* place for just long enough to beat the snot out of him! He ran off, most likely to hide from Drackiss and Thive…Now that is enough deep talking for today. I have quite a bit of work to do and as a matter of fact you will in a few months as well. I want you and your team to take the next six months and relax. Go see the beautiful sights of the galaxy and have some fun. I am going to be sending Warbick to fetch your father, as well as your friends Zack and Penny when the time is right—which should be right about when your vacation is over. Now I want to stress this so you understand the importance of this little break I'm giving you. You may well not get a chance at a vacation *ever* again. Even if you do I dare say it will be a *long* time from now. So use this time to bond with your team through more than just toil and hardship but in joy as well. This will help you all, and keep your minds pure and innocent for as long as possible! When you get back you will have to interview quite a lot of folks who want to join your task force. You will need to decide the ranking system you wish to use and who is at what rank. So that may be fun…it may also be difficult. But that is later. By now Warbick has already told the others and they should be getting things ready. Go pack your things, and I will have the droids take your bags to the landing pad."

"The landing pad? We *have* one of those?"

"Yes, and Alex was kind enough to purchase a ship for the task force to use. For the time being though it will be how you all get around. Far cheaper than taking gates everywhere, now get moving!" Michael left the room and Warbick came in from a door near the back of the room.

"You didn't tell him about his vision, why?" Dojee looked at Warbick and smiled lightly.

"Because that is information that neither he, nor *any* of us are ready for…"

‿

So they all made there way to the landing pad. It was located on the roof of the headquarters and was very big in true Asendor style. They all stood on the pad in the cool morning breeze. Spring was starting to fall on the planes and Michael could smell sweat flowers starting to bloom. Blaze shivering a bit, even though it was far warmer than it was on their trip. It was still chilly up on the pad, and they were not dressed for it. Michael quickly got a jacket out of his bag before the droid could stow it on the ship, and he put the jacket over her shoulders. She gave him a warm smile and a quick kiss. Conshen Saw this and must have thought it looked like fun because she immediately started kissing Foeseth, who was in no way bothered by this. Alex looked over to Eliza, sprayed some mouth freshener, and walked over to her to try yet again to hit on her. He thought she would be in a kissing mood as well—she was not—Kujex gave him a nod and he started talking to her. From where Michael was standing he couldn't hear what was being said, but in less than a minute Alex was carrying all of Eliza's bags on the ship for her. Kujex was just about rolling with laughter, and the rest of the team boarded the ship.

It was a nice ship and very big, which was good because they were going to need space to move around on this thing for the next six months. They strapped in for take off and Michael looked out the window. As it happened Able was a skilled pilot and took the job happily. As they took off Michael watched the castle disappear under the clouds and at last it was gone. Michael felt strange, he had not been at the academy for a full year even and still it felt like leaving home, but that wasn't the case. Only his dad, Zack, and Penny being there would make it complete and that would happen soon enough. He looked around the ship at all the people that were now his crew and realized they were his home too! He didn't know what they were going to do on this break, but somehow he knew it was going to be an adventure all its own.